A HARD BARGAIN

"What's to stop me from getting rid of you, taking the plate and finding the treasure for myself?" Rayce asked in a soft growl.

Her eyes met his for a brief moment and then Tru pursed her lips. "Someone at the Institute knows my mission. If he doesn't hear from me at regular intervals, he'll call in the authorities and launch a full-scale investigation."

Rayce tapped his fingers lightly on the table. *Everything.* She'd planned for everything and backed him into a corner.

He pulled himself up from his seat, slowly and deliberately, with absolute menace. Tru's eyes widened marginally, but she didn't back down even as he bore down on her. He moved within centimeters of her face. His voice was low, hard. "Then I guess you've got a deal, *partner.*"

But he couldn't figure her out. First she'd threatened to ruin him; then she wanted more. The woman had no fear. A thought struck him.

Maybe she did have a weakness.

"On one condition."

She frowned. "Wh

"A kiss a day. Ever takes. When I say, w

Other *Love Spell* books by C. J. Barry:
UNEARTHED

UNRAVELED

C.J. BARRY

LOVE SPELL

NEW YORK CITY

*Dedicated to my wonderful parents, Tom and Jean,
who always encouraged me to shoot for the stars.*

LOVE SPELL®

October 2003

Published by

Dorchester Publishing Co., Inc.
200 Madison Avenue
New York, NY 10016

ISBN 0-505-52562-3

The name "Love Spell" and its logo are trademarks of Dorchester
Publishing Co., Inc.

Printed in the United States of America.

Visit us on the web at www.dorchesterpub.com.

ACKNOWLEDGMENTS

I owe my gratitude to many great people: Chris Keeslar and everyone at Dorchester Publishing; my terrific agent Roberta Brown; the Purple Pens; the CNY Romance Writers; the Lollies; my dedicated critique partners Cactus, Patti, Joyce; co-workers and cyberfriends; the Romance Writers of America; Susan Grant; Catherine Spangler; and every one of my loyal readers. I also thank the tarot card lady in New Orleans who told me that I needed to go home and finish this book. And, as always, I am deeply grateful to my family: Ed, Rachel and Ryan. Thank you all. I couldn't have done it without you.

UNRAVELED

Chapter One

Tru took a deep breath and stepped through the battered doorway. A drinking glass shattered against the wall behind her, splashing its lime green contents across one leg of her silver bodysuit. A chorus of roars burst from the far corner of the saloon. Tru froze as The Rough Cut attacked all of her senses at once. The noise, the smell, the visual were overwhelming. In her mind she fought to make order of the chaos before her.

Noise demanded attention first. An ebb and flow of hearty masculine bellows deafened the dreadful music straining above the discord. Jeers, cheers, rants—they all melded into a raucous symphony.

The smell, well, she didn't even want to analyze that. Her nose would never be the same.

The visual would take a bit longer to sort through. The four dilapidated walls were a patchwork of crudely attached composite board marred by vulgarities in every alien language. A serving bar stretched the length of the far wall, manned by a single burly saloonkeeper. A haphazard collage of tables and chairs in various stages of ruin littered the rest of the place.

Then there was the patronage. Tru caught glimpses of scars, matted hair, missing teeth and something furry in the corner that she was trying hard to ignore. Men huddled over small tables, heads close, grunting and chortling, watching her.

Lovely place. And to think that in all her twenty-nine years she'd never been in a saloon. Nice to know she hadn't missed a thing.

Over the general racket and chaos, Tru scanned the saloon and spotted the man she had come to see.

She made her way through the crowded tables and overt looks to where he sat at the bar, his back to her. She slowed as she got closer and he got bigger. Standing behind him, looking at those broad shoulders, she nearly changed her mind about the whole idea.

What did he eat?

She shook off the thought and spoke up. "Excuse me. Rayce Coburne?"

The man before her turned leisurely on his stool and propped his elbows on the bar. Tru froze as brilliant blue-green eyes drilled into hers. They were hypnotic, a stunning complement to the black hair that hung carelessly over his forehead. Finely chiseled features under smooth, bronzed skin fashioned a rogue's countenance. He lounged on a barstool amid the barrage of foul language and stench of alcohol, looking completely at home. She couldn't tell how tall he was, but he was solidly built. Big arms and shoulders stretched the seams of the supple gray jacket he wore. His white shirt-collar was open, revealing a golden brown, powerful chest. Strong leg muscles bulged through the light fabric of the black pants. Even though she'd seen images of him, the live, up-close version proved far more daunting.

He gave her a long once-over before breaking into a slow, lazy smile.

"Have a seat," he said in a soft growl of a voice that burned into her memory long after he showed her the empty stool beside him.

As she sat down, she was keenly aware of his eyes scanning the length of her body. *Talk about distracting.* Her pulse quickened; her palms began to sweat. She rubbed her hands on her thighs. The worst part was that he hadn't done a thing except offer her a seat.

Annoyed at herself, Tru straightened. After all, he was only a man. A man who would soon work for her.

Boldly, she met his gaze. "What are you drinking?"

Coburne narrowed his eyes. "What are *you* drinking?"

She hadn't planned for that. She never drank, but she wasn't about to admit that to him.

"Safin," she said quickly. It was the only intoxicating drink she knew of.

His eyebrows went up—in respect, she thought. She hoped. He held up two fingers to the saloon-keeper who nodded back.

The drinks appeared immediately and Tru picked up her glass as if she did it all the time. She took one small sip. Nice. Pleasant. Cool. She took a

3

big sip and stopped breathing. Cool turned to heat in a flash that shot from her hair to her toenails. It was all she could do to stay on her seat.

Coburne chuckled softly next to her. Through the tears in her eyes, she watched in awe as he downed his drink in one swallow.

He immediately ordered himself another. Tru grimaced. She'd better get to business before he drank himself into a stupor.

"My name is Tru Van Dye and I have a business proposition for you," she stated firmly.

He stared at her for a full minute before answering. "How much?"

Tru blinked. "Don't you want to know about the job first?"

He laughed low over his new drink. "I know the job. How much?"

She frowned. "I thought 5,000 credits up front would be fair. We can negotiate the rest later."

Coburne choked on his drink. He gave her a hard look and then glanced around behind her. "For just you?"

Sensing that she was missing something quite significant, Tru replied carefully, "Yes. I'm good for the credits."

He blasted her with another killer smile. "You better be good. I don't pay that much for any woman."

Tru's mouth dropped open in comprehension as his smile turned sinful. The air changed around her, growing hotter and more sultry. Coburne moved fast, slipping his hands around her waist, pulling her up out of her seat and against him. She gasped as her body made hard contact with his.

Oh, dear. This was not going at all as she had planned.

He lowered his face to hers and murmured, "Okay, lady. Let's see what a man can get for 5,000 credits these days."

Incensed out of her initial shock, she shoved against his chest and stepped back a fair distance from him.

"I don't believe this," she said with what she considered exceptional self-control, under the circumstances. "You aren't paying for me. I want you to work *for* me. I am a client, not a street moll."

By now, the entire saloon had seen and heard their conversation. The peal of male laughter hit her ears like a slap.

Coburne grinned wide and crossed his arms. "I think I prefer to be the client."

Another roar of laughter. The heat of humiliation stung her cheeks. At that precise moment, she knew that her carefully crafted plan had failed beyond all repair.

Disgusted with herself and him, she turned and stalked around the tables for the door. She'd blown it. And as far as she was concerned, there was never an excuse for failure.

Nothing less than perfection, Tru. Her father's familiar maxim mocked her.

She felt Coburne's hand on her arm just as she exited the saloon. Effortlessly, he spun her around to face him and pinned her to the rough outside wall of the saloon. Before she could protest, his mouth covered hers with a scorching, staggering kiss that made her knees buckle.

The kiss turned to pure liquid heat stronger than

any drink, pouring through her veins and igniting sensations she'd never felt before. No man had ever kissed her this way—all wicked and decadent—putting his whole being into one, sole purpose. It was her first full-body kiss. *So, this is how it felt to be seduced by a rogue. No wonder women fell at his feet.*

His body pressed against hers and suddenly she felt as if the oxygen had been sucked from her lungs, replaced by something hot and volatile, ready to explode. She actually shuddered from the intimate onslaught, unable to find a single weapon with which to defend herself.

Not in the original plan at all.

For the first time in her life, her body utterly refused to listen to her mind, not even when he broke off the kiss. His lips were now making their way down her throat leaving a fiery trail and moving still lower. But when he reached her breasts, she froze. Too real, too close. Panic gripped her as she pushed him away. He stood back, staring at her in confusion.

Quickly, she said, "Computer: End program."

Rayce Coburne and his heat faded away as the virtual-reality simulator powered down. Even though only her mind had actually been in the program with Coburne—felt him touching her—the residual tremors still skittered through her nerve endings. The VirtuWav was a marvel in technology, and hell on one's senses.

Tru floated down the simulator's tube of buoyant gases until her feet were back on solid ground. As the blue shield lowered around her, she tucked her hair back into its tight chignon and tried to compose herself.

She glanced up at her elderly colleague waiting at the VirtuWav control panel. All she could see of Majj Noa Leeberfinger behind the console was his shocking white hair, ruffled and chaotic, as if trying to escape his head. That head housed a brilliant mind. Too bad she'd wasted his effort. How was she going to break the news to him that she'd miscalculated badly after he'd spent the past month building this exercise for her?

Noa squinted at her as she stepped out of the VirtuWav. "So? How did it go?"

Tru joined him at the console and gave her old friend a weak smile. "Not quite as well as I'd hoped."

The older man's gray eyes widened in rapid panic. Tru patted his arm and added quickly, "It's not your fault. I took the wrong approach. I've got it figured out now." She didn't, but she'd think of something between now and the time when she needed to confront the real Rayce Coburne.

Noa fell in step beside her as they made their way out of the VirtuWav lab and down the corridors of the research building. Tru shortened her stride for the diminutive elder, his shoulders hunched forward as he limped along. His silver jacket hung like a sheet from his thin body. Although his mind was as sharp as ever, he seemed to be moving more slowly these days.

"I used all the information I could find to replicate Coburne," Noa said apologetically after they'd cleared security and walked out into the waning daylight.

C. J. Barry

Tru narrowed her eyes in concentration. "I think Coburne is satisfactory. Perhaps a change of venue is in order. Somewhere they don't serve drinks."

Noa shrugged. "I suppose I could alter the program, but you realize, everything must be as realistic as possible. His world is not like ours, Tru. It is different, unpredictable—with life forms who act randomly and recklessly with no forethought to consequences of their actions. I went on the outside once." He gave a hard shudder, as if reliving a memory.

Tru glanced across one of the many pristine courtyards of *their world*—the Majj Institute where she'd spent her entire life. White stone buildings and towers around the perimeter gleamed pink in the late day sun; so mirrorlike you could almost see your own reflection. Almost. The silver uniforms they wore blended in so well, a person all but disappeared into the Institute walls.

The landscaping was equally immaculate. Not a stray leaf on the stone pathways, not a shrub out of place, not a dead bloom to be seen. The flowers were perfect, every one of them exactly like the next.

Tru gave a practiced nod to a pair of female colleagues passing by, the full Majj crest on their uniforms gleaming in the setting sun. She looked down at her honorary token crest and tightened her jaw in resolve. Yet another reason why she would not fail. Before this term was out, she would have her full Majj crest. She waited until the women were out of earshot.

"I've spent the past year working on this project,

8

Noa. I will not fail. Rayce Coburne is just a man. No more, no less."

Noa shook his head. "Not like other men. Not like anyone here. He is rash, impulsive, dangerous—"

Tru interjected, "He may be all that but he's also very good. I need this coup. If I don't produce a major discovery and secure my own Charter soon, they will kick me out of the Institute."

Noa winced visibly. He knew, as she did, that individual achievement was the only way to stay at the Institute past the age of thirty, regardless of birthright. The administrators did not back losers.

He offered, "You don't have to worry about that for some time."

She gave him a wry smile. "You've earned your place here. The VirtuWav would not exist today if it weren't for your research. I don't have such a luxury. And I don't have a lot of time. Besides, this is for me. My right, my Charter. I can't hide behind my father's past successes any longer."

"You helped him with those successes," Noa reminded her with a scowl.

She shook her head. "You know it's not the same."

"But Coburne?" Noa raised his voice in frustration. "He's nothing but a commodities broker, a common mercenary. There wasn't another choice in the entire galaxy?"

Tru pursed her lips. It wouldn't do to tell Noa that she'd found Coburne's name in her father's belongings. Noa and her father had never seen eye to eye.

"Coburne is an acquisitions specialist, and a good

one. No other man met my criteria. He can obtain any article a client desires. He is well-connected, discreet and fearless," Tru said firmly. "And, as far as I can tell, he has never failed to satisfy his clients." She flinched at her choice of words.

Noa grumbled something low and then asked, "So what if Coburne refuses your request?"

Tru smiled to herself. "He won't. We know he needs the credits. Every man has his price."

They passed through the yawning archway into the Majj housing complex where their paths split. Tru came to a halt. Noa stopped in front of her, shaking his full head of white hair.

"Don't be too certain, Tru. You can't underestimate him." Noa looked down at his feet for a few seconds and then added, "You've heard that he . . . likes the women?"

The heat rose suddenly in Tru's cheeks. "Yes. That fact came across particularly well in your program." She cleared her throat. "Don't worry. I can handle him."

Noa's cheeks were red, as well. "I certainly hope so. When do you leave?"

"As soon as the meeting arrangements are complete with Coburne."

He frowned. "I hope those exit documents I fabricated for you work. If anyone checks the approval stamp . . ." His voice trailed off.

Tru smiled at him. "I'm sure they will be fine. Everything you do is perfection." Then she paused. "I probably won't see you again before I leave," she said quietly. "Thank you, Noa. For all your help and faith."

He stuffed his hands in the pockets of his silver

jacket and shrugged his shoulders. "Nonsense. You don't need any help from an old man."

"I will always need you." Then she lowered her voice. "And don't forget to care for my flowers."

He rolled his eyes to the sky. "You still have those? Why do you bother? They are nothing but rejects."

Tru corrected him, "They are *unique*."

Noa threw up his hands in defeat. "If you say so. I'll do my best not to kill them all. You know I don't do well with living things."

Tru smiled warmly and resisted the urge to hug him. That would never do on the Institute grounds. "You are my only friend."

He gave a terse grunt. "Then I pity you and me because you are mine, and we both should have more." He stared at her for an awkward moment. "Be careful, Tru."

"I will," she whispered. He nodded once and turned down the walkway to his residence.

She watched until he was out of sight and then headed in the opposite direction. She hated lying to Noa, but there was no way she could tell him her ultimate plan or he never would have forged her exit documents so she could leave the Institute. But she had no choice. Her mission couldn't be completed in a VirtuWav or through the Institute's archives. This was to be a mission like no other, with a reward far greater than granting her a Charter to stay here. She would be bringing history alive.

She smiled proudly. The Majj had single-handedly obliterated entire diseases, developed life-saving treatments, created new computer technologies, documented lost civilizations and much more for the good of billions. It was her life's calling.

Nearing her apartment, she spotted a frail-looking plant beside the walkway, its yellow flower head drooping toward the ground while all the other plants' blossoms looked up. Tru stopped in front of it and gave a quick look around. Seeing no one, she stooped down, sunk her fingers into the soil around the roots, and lifted it out of the ground. She filled the hole it left and made her way into her apartment with the plant.

Once inside, she walked directly to her bedroom, past the blinking messages on her console, past the new travel bags packed and ready. Against the glow of the sunset, she studied the small plant.

"Today is your lucky day, my little *roxius gernilium.*"

Humming softly, she placed it in the long planter that took up a quarter of her bedroom. Then she stepped back to admire her secret garden thriving and crowding the box. Each one she'd saved from the master gardener's wrath ever since the day she had watched him yank a poor plant out of the garden simply because its flowers were too large. Not like the others. Genetically imperfect.

But to her, they were beautiful, courageous, daring to be different. And worth saving.

Tru looked over the plants and out through her bedroom window, which framed the red setting sun of the planet, Koameron. The Van Dye building sat prominently on the grounds, its silhouette black against a crimson twilight sky. The building was named for her father, the long-time head administrator of the Institute.

Sadness settled over her. Life had never been the same since his death last year. So much had been lost, so quickly. Her world had changed forever.

Absently, she pulled the clips from her hair, letting it fall the length of her back. As she untangled the long tresses, her mind wandered, analyzing each mundane event of the day and then tossing it aside. When she'd ferreted out the nonsense, she concentrated on the current problem—Rayce Coburne. Her fingers paused in her hair.

Based on the results of the virtual-simulation exercise, a more professional approach to Coburne was definitely in order. She wanted no mistaking who she was and who would be in charge of this project.

Then she grimaced. And she should probably offer him more credits than the average street moll could command.

As she watched darkness descend over Koameron, she realized that Noa was right about one thing: Coburne wasn't like other men. At least the ones she knew. The men at the Institute were intellectuals, inarguably the top experts in their chosen fields. Cerebral equals. An academic challenge, she could handle easily.

But Coburne was not cerebral. He was something far more dangerous, something she had little experience with.

Rayce Coburne was physical.

Nice day for a space walk, Rayce thought as he floated out of the escape hatch of his spaceport and into the great abyss of deep space. His suit boosters eased him silently through the vacuum until he was about fifty meters out. Then he turned around to take in the vision of his spaceport.

If a spaceport could be called beautiful, then this one was all of that. Like a beacon, it glowed gold and silver against the black of space. The massive center disc housed the majority of the station's internal systems, public trading areas, entertainment arenas, offices, and the extensive gardens. Smaller discs rose above and below the main level symmetrically, covered by gold-tinted viewports. They contained the private auction and meeting rooms, restaurants, services, spas, shops and private guest quarters—every room with a one-of-a-kind view of the stars.

He couldn't help but smile. With her perfect proportions and stunning spaces, she was a rare beauty among man-made spacecraft, and she was all his. Well, his and Gil's and half a dozen very anxious, very inquisitive investors'.

He tapped the side of his helmet.

"Can you hear me, Gil?"

The comm crackled next to his ear and the voice of his partner and best friend came through. "Yup. You really don't have to be out there, Rayce. These guys know what they're doing. That's why we hired them."

Rayce maneuvered himself so he could watch the small crew of workers in spacesuits handling the cone-shaped stabilizing engine below him. About one hundred meters away, a tow barge was pushing the giant engine toward his spaceport where it would be installed.

"I hear you, but we've got a lot of credits invested

in that engine. Patch me into their communications," he told Gil.

The comm came alive with the head supervisor's raspy order. "Easy, boys. Nice and slow. Chazer, are you ready for us?"

Rayce glanced toward the lone man attached by a tether to the bottom edge of the spaceport near the insertion point of the engine. Chazer waved an arm over his head and answered, "Ready here."

The barge continued along at an excruciatingly slow pace toward its intended target with the replacement engine in front looking like a giant needle about to inoculate someone.

Gil muttered to Rayce privately, "Well, this could take all day."

Rayce grinned. Gil was usually the patient one.

Suddenly, flames shot from the rear of the barge and it gave a jerk, bumping the engine hard.

Rayce heard the supervisor yell. "Burn out. All stop!"

But it was too late. The giant engine bounced back against the barge and then careened forward, snapping the leashes and freeing itself. Rayce watched in grim dismay as the engine slid toward the lower level of the spaceport—alone and unencumbered.

A chorus of shouts went up, everyone calling out orders at once. From his vantage point above, Rayce could see the trajectory and knew there was no way any of them were going to stop the engine from crashing through the outer hull.

"Gil, clear Level 12, now!" he shouted into his comm.

Then he heard something that chilled his blood.

15

The supervisor was screaming, "Chazer, get out of the way!"

Rayce looked down. Chazer hadn't moved from his position, and the engine was heading straight for him.

Chazer screamed back in the terrified voice of a man watching his own death. "I can't release my tether! It's coming at me!"

Rayce spun in his suit and flipped his boosters on high. He dove head-first at full speed on an intercept course with the engine.

A few seconds later, Gil's voice came over the comm. "Uh, Rayce. Exactly what are you doing?"

"I don't think you really want to know, Gil."

As Rayce sped toward the moving engine, he tried to calculate the impact point. If he struck the engine too close to the back end or front end, it would go into a slow spin and still hit Chazer. He needed to make contact at the precise location and angle to alter its course without sending it out of control.

"Rayce," Gil said nervously, "this isn't funny. You will never survive a collision like that."

Rayce ignored him. He was closing fast, the engine looming large, moving silently through space. Another fifty meters. He adjusted his angle.

"You crazy bastard," Gil muttered. "The medic is *not* going to be happy to see you again."

As if Gil wasn't enough, Chazer was screaming in earnest now. Distractions everywhere.

Rayce ordered, "Gil, cut all communications."

"Forget it," Gil came back hotly. "I'm staying with you."

Thirty meters. All he could see was engine. It

looked like a damned mountain. "Fine, just cut out everyone else."

The screaming stopped abruptly, giving Rayce the extra concentration he needed. Even Gil stayed quiet, for once.

Ten meters. Rayce gritted his teeth, veered hard right on a parallel intercept with the engine and closed his eyes.

There was a sickening crunch as man met metal. The impact was much harder than he'd expected, slamming his head against the inside of his helmet. His shoulder buckled and pain shot down his left side. A loud hiss whistled in his ears and yellow sparks streaked across his head. Through it all, he squeezed the booster controls for the few seconds he connected with the engine, hoping it would be enough to alter the engine's course. Then he ricocheted off and spun away. A few seconds later, the outer hull of the spaceport appeared in front of him. He slammed into it full force and bounced off into space with a heartfelt grunt.

Then he flopped slowly, head over heels, just catching a glimpse of the engine as it glided harmlessly beneath the spaceport. *Success*.

But he was cold now and the sparks in his head were amassing into one giant halo before his eyes. Above the thunderous hissing in his ear, a female voice repeated a warning, a breach of some sort. She sounded so far away.

He grinned. He'd always wanted to meet the woman behind that sexy voice. As he rolled, deep space surrounded him, the millions of stars like pinpoints in a celestial tapestry. The sparks converged in a great white crescendo, and then everything went black.

Chapter Two

"He's coming around now," Rayce heard the medic say through the fog. Everything else sharpened in jarring surges—the med center, the bright lights, the smell he hated so much and Gil's homely face, looking extremely displeased. A red aura of closely cropped hair surrounded Gil's head, making his face look even longer and more unhappy than it was.

Rayce groaned and tried to roll over. A bony hand held him down.

"I don't think so, hotshot," Gil said with a voice that matched his sour expression. "You get to spend some time in the med center for this one."

Rayce grimaced and relaxed back on the table. "Who's the boss here?"

Gil crossed his arms. "I am, considering you have a concussion, space sickness and a broken collarbone."

"Shit," Rayce muttered and glanced down at the wrap on his left shoulder.

"Next time you pull a stunt like that, I'm not going to come out and get you," Gil scolded.

Rayce rubbed his head. It hurt like hell. Apparently, it wasn't as hard as people kept telling him. Then he gingerly rolled up on one elbow and looked at Gil.

"Is Chazer all right?"

Gil threw up his hands. "You didn't hear a word I said, did you? Yeah, he's all right, except that he ruined a perfectly good pair of space pants."

Rayce chuckled at that, even though the pain nearly brought tears to his eyes.

Gil shook his head. "It's not funny. What the hell am I supposed to do with a half-renovated, 300-room spaceport if you get yourself killed?"

Rayce pushed himself to a sitting position with a loud groan. Gil hovered over him, as usual. Rayce shook his head and thanked his lucky stars yet again for having a friend who gave a damn. In all the ten years they'd been partners, all the dangerous situations they'd been in, Gil had bailed him out more times than he could count. But by far, this spaceport was the biggest gamble they'd ever taken together. He wasn't about to let Gil down.

"Where is that engine?"

In disgust, Gil said, "Retrieved and installed."

"It works?" Rayce asked.

"Yes," Gil rubbed the back of his neck. "Now we just have to figure out how to pay for it."

Rayce swung his legs off the table and stood. A swarm of sparks threatened to drag him back under. Gil held him up as Rayce grimaced under the fog of the healing-accelerator drug, Aritrox. He hated the drug but knew it was necessary if he wanted to get back to work. Thankfully, his head cleared in a few minutes.

"How long have I been out?" Rayce asked Gil as he balanced on his own two feet.

"Twelve hours. I'm serious, Rayce. You have to stop playing hero. One of these days, you aren't going to be so lucky."

Rayce grunted. So, this was *lucky*. He nodded thanks to the medic and limped out of the spaceport's med center with a sulking Gil in tow.

"I don't suppose it would do me any good to tell you that you need to rest," Gil mumbled.

Rayce grinned. It was like having his mother aboard.

Suddenly, a giant, black, furry, fifty-kilo beast appeared out of nowhere and ambushed him, knocking him flat against the near wall while licking his face with a fat, wet tongue.

Rayce winced as a new blast of pain shot through his shoulder.

"Down, Elvis," he scolded firmly. The dog obeyed immediately and gave an excited bark wagging his tail with gusto, eyes wide and alert.

Gil shook his head. "Nothing can be *that* happy all the time. Can't you medicate him or something?"

Rayce grinned and scratched the dog's head. "He just needs to grow up a little."

"Grow up?" Gil choked. "He's been doing nothing but growing for the past six months and he still hasn't filled his feet."

"Paws," Rayce corrected. "He's only a year old, still a baby."

"That's the biggest, smelliest, most unruly baby I've ever seen," Gil muttered.

Rayce watched the dog snap his mouth at a bug flying by. "He's learning. He'll settle down in a year or two."

"A year or . . ." Gil gasped and pointed an accusing finger at the dog. "He's going to be like this when we are operational? I don't want to hear it the first time he jumps on a guest and lays them out flat."

"You wouldn't do that, would you boy?" Rayce said to the dog. Elvis wagged his entire rear end in agreement, his whole body gyrating.

Gil looked disgusted. "What kind of name is Elvis, anyway?"

Rayce shrugged. "Tess named him after some Earth singer."

"I still can't believe she dragged that monstrosity off Earth, halfway across the galaxy thinking you couldn't live without him."

"She's a good friend. What was I going to do, refuse?" Rayce grinned at the happy animal. "Besides, he kind of grows on you."

Gil pointed to his boots as if he hadn't heard a single word. "And another thing. We need to talk about this problem of him launching into full-boot-destruct mode. I can't afford to keep replacing mine."

Rayce chuckled and resumed his trip to the office with the dog prancing at his side. "You never know. Maybe that's a great honor in Earth-dog society."

"Very funny," Gil mumbled. They walked in silence for a few seconds before Gil said casually, "By the way, while you were indisposed, I received a communiqué for you."

The door to Rayce's office slid open for them. Rayce headed straight for the lav and shower. "What kind of communiqué?"

Gil took a seat at the office console and Elvis plopped his head up on the table next to him.

"It looks like a job." Then he muttered, "But I don't think you're in any shape to take it on."

"Now, what makes you think that?" Rayce said as he entered the lav. "I feel great."

Gil snorted. "Just because you've got more lives than a samaratt, doesn't mean you're immortal, you know?"

Rayce turned on the spray and muttered, "Believe me, I'm feeling very mortal at the moment." With great care and some silent swearing, Rayce pulled off his clothes and stepped into the shower. He hung his head as the spray of water sloshed over his battered body. Another near-death experience. Gil was right. He had to stop doing this. Precisely the reason this spaceport must open. Legitimate businessmen rarely got their asses kicked.

While the water soothed him, Rayce listened as Gil chattered on about the spaceport, how far behind schedule they were, how short of credits they were, how much more needed to be done. Rayce took a deep breath. If they didn't open for business in two months, he would lose everything. He'd tapped all his sources dry. He needed credits and he needed them fast.

He exited the shower and stood naked under the dryers, letting their warmth caress his body. Already he felt better, his head had cleared and the space sickness had dissipated. The collarbone would take longer.

After pulling on pants, he walked over to where Gil sat at the table with the communiqué displayed before him. Gil turned to Rayce, "Here it is."

Rayce leaned over and read the communication off the Galactic Net.

Would like to meet you to discuss a business proposition. Excellent pay. Confidentiality requested. You may reply to this address with a time and location. No saloons, please.

Majj Van Dye, Majj Institute

"So what's this guy got against saloons?" Gil questioned.

Rayce ignored him and frowned. "Majj Institute."

Gil grimaced. "Yeah. Look, I know they're bastards and all, but we really need the credits, Rayce."

Rayce growled as old, familiar bitterness filled the pit of his stomach. "Forget it, Gil. I don't work for the Majj. I can't believe you even asked."

Gil swung around on the chair to face him. "I asked because we have no choice."

"I'll find the credits some other way," Rayce countered.

Gil shook his head. "No time and no other offers. All our old clients have found new acquisition specialists. And we've got investors and creditors breathing down our necks, a trading spaceport renovated to the point of no return, and families to feed. You aren't the only one hanging here."

Rayce clenched his fists. Unlike most of his prior

projects, he wasn't alone this time. Every person aboard this spaceport had bet on him to pull this venture through.

"Fine. But I'm not smiling," Rayce grumbled.

Gil turned back to the console. "Whatever. Just go easy on the guy. You know those weird geniuses can't function in normal society."

Rayce crossed his arms over his chest. "Right. Us poor *gruners* are too crude for their delicate egos. So, what's a Majj need with me? They never leave that Institute."

Gil smirked. "No kidding. That's cause no one else can understand what the hell they're saying."

"Set up a meeting here," Rayce said. At least he'd be on home territory.

"Done," Gil said, tapping the last of the commands in. "I set a meeting two days from now. That should give him plenty of time to get here."

Gil leaned back in his chair and grinned at Rayce. "Well, at least this sounds like a safe, easy job for a change. You may even finish it without a scratch."

Rayce snorted. "Don't count on it. My acquisition jobs never seem to turn out the way I plan."

Gil shook his head. "Plan. Now there's a word I don't hear you say too often."

"I always have a plan," Rayce shot back indignantly. Well, most of the time it was true.

Gil gave him a look of total disbelief. "Yeah? And how come in all the time I've worked with you, I've never seen one?"

Rayce shrugged. "It changes."

"We gotta work on your definition of a plan," Gil said with a laugh. "You can't run your life on luck.

We were fortunate to survive some of your little adventures."

After a few quiet moments, he added, "Sorry about the Majj, Rayce." Then he brightened and grinned wide. "But at least they're loaded. You might even be able to pay for that new engine."

"We'll see. I have yet to see a Majj bloodsucker part with his credits."

Gil pushed out of the chair and slapped Rayce on his good shoulder. As he headed for the door, he added, "And try not to scare him off. Van Dye is probably some little old man with a bad heart."

After the door slid shut behind Gil, Rayce eased into the chair and read the message one more time.

"I hate this, Elvis," he said. The dog's ears perked up and he gave a soft whimper of sympathy. Rayce absently rubbed the dog's soft head.

The Majj. They touted themselves as the salvation of humankind, the leaders in technological advances. And they accomplished it by selling their discoveries to the highest bidder, regardless of the suffering the *gruners* endured waiting for the innovations.

Under any other circumstances, he would tell the Majj to go to hell. But not today. Today, he needed credits.

Rayce blew out a long breath. By rights, he was a wealthy man. However, at this point he had very little to show for it. Every credit was tied up in resurrecting this old spaceport. Converting it into the sector's only luxury trading spaceport had taken more monetary resources and more time to get rolling than he'd anticipated.

He stood up and walked to the spacious viewport

with its panoramic sweep of deep space. The space-port revolved at a crawl, promising a different star-studded display at every glance. He loved it here, loved planting his two feet on something he con-trolled. For once in his life, to possess something he didn't have to beg, lie or steal for. More than any-thing, he wanted this spaceport to be *his*. He just needed a little more time. The last thing he wanted was for his investors to catch wind that he was run-ning low on funds.

He glanced back at the message and shook his head. It was either a lucky break or the job from hell. Next to the display, Elvis cocked his head at his master and thumped his tail.

"I'll do it, Elvis," Rayce said, turning back to the stars. "But I sure as hell don't have to be happy about it."

Tru frowned as her transport set down with a thud on the landing deck of the old spaceport. The land-ing bay looked like a small bomb had exploded re-cently, and no one had noticed.

The pilot grinned at her, revealing a jagged line of bluish teeth. He chattered rapidly, conveying something she assumed to be, "We're here." She'd spent the last four hours with him and had yet to determine his dialect, despite the fact that she con-sidered herself an expert in the field.

With a blue grin, he sprung out of his seat and headed to the back hatch. Tru grabbed her travel bag, followed him to the back, and exited the trans-port.

The smell of burning metal and lubricants stung her nose. Wires hung from the walls and ceiling above her. She didn't know a lot about spaceports, but she was relatively sure that she wasn't supposed to be seeing bare wiring. A horrendous screeching noise emanated from within the craft, the unmistakable sound of metal grinding metal. Tru blew out a breath.

"I guess I should have been content with the saloon," she muttered.

"Can I help you?"

Tru turned to the reedy voice. A tall, lanky man approached, bobbing as he walked. Red hair, long face, no chin. Definitely not Coburne.

He stopped in front of the pilot expectantly. Tru cleared her throat and stepped forward. "I am Tru Van Dye. I'm expected."

His mouth dropped as he looked at her face, then at the pilot, then to her body, then back to her face. Obviously, she wasn't what he was expecting.

He recovered from whatever crisis he was having and grinned. "Gil. Rayce's partner. Nice to meet you. This way." He swept a hand toward the exit.

She turned to the pilot and whispered, "Stay here and don't leave until I notify you."

The diminutive man nodded enthusiastically about a dozen times, smiling all the while. Tru figured he hadn't understood a word she'd said.

She hiked the bag over her shoulder. About halfway across the landing bay, she caught up with Gil's long stride. They turned down a wide corridor and headed toward the center of the spaceport.

He waved a hand around the disaster and said, "Sorry for the mess. We are in the middle of renovations."

Tru smiled and nodded. Yes, she could see that.

She also knew that renovations cost credits. That much she was counting on. What she didn't expect was the room that Gil led her into. She stopped dead and pulled a long breath. *Oh my*. What a beautiful place—all mirrors and silver metal. Shards protruded from the ceiling and walls, so well-placed that the space itself changed with every step she took. A living, breathing room.

A screeching wail from a far corner forced her to cover her ears. She watched Gil cross the room and approach a man in heavy coveralls, welding a grinder. The man lifted the shield over his face and they talked for a few seconds. Then the man turned to her.

His eyes met hers and she felt it exactly as she had in the VirtuWav—sudden panic mixed with uninvited anticipation. And those blue-green eyes, so dazzling, they drilled into her, through her. She gave him a small smile but he didn't return it. In fact, he didn't look particularly happy to see her at all.

Never taking his gaze off her, he set down the grinder and released the fasteners of the coveralls. They dropped around him, revealing a bare chest and pants. A bandage covered his left shoulder. Muscles, skin, everything was a blur as she realized he was walking toward her.

She licked her lips. *Physical. Definitely physical.*

"Rayce Coburne," he said curtly. Tru blinked at the familiar drawl. Noa would be happy to know that he got the voice perfect.

"Tru Van Dye," she responded and waited for the rest of the words to follow. However, the whole mind-mouth coordination effort had stalled. He appeared much different than in the VirtuWav. With his hands resting on his hips, no shirt, all that skin and muscle, he looked even more uncivilized, dangerous and, unfortunately for her, very distracting.

"I'm early," she babbled and winced. Now there was a professional opening.

He crossed his arms, studying her. "No problem. I like surprises."

She frowned. She didn't.

"We can discuss your business in my office," he said as he turned and walked out of the room, leaving her and Gil standing there. She stared after him. *How positively rude.* The man obviously had *no* manners. This was not the reaction she was expecting from Coburne, certainly not based on the hands-all-over-her, give-me-your-body VirtuWav exercise.

She glanced at Gil, who smiled at her weakly and nodded toward the exit. Tru pursed her lips and preceded Gil down the long, empty corridor. She'd planned for everything. Everything. Had done her usual thorough research. Something definitely wasn't right. She wished she knew what it was she'd missed.

Rayce showed Tru into his office with Gil following, and the door slid shut behind them. He waved a hand to the table in the center of the room.

With willowy grace, she walked over and took a seat. He shook his head. Gotta love those Majj Institute uniforms—nothing but a silver second skin from neck to ankles. It was a damn miracle they got anything done.

Long legs, high breasts, slender hips, silky blonde hair knotted tightly to her head, but he could tell

C. J. Barry

there was a lot of it. Tall, sleek, built for speed. Just like his ship.

He grabbed a shirt off a nearby chair and put it on, aware that she was watching him intently. The rest of him might be miserable but at least his ego was happy.

He took a seat next to Gil across from her and tried not to stare at those smoky gray eyes, the full lips, and the face of a classic beauty.

He slanted a glance at Gil, who lifted an eyebrow in response. *So much for the old man with a bad heart.* She didn't fit any Majj stereotype, physically. But a Majj was a Majj and it didn't matter if she was an old man or drop-dead gorgeous. They were all equally ugly on the inside.

"So what can I help you with?" Rayce asked.

She tapped a perfect fingernail on the table. She cast Gil a worried look. "You realize this must remain absolutely confidential."

Gil looked at him but he already had a hand up. "*Everything* we handle is confidential."

She took a deep, deliberate breath. "I have a rather unusual quest. I need immediate transport and a guide."

Rayce stilled.

"I generally work alone," he said tightly.

Gil kicked him under the table.

Rayce grimaced and gritted out, "But I suppose I can make an exception in this case. To where?"

She shifted in her chair. "The city of Jabe Ku on Curzon."

Gil groaned for all of them and leaned forward. "I'm sorry to tell you this, but Curzon isn't exactly the most friendly place for outsiders."

30

Tru swung her gaze to him. "I know. That's why I need a guide."

"More like a bodyguard," Gil muttered, rubbing his head.

Rayce added, "Outsiders are considered pests to the Curzons. Unwelcome, abused or worse. It's dangerous territory."

Tru challenged him. "Are you telling me that you are afraid to take me there?"

Rayce grinned at her. "I guess that depends on how much you pay me."

She licked her lips and he watched the pink tongue disappear. Damn, if it wasn't the outfit, it was something else.

"30,000 credits up front, plus expenses. I can give you verification of funds."

Gil sucked in a breath next to him and Rayce knew why. 30,000 credits was a lot, even for a jaunt to Curzon. Enough to cover payroll this cycle. But he wasn't biting just yet, no matter how many times Gil kicked him.

He leaned toward her. "So I get you onto Curzon, then what?"

"I run a test to verify a hypothesis," she stated. "It shouldn't take more than a few minutes."

Rayce's eyebrows went up. *A test*. Now this was getting interesting. "What kind of test?" he asked.

She donned a faint pout. "Nothing dangerous, I assure you."

He grinned and crossed his arms. "You'd be surprised how often I hear that. I'll need something a little more specific."

"I want access to the pyramid at Landwehr Square."

Rayce squinted his eyes. "How much access?"

She tapped a fingernail on the table as if she were growing tired of his questions. Too bad.

"I need to climb it."

Gil burst out laughing. Rayce gaped at her. Now, who would have thought, by looking at her, that she was crazy?

Tru never took her eyes off him. "I know it sounds unusual, but I'm working on a very significant theory."

Rayce couldn't help himself. "What the hell kind of theory involves climbing a giant pyramid in the busiest section of Curzon?"

She pursed her lips. "I can't give you any more information than that until I run the test. If my theory works, then we can negotiate for whatever the rest of this mission entails."

At the mention of potentially more credits, Gil stopped laughing.

"Sixty thousand credits," Rayce said, narrowing his eyes.

She didn't even hesitate. "Agreed."

Chapter Three

As she expected, the transport driver was gone when she returned to the landing bay. Her gear was stacked haphazardly in a pile. Tru blew out a breath. Why did she have the feeling that she was trapped in the predator's den?

Gil reached for the two bags and hefted them easily. "I'll show you to your room. It'll take Rayce some time to arrange entry onto Curzon for the two of you."

Tru picked up the last small bag and fell into step beside him as they entered the corridor. "And then what?"

"You'll take Rayce's transport to the planet," Gil replied. They stepped into a lift and Gil gave the computer their destination.

She frowned. "Just the two of us?"

Gil shrugged. "It's a small ship. It'll accommodate two people but only needs one pilot. Is it a problem?"

33

Tru stared straight ahead. "I get the feeling he'd rather work alone."

Gil grinned. "He's a bit of a loner, yes. But at least having you along should keep him out of trouble."

Tru frowned. She didn't like the sound of that. And she didn't believe him. There was more to it. Coburne had a problem with *her*. A personal problem. She could feel it.

They exited the room into a glorious corridor. Tru nearly lost a step. This level was a striking contrast to the unfinished rooms she'd seen on the last level.

"Here are your quarters." Gil stepped aside to let her enter the room first. The first thing she noticed was the bouquet of flowers, arranged in a beautiful green vase. Behind it, a great expanse of deep space and stars in the floor-to-ceiling, wall-to-wall viewport, more beautiful than any mural. She absorbed the rest of the room's luxury accommodations: The hues of blue, the perfect proportions made the room a work of art in itself.

"Who designed your interiors?"

Gil smiled. "I did. Like it?"

She turned to him in amazement. "You're very good."

He blushed. "Thanks." Then he brightened. "Do you want a tour of the place? There's nothing like this spaceport in the whole sector. We'll have galleys, recreation areas, spas, shops, VirtuWav banks, the gardens—"

She blurted, "You have gardens?"

Gil grinned. "An entire section of Level Two. Flowers for the rooms and greens for the restaurants."

"I'd love to see it," Tru said with reverence. Then she frowned. "You don't kill off the imperfect plants, do you?"

Gil looked surprised. "Why would I do that?"

Tru gave a sigh of relief. "Wonderful. When do I get my tour?"

"I'll give the tour." A sharp voice cut in.

Tru spun around to find Rayce propped up against the open doorframe. He regarded her coolly. Her smile stayed. Damned if she was going to let him intimidate her.

And she would have stayed cool if a big, barreling fur ball of a creature hadn't come hurtling at her at that moment, all muscle and strength and black as deep space. Her entire body froze as a broad head and chest, wide snout, big ears, big teeth, big everything skidded to a stop in front of her just before he shoved his nose into her crotch.

She pushed him aside. Her hand came back covered with saliva. Tru asked Rayce. "What is it?"

He wore a smug grin. "Canine dog, a Black Labrador from Earth. Meet Elvis."

Hearing his name, the beast immediately let out a sharp, loud yelp. Then looking pathologically happy, he made himself at home by planting himself on the floor next to her feet and leaning all his weight against her leg. He looked up at her with a long, wet tongue hanging out of his mouth. Although he was huge and clumsy and far too friendly, he appeared mostly harmless. Except for the big teeth. And the tiny brain.

Tru stepped to the side. The dog moved with her. "How do you get rid of it?" she asked.

Gil huffed. "Good luck. When you find a way, let

me know." He smiled at Tru. "I'll see you at dinner."

Then he left the room, whispering something to Rayce as he passed by. Rayce just stared at her. She stared back. Elvis drooled on her foot. Well, this was wonderful.

"I got us an entry pass onto Curzon. It's a one-day trip each way. We leave tomorrow morning." He shoved off the door and approached her. As the door slid shut behind him, she fought the urge to run. With Gil gone, she could feel the full brunt of what she'd only sensed during the meeting. Tension. No, not tension. Anger, directed at her. What did she ever do to him? She was paying him well, so what was his problem?

She crossed her arms. Now *she* was angry.

"Thank you. I assume you also checked my account?"

Rayce stopped in front of her and grinned.

"I did," he replied. "Now we have to discuss a few rules."

Rules? Who said anything about rules? This was *her* mission.

"What kind of rules?" she asked slowly.

"The kind that I give when I don't know what my client is getting into," he responded. "I usually work alone. But now I have you, so we have to have rules."

She glared at him. "Does one of these rules have anything to do with being civil?"

He crossed his arms like hers. "No. You picked the wrong man for that."

"So tell me," she asked with growing impatience.

"If you dislike me so much, why did you take this job?"

He shrugged. "I need the credits. Why did you choose me?"

She muttered under her breath. "Short list."

He stepped up to her, his blue-green eyes blazing. She could feel the control he was exerting, holding something back. What?

His voice was low. "I'm serious. There are a lot of men out there who do acquisitions. Why me?"

She seethed. He was as relentless as that damn dog. "I did my research. Based on your previous dealings, you seem to be well-respected and trusted by your clients. You've never failed to deliver a product. A perfect record. Satisfied?"

He flashed a predatory smile. "What? Nothing about my rakish good looks and devastating charm?"

"No." She smiled sweetly. "I see why, now."

He smirked at that. "I did some research, too. Can't seem to find a thing on you."

She stiffened. "We tend to keep a low profile at the Institute."

"Uh-huh," he said, obviously not happy with her answer, even though it was the truth. The Institute had its own short list.

He narrowed his eyes. "Here are the rules. You do exactly what I say, when I say, with no questions asked. Once we reach Curzon, you don't leave my side, you don't wander off, you don't talk to anyone. Don't even make eye contact."

Her mouth dropped at his audacity.

His eyebrows went up in warning. "It's either follow the rules or find someone else. And I guarantee that you won't find another guide crazy enough to take you to Curzon."

He wasn't going to make this easy. Damn, she needed to get to that pyramid and she didn't have time to find another guide.

"And I've got a rule of my own," she countered.

A corner of his mouth kicked up. "You can try."

She nearly smacked him. Instead, she blurted out, "Don't touch me."

She was almost as surprised as he was. Where did that come from? And then she knew. The VirtuWav. *Oh, damn. This was becoming a worse disaster than the exercise.*

He drew back, regarding her with open disbelief. Then she watched the rapid transformation to hatred once again.

"I forget that us *gruners* aren't good enough for a Majj."

She blinked at him. What was he talking about?

"No, that's not—"

He raised a hand, cutting her off. "Don't worry. I won't even get close."

She wanted to tell him that he'd misunderstood her, but his bitter expression stopped her. A quiet resolve stole over her. Let him think what he wanted. What did she care? Obviously, they weren't going to be friends for life.

"Will there be anything else?" she asked, wanting nothing more than to be left alone. Already she was dreading the prospect of being trapped in a small transport with him for any length of time.

"One more thing." He scanned her critically. "You can't wear a Majj uniform on Curzon. We'll need to be as inconspicuous as possible."

She lifted her chin. "I don't *have* anything else to wear."

His eyes met hers and a slow smile crossed his face. "No problem. I'll take care of everything."

As he turned and left, she realized that's exactly what she was afraid of.

Over his shoulder with the beast in tow, he said, "I'll come back in thirty minutes for that tour. Be ready."

Tru glared at the door after they had exited, trying to figure out exactly when and where she had lost control of *her* mission.

She tossed her bag on the bed, sat down beside it and rubbed her temples. She should have listened to Noa, should have found a few more names. It was too late now. For some unknown reason, Rayce hated her. She couldn't think of a single reason why. And why did he call himself a *gruner*? What was all that about?

She reached into her bag for her personal datapad and pushed a preset. Seconds later, Noa's gaunt face appeared in the window.

"Greetings, Tru." He seemed relieved to see her whole.

"Greetings, Noa. Miss me?"

He grinned. "You're my only friend, remember?"

Tru laughed. "I can always count on you to make me feel appreciated. It looks like our two-way comm units work fine. Are you sure no one can pick us up?"

Noa snorted. "You forget who you are talking to, my dear. Creating a perfectly secure channel using multi-phase shift transponders is child's play." The old man grinned. "So how did your meeting go with Coburne?"

Tru gave him her brightest smile. "I'm on my way to Curzon."

Noa's eyes widened, his expression dropped. "I thought you were going to give the plate to Coburne and he would go alone? Curzon is no place for you, Tru. Do you have any idea how Curzons feel about outsiders?"

Tru held up her hand. "I know. It's only for a few days."

"A few days!" Noa gasped. "You planned this all along, didn't you?"

Tru winced. "I'm sorry, Noa. I can't trust Coburne with the plate. It's too valuable."

"I knew I shouldn't have forged your egress off the Institute," Noa muttered. Then he gave her a sharp look. "I only got you a two-day pass, Tru. Two days. You were supposed to meet with Coburne, send him on his way and come back. Do you know how much trouble you are going to be in with the administrators? You know the rules about leaving the Institute."

"I understand the rules. I have no choice."

Noa sighed deeply in resignation. "Is all this worth it? You couldn't find an easier project?"

"Noa, if I come back to the Majj Institute with the Curzon Collection, I'll be guaranteed a permanent Charter. They would never turn that down."

"And if you don't find the Collection?" Noa asked.

"Then I won't come back," Tru said simply. "My Majj career will be over. I don't have time to research another project before next year."

"You'll be banned from the Institute," he said bluntly.

"Yes," Tru replied. Worse than banned—excommunicated and humiliated. The disassociation process was horrendous, stripping a Majj of everything that meant anything. A fate worse than death.

For a few moments, Noa said nothing. "Then find the Curzon Collection." His expression softened. "Find it and make yourself a name. I'll cover for you as long as I can."

Tru smiled. "Thank you, Noa."

"Yeah, yeah," he mumbled. "But you must keep a low profile, Tru. I mean it. If the administrators find out you are loose, they'll have my head as well as yours."

Tru bristled. "Don't do that for me. I won't have you ruined for my sake."

He grunted. "I'm an old man. What are they going to do to me?"

Tru flinched. She didn't even want to consider that.

Then another thought struck her. "Noa, have you ever heard of the term *gruner* used at the Institute or in the archives?"

His expression changed to confusion. "*Gruner*? No, can't recall that term anywhere. Why?"

She shook her head. "I'm not sure. Coburne used it to describe himself. It must be a slang term."

Noa agreed. "So how close is the real Coburne to my program?"

Tru clenched the datapad, recalling Coburne's heat in the VirtuWav and his icy reaction here.

"He looks exactly as he did in your program."

She gave him a wide smile. "So, how are my plants?"

"Alive, but don't be gone too long." Noa frowned deeply. "I don't think they like me."

Tru laughed. "Noa, they're plants, not people. They can't like or dislike you."

"Well, they seem to be changing color," he looked back at her hopelessly.

Tru grimaced. "I'll contact you again after Curzon."

"Safe travels, Tru."

She signed off and tossed the comm unit on a nearby table. She fell back on the bed and stared at the ceiling. This whole project had seemed much smaller and simpler when she planned it on Koameron.

And the VirtuWav exercise, what a waste *that* had been. No help whatsoever. If Coburne had any heat in him, she'd never see it. Not that she wanted to, but she'd prefer heat to what she was getting now. How could Noa have been so far off? Perhaps it wasn't Noa's program, maybe it was her. Maybe Coburne didn't like her demeanor or the way she looked or dressed. He certainly wasn't about to kiss her. At least she didn't have to worry about that. She stopped short.

"I don't believe this," she muttered under her breath. She was obsessing about a simulated kiss from a simulated man in a simulated world. There was a first . . . and last.

Tru sat up and reached back into the bag for a soft pouch the size of her hand. She slipped the heavy, square plate from the pouch and felt its familiar hum in her hand. She wrapped her fingers around it. Such a simple little piece. Who would guess it was the key to the entire mission?

She placed it back into its case and tucked the pouch beneath her belongings. She was on her way and that's all that mattered. She'd deal with Coburne's attitude and any other obstacles in her way.

There really was no other choice.

She was well past the point of no return.

Rayce walked into Gil's office and slammed the datapad on the table. At his computer, Gil jumped half a meter. Elvis put his tail between his legs and hid under the table.

Gil glanced up at Rayce. "What's *your* problem?"

Rayce dropped into a chair and set his feet up on the office table. "Nothing. Things couldn't be better."

Gil's eyebrows went up. "This wouldn't happen to have anything to do with our new client?"

Rayce glared at him. Gil raised a hand.

"Hey, I'm just trying to figure out what you are so mad about. You get to spend two days, maybe more, alone with a gorgeous, intelligent woman who's paying you an obscene amount of credits to escort her around the sector. Tell me where the problem is."

"If you think it's so great, why don't you take her?" Rayce drawled.

Gil laughed. "Oh yes, my Amaii would love that. Besides, Tru wants you. Don't ask me why, considering your lousy manners."

"Nothing wrong with my manners," Rayce replied. "I just don't choose to use them."

"Well, *I* think you're annoyed because you finally

met a woman who can resist you," Gil said with a snicker.

"I wouldn't touch a Majj if you promised to finish this station on time."

"Well, Majj or not, she's a good client, Rayce. Don't blow it. This job could have a big payoff. She didn't even flinch at 60,000 credits."

Rayce sighed and crossed his arms. "I know. I'll be a good boy." He glanced at Gil. "Are you going to be able to hold things together here while I'm gone? It could be a while, depending on whatever crazy theory she's got in mind."

Gil nodded. "I can handle a few nosy investors. Levels Three through Five look pretty decent. I can give them a token tour to keep them fat and happy. You just keep those credits coming."

"She's hiding something," Rayce said after a few silent seconds.

Gil continued his work. "Can't argue with you there."

"I plan on finding out what on the way to Curzon," Rayce said firmly. In fact, he was looking forward to that particular part of the mission.

Gil shrugged. "So maybe she's hiding something. Everyone has secrets." Then he turned to look at Rayce, lifting an eyebrow. "I've known you for ten years and you never did tell me what you have against the Majj."

Rayce set his jaw. "Not a thing."

Gil gave a snort of a laugh. "Right. I've never seen you act like this before, especially with a beautiful woman. I know the Majj are a little eccentric and over-priced and greedy but hey, everyone's greedy these days."

"It's more than simple greed. We are talking lives, here. They don't care about anything except filling their vaults," Rayce hissed. Then he glanced at Gil's concerned expression and blew out a long breath. He was going to have to control himself. "Don't worry. I won't let it get in the way of the job."

Gil nodded and turned back to his station. "If I were you, I wouldn't dump Tru in with all the other Majj. She seems like a real nice lady to me."

Rayce laughed cynically. "Don't let her act fool you. All Majj are the same. Credits rule."

He glanced under the table to find Elvis looking up at him. Rayce smiled. Watching Tru sidestep, dodge and generally try to shake the unshakeable animal during the spaceport tour had been worth the effort. He'd bet it took a lot to rattle a Majj.

Rayce stood and headed toward the door. "If you need me, I'll be in my office."

Gil looked after him. "Getting ready for Curzon?"

Rayce glanced over his shoulder. "No. I'm going to do some more digging on our new client."

Tru would be forever grateful to Gil for agreeing to join her and Rayce for dinner. She was equally grateful that the dog-beast was not dining with them. There was something very unnerving about an animal sniffing around your body parts while you were trying to eat. She'd bet that Coburne had purposely brought the animal along on the tour just to fluster her. Fat chance. Van Dyes didn't fluster.

She glanced over at Rayce to find him watching her again and she returned to her meal. He'd hardly

45

spoken, apparently content on scrutinizing her to distraction, much as he'd done during the spaceport tour. And what a tour it was. She hated to admit it, but she'd never imagined such an ambitious undertaking. Nothing in her research on him had prepared her for the sheer scope of this project or how very much involved with it he was. There was no doubt in her mind that although Gil was his partner, this was Rayce's dream.

Even with his surly attitude, she could hear the pride in his voice as he showed her the place that would be an all-encompassing trading post and gambling center. The plans were well thought out, capable of accommodating a variety of humans and near-humanoids with luxurious rooms, spacious trading halls, and entertainment of every sort. Even the restaurants would be first-rate.

It was a magnificent project. Rayce was proud, and rightly so. Who would have imagined that he could have these kinds of aspirations? Certainly not her. But there it was, each room more spectacular and unique than the last. No wonder he needed so much capital. Nothing was less than first-rate. This was going to be no ordinary trading post.

And the gardens. She gave a silent sigh. Stunning, wild, chaotic with plants barely kept within their borders. More blossoms than she'd ever seen in one place piled on top of each other, rambling freely and happily. A perfectly eclectic and blissful garden. Even the dog loved it. Maybe he wasn't as brainless as she thought.

"So this is your first time off Koameron?" Gil asked her, chewing on a mouthful of food.

She smiled at him seated across from her. "Yes.

We are able to conduct all of our research and development at the Institute regardless of specialty."

Gil nodded. "So what's your specialty?"

"Alien cultures," she answered.

Gil stopped chewing and frowned. "Alien cultures. That must be kind of tough if you don't travel much."

She laughed lightly. "Very perceptive. Luckily, the Institute's computer archives are quite extensive. But I'm very excited for the chance to see first-hand what I've spent years studying."

"How many years?" Gil asked between bites.

"I've been the research analyst for my father since I was ten," Tru replied. "His specialty was economics—domestic and foreign. I never saw a man so passionate about his work. He worked constantly, almost non-stop for the past forty years."

Gil stuffed another morsel into his mouth. "Huh. Ten? You must be pretty smart."

She smirked. "Convenient, actually. My father completed many major projects, some of which weren't in his specialty. I picked up those, learning the field as I went."

"Interesting," Gil nodded. "Don't you think so, Rayce?"

She turned to Rayce and waited. He considered her for a moment before answering. "Fascinating."

Tru drew a deep breath. It was going to be a very long, very quiet trip to Curzon.

She gave Gil a smile. "The meal is excellent. My compliments to your galley crew."

He grinned wide. "Wait until we get a full staff in here. We'll have the finest restaurants in the sector."

"I believe you." She pushed her plate back and stood up. "Well, tomorrow is a busy day. If you'll excuse me, I will retire."

To her dismay, Rayce pushed back his chair and stood with her. "I'll escort you."

She bristled, meeting his stunning eyes over the width of the table. "That's not necessary. I'm perfectly capable of finding my room."

He gave her a predatory grin that sent a little shiver down her spine. He was already around the table and by her side.

"I'm heading that way myself."

Tru tried but she couldn't think of another way to shake him. "In that case, good night, Gil."

Gil looked from her to Rayce and back again. "Yeah, sure."

Rayce put a hand to her back and turned her toward the door. The heat of his warm hand on her back stopped her cold. Their eyes locked—hers in panic, his in surprise. Then he abruptly withdrew his hand, the old irritation returning in a flash.

She tried to say something but no words formed. A great time for her brain to quit on her.

"You first," he said coolly, stepping away from her.

Tru led the way, the doors opening and closing automatically for them. Next to her, he walked silently, brooding. She thought she had sensed him loosen up a little during the tour and dinner. But it was gone now. Three days of this. She'd never survive.

Just as she was about to enter the safety of her room, Rayce's hand closed around her arm. She froze in place as he pulled her to a stop and moved near, his eyes holding her hostage. His scent rolled over her, flooding her senses.

"You should know that my ship is small," he said softly.

She wasn't sure if that was a statement or a forewarning. "Yes?"

"We may bump into each other once in a while."

He was so close, just like he'd been in the VirtuWav. But he was sober now—serious and infinitely more dangerous. His eyes locked on hers and the heat she'd experienced in the VirtuWav swept over her. It was her, not him, she was sure. How could her body betray her like this? He didn't even *like* her.

His gaze dropped to her parted lips and her breath came out in little puffs. She should say something, anything to escape. Instead, her body was singing, exposing her vulnerability.

"Okay."

His eyebrows went up at her strangled response. Tru's eyes widened in dismay. Clumsily, she stepped out of his grasp and bumped against the wall behind her.

"I understand the situation. It shouldn't be a problem," she amended with as much dignity as she had left in her. She stepped in front of the door, it opened and she backed into her room. "Good night."

His hands were on his hips, his gaze intent as the door closed between them.

Rayce stood outside her room for a few minutes, trying to figure out what *that* was all about. He turned and headed toward his office.

He could have sworn she looked scared to death.

Why? He hadn't done a thing to intimidate her. He stepped into the lift and gave the computer his destination. Well, maybe he'd intimidated her a little, but he wasn't going to play games onboard *Miranda*. The ship *was* small. They *would* bump into each other. He wasn't about to apologize every time he touched her.

The lift doors opened and he made his way to the office. She wasn't what he expected, but that didn't mean that when it came right down to it she wasn't a Majj through and through. They all worked toward one goal—to make the greatest profit on every discovery.

And she was even more guilty. Thanks to some creative breaking and entering into the Majj Institute's computer archives today, he'd finally found something on her. Or rather, on her father. Sashel Van Dye had been the most influential principal in the Institute's history. Responsible for shaping much of the economic and financial policies in the past thirty years. Responsible for keeping the discoveries from the hands of those who needed them most. Responsible for countless deaths in doing so.

And as his assistant, Tru Van Dye had helped him. She'd admitted to that tonight. Except for her name listed as Sashel's daughter, Tru Van Dye didn't exist. Nor did most of the Majj. They had no individual identities, instead living under one umbrella. He'd only uncovered a few names, all of them high-profile members. He knew there had to be thousands of them living at that Institute. It was as if the Majj were one, cold, driven entity that lived on and on.

Rayce stalked into his office. He'd finish this trip

to Curzon and that would be it. He'd seen her account. She didn't have enough credits to make it worthwhile for him to continue whatever crazy ideas she came up with. And there wasn't another damn thing she could offer him to make him change his mind.

His comm unit beeped softly.

"Yes?"

It was a deep, booming voice that answered, "So how're the ladies treating you, son?"

Rayce gazed at his father through the comm viewer. The man hadn't changed in ten years, still grinning, still youthful under the gray-shot black hair and brilliant blue eyes. And as usual, Quin Coburne got right to the important stuff. "Fine. You?"

"Eh, your mother can't get enough of me."

Rayce shook his head and laughed. "You wish."

"Yeah, I do," his father chuckled. "But what can I say, I'm crazy about her. She's been pestering me to check on you."

Rayce took a seat at the table and leaned back so his father could see him better. "Tell her I'm fine."

"I always do."

Rayce nodded. "So how's business these days?"

"Oh, we get by."

Rayce tried not to frown. He knew what that meant. Time to send his mother a small infusion of credits. Unlike his father, she'd know how to use it wisely. He only wished it were more. Enough so his parents could retire like they were supposed to at their age before the hours at the family business killed them. Especially after he'd left them to fend for themselves.

Rayce said, "That's good. And the rest of our relatives?"

" 'Bout the same. Births, funerals, it all evens out. How's that spaceport of yours coming along?"

Rayce cast a quick glance around at his point-of-no-return work-in-process and lied, "It's almost finished." And changed the subject. "Don't tell Mother, but I'll be out of touch for a few days. I have a quick job to do."

"Oh? Thought you were out of that line for good."

He shrugged, "I can always use the extra funds. Besides, this is an easy one."

"Uh-huh. And how is that?"

"My client just needs a guide to take her to Curzon."

His father's dark eyebrows went up. "Really? A woman?"

Rayce groused. "And she's coming with me."

There was a pause. "Not Gil?"

"And she's a Majj." Rayce gritted out the last word.

"Interesting."

Rayce scowled at his father. "Did you hear me? I said she's a Majj."

His father replied, "I heard you. What is she doing off the Institute? They stick pretty close to home. In fact, I've never heard of a Majj leaving that Institute of his own free will. So, is she pretty?"

Rayce leaned forward. "She's a *Majj*."

His father sighed loudly. "Rayce, the Majj didn't kill Miranda."

Rayce swallowed the bitter taste of old memories. "Like hell they didn't."

His father's voice lowered. "It wasn't the Majj's fault that we didn't have the credits for her treatment."

"It was *their* treatment and *they* held it up in pricing negotiations with the planet leaders while our people died. I'd call that their fault."

His father shook his head. "Bad timing, Rayce. We did get it eventually."

"Too late. Too late to save Miranda," Rayce snapped.

"I know. But no one said life is fair. You can't let anger control you," his father replied.

"Nothing and no one controls me."

"Maybe. Only problem with that is you don't end up with anything worthwhile. Let it go, Rayce."

"I can't. No one cares that she's dead."

"That's not true." His father's voice broke a little and he looked away.

Rayce rubbed his face with his hands and exhaled hard. He shouldn't be doing this to an old man who understood full well what grief was. "I know. I didn't mean it that way. I miss her."

His father nodded. "We all do. So, does this Majj have a name?"

Rayce blinked at the quick subject change. "Tru Van Dye."

His father looked intrigued. "Van Dye. That sounds familiar."

"It should. Her father was the head administrator for thirty years."

"Ah yes, you're right. She must be one smart woman. Pretty?"

Rayce reached for a nearby bottle of Safin. "Gorgeous, actually."

"Is she good company?"

He poured himself a drink. "When she's not trying to tell me what to do."

"Ah. I like her already. When do we meet her?"

Rayce nearly choked on his first sip. "You don't. We complete her mission and she's gone."

"I see. So I take it you aren't attracted to her?"

"No."

His father chuckled. "Well then, that would be a first."

Rayce drained his glass. "You know, I wish I was half as lucky with women as everyone seems to think I am. I'd be delirious."

Quin gave a booming laugh. "Don't expect me to feel sorry for you. Besides, you only need one woman to make you happy."

Rayce shook his head. "Yeah, well I'm not looking. I've got a business to open in two months."

"Do you think that business will make you happy?"

Rayce glanced at the bottle of Safin and then pushed it away. "Believe me, I'll be the happiest man alive if I ever get this place opened."

His father gave a long hmmm. "And then what?"

Rayce stared at his father for a moment and felt suddenly very tired. "I'll let you know when I get there."

Chapter Four

Tru walked through the back hatch door into the large cargo bay and then stepped into the crew section of Rayce's ship and stopped dead. He'd warned her that *Miranda* was small. What he'd failed to mention was that it was impossibly small. There was no way that this ship was built for two people.

She snaked her way through machinery and equipment, past what she assumed to be a lav and tiny galley and between twin consoles that ran the length of the living quarters to the cockpit and two seats. Everywhere she looked, lights and controls blinked back at her. There wasn't a spare centimeter anywhere.

She closed her eyes. This trip was going to be insufferable.

Rayce boarded behind her, carrying several bags and pouches, including her small bag. He moved through the ship easily despite his size. She stood in the narrow aisle and watched him stuff the bags into walls, cabinets and only heaven-knew-where, because she certainly didn't.

He looked at her suddenly, catching her mid-stare. "I packed some clothing for you. I assume you brought everything else you need."

She nodded, feeling suddenly suffocated. He blocked the exit completely. The ship was suddenly too small, too closed up, too warm. And he was too damned substantial.

Rayce frowned at her. "Are you all right?"

Tru swallowed, fighting back her misgivings. "I'm fine. When do we leave?"

"Now." He slammed a cabinet shut and locked it down. "Take the seat on the right and strap yourself in."

Tru slid into the seat. Straight ahead, the shuttle bay doors opened, revealing star-studded space. She concentrated on it, trying to push aside the flood of helplessness she felt. She suddenly became very aware of her situation. Trapped in a small ship for twenty-two hours with a very large, very rude man and absolutely nothing to do. And that was just the first leg.

Rayce dropped into the seat next to her, strapped down and began the launch sequence. She watched in fascination as his big hands flowed over the controls with such familiarity. He had nice hands, large but not unwieldy. Long fingers . . .

They stopped.

She snapped her gaze to his as he looked back at her intently.

"You aren't strapped in," he said evenly.

She stared into his dazzling eyes fringed by black hair, not more than a meter from her, and felt the heat rise in her cheeks. Then she quickly looked down and wrestled with her harness. Why was it every time she got caught in his eyes, she became a complete idiot? All that education, all that intellect, reduced to inept fool with one look.

Thankfully, the harness clicked together. Then Rayce's hand was on the center strap, just below her breasts. Tru sucked in a breath and held it as he yanked hard on the harness.

"Just checking," he said when she turned to him.

"Warn me next time you do that," she said, finally exhaling.

"I warned you last night," he drawled. "You said it shouldn't be a problem."

She hated it when he drawled. She glared at him in some semblance of protest but he was already busy talking to Gil on the comm.

Then the engines whined, the ship lifted off the floor, shot past the shuttle bay doors and out into deep space.

The entire galaxy lay before them in all its beauty. Tru smiled slowly. This part, she'd never tire of. After spending her entire life on Koameron, deep space intrigued her more than anything. There was something very significant about feeling part of the big, wide universe.

Then without warning, the small ship spun upside down and around in a tight spiral. Tru gripped the armrests and gasped loudly. The ship then dove, twisted, dove again, and spun. After a full minute of impossible maneuvers, she had no idea whether they were upside down or right side up, nothing to gauge their position against. Then, just as suddenly, the ride flattened out. All she could hear was her heart pounding in her ears.

She turned and pinned Rayce with a glare. "What the hell was that all about?"

He was grinning now, working the console. "Just wanted to see what kind of stomach you have."

Before she could respond, her head snapped back, and the stars streaked by them as the small spacecraft jumped to hyperspace. She stared out the viewport until there was nothing to look at.

"That wasn't funny," she finally said, gritting her teeth. Not a good way to begin a mission. Of course, it wasn't like it had been that great up until now.

She heard Rayce unstrap himself and looked over. He was facing her, one arm resting on the back of his chair, the other on the console in front of him. His eyes were locked on hers with enough intensity to make her flinch.

"Now," he said, very softly. "I want the rest of your story."

He could tell he'd surprised her, could see the shock in her face. She'd never make a good gambler, couldn't lie, at least not to him. That was to his advantage. He was very good at finding advantages.

"I don't know what you mean," she said and licked her lips.

Lie.

One corner of his mouth kicked up and he leaned into her, just because he could. "I want to know what you left out back there at our first meeting. All of it, lady. Or this is going to be one very short mission."

"Do you treat all your clients this way?"

"You're changing the subject."

"Damn right." Her face was flush with color, anger making her even more striking than she already was. He wasn't blind. He knew a beauty when he saw one.

She raised her chin. "Even if I told you, you wouldn't believe me."

"I hear a lot of crazy stories in my line of work. Try me."

For a long time, she just studied him. He could almost see her brain working. A bad sign. She probably never did a thing without analyzing it first, considering all the angles, preparing for all the possibilities. Bet she had a plan for everything. No wonder she and Gil got along so well.

"I need to get my bag from the back," she said finally.

He paused and then leaned back just far enough to let her out. She slid out of her seat, very careful not to brush against him but close enough so he caught a whiff of a subtle perfume. He inhaled sharply. It rocked him, woke him. He shook it off. One sniff—pathetic. He'd been celibate for too long.

Rayce released both seats so they swiveled toward the back, the position they'd stay in until twenty-two hours from now when he brought them out of hyperspace. He ordered the table up. A round circle rose from the floor between the chairs. Then he watched Tru rifle through her bag.

She was concentrating, he could tell by the little crease between her eyebrows. He'd never seen such perfect skin—ivory, clear, probably very soft and supple. And a lot of it. She was nearly as tall as he was, but those legs seemed to go forever. The silver uniform left little to the imagination although his was working pretty hard. *Damn*, he shook his head. *Forget it. A Majj, of all people.*

She returned, her hips negotiating the tight quarters gracefully, but he pretended not to notice.

Instead, he zeroed in on the little pouch and datapad she was carrying. She slipped into her chair and opened the pouch. Out slid a flat metal plate about ten centimeters by ten centimeters. Tru held it out to him.

Race took it. Besides being a perfect square, it was heavy, warm, and thick. An "X" ran from corner to corner. Small triangles were etched at each corner, and at the center where the lines intersected. But there was something else. He set the plate on the table, studied it, listened, and then picked it up again.

His eyes met Tru's. "It hums. Energy matter?"

She gave him a little smile. "No. The metal seems to resonate only when held by a human. An energy conduit, I believe."

He held it up to the light, studying the surface. "Where did it come from?"

"I don't know," she told him, shaking her head. "I wish I did. I found it among my father's effects after he died."

He gave her a skeptical look but she didn't even blink. *Truth.* Did she know how easy she was to read?

"I also found this," she passed the datapad to him. He recognized the image on it—a rudimentary starmap.

Tru leaned back in her seat. "I believe my father

started a quest for something that I'd like to finish."

"A quest for what?"

"I'm not sure." She stared straight ahead in concentration. Then she picked up the plate and turned it over in her hands. "But this is the key. I'm positive."

He studied her for a minute. She was either brilliant or crazy. He really hated working for crazy clients. "Why the pyramid on Curzon?"

"Have you ever seen an aerial view of a pyramid?" she asked, lifting a delicate eyebrow.

"I never really paid attention. Why?"

She held up the flat plate with its "X" facing him. "It looks just like this."

Then he saw it. Just as a pyramid would look from above. Okay, so she was brilliant. But that didn't mean she couldn't still be crazy.

He eyed her. "And you think that you're going to get your answers by climbing the pyramid?"

She laid the plate flat on the table. "Actually, there's more than just the climb. Did you know that the pyramid at Curzon has no cap stone?"

Her eyes met his, clear and bright. For a second, he forgot what they were talking about, only that her lips were perfectly shaped. He shook it off. *A client.* That's all he could think about. A lot of people were relying on him. Everything else was irrelevant.

"No, I didn't."

She nodded. "The top ten centimeters are missing." Then she pushed the plate toward him and smiled smugly. "That just happens to be the exact size of this plate."

He glanced at the plate, and then back at her as

the realization settled in. Maybe she was just plain brilliant.

"So what's going to happen when you place the plate on the pyramid?" he asked.

"*That* would be the test. I really have no idea what will happen. Hopefully something that will lead us to the next step."

He frowned. "How can you be so sure there is a next step?"

"I can't. I have no proof, no real hypothesis." She tapped her fingers on the table. "All I have is a gut feeling." She glanced over at him. "I'm sorry. It's a poor reason."

He snorted lightly. "Sounds perfectly logical to me. I happen to live my life on gut feelings."

"I don't," she whispered, tracing the plate with a slender finger. "So how will we get to the top of the pyramid?" she asked, looking at him intently with soft gray eyes.

He shifted in his chair. "Good question."

"Holodeck up," he told the computer.

A cylindrical, mesh grid rose up from the table top about two meters.

"Show me Curzon. Jabe Ku. The pyramid at Landwehr Square."

The planet of Curzon appeared first, then zoomed in on the city of Jabe Ku, and finally exploded into a visual image of Landwehr Square. The pyramid sat in the center of the square.

Rayce nodded toward the holographic image. "This is the latest visual shot of the pyramid. Computer, rotate image."

Tru leaned toward the grid, her frown glowing in the blue light. "What's that on the top?"

Rayce ordered, "Computer, zoom in twenty percent."

The image enlarged. He squinted at it. "Looks like a platform built around the top of the pyramid."

She cast him a quizzical look. "Why?"

Rayce watched the image turn slowly. "Computer, stop rotation." He glanced at her. "That's why."

Her face dropped as she saw it, too. Along the center of the pyramid—bottom to top—a stairway had been attached.

"They turned it into a tourist attraction," she said sadly.

"And knowing the Curzons, you can bet it's not free," he added grimly. "At least, the stairs will get us to the top. Computer, zoom in on the pyramid's apex."

The top of the pyramid appeared, filling the grid. The platform sat like a hat atop the pyramid's four sides. Rayce studied the part of the pyramid still exposed—the pinnacle.

"Can we reach the apex?" Tru asked quietly.

Rayce shook his head. "Not sure. Computer, calculate the approximate distance between the platform floor and the apex."

The computer responded, "Four meters."

He winced. Too high for either of them to reach.

Tru knew it too and blew out a long breath. "So what do we do?"

He ran a hand through his hair. "I'll come up with something. I brought two Curzon outfits and makeup."

Tru looked up in surprise. "Do you think we can pass for Curzons?"

He shrugged. "They are humanoids, too. I don't see why not. I wished I'd had time to undergo a Curzon language interface before we left the spaceport."

"Don't worry about it. I know Curzon."

He swung his gaze around. She stared into the holodeck. Of course, she would know the Curzon language. She planned everything. She probably had her entire life mapped out.

"Good. You can tell me what the locals have to say. Holodeck down." The grid lowered.

There was a long moment of silence. Tru rubbed her hands on her thighs. She cleared her throat. "So. What do you do when you are here alone for a long flight?"

He crossed his arms, enjoying her obvious unease. "Read, mostly. Cook, some. Sleep, a lot."

At the mention of sleep, her head popped. Ah, he wondered when she'd entertain that small technicality. He waited.

Her gaze swept the tiny cabin. "Where *do* we sleep?"

He grinned. "Computer, lower both bunks."

Tru jumped as the wall over her shoulder opened up and dropped down into a bed. His bunk dropped down beside him as well. He wanted to laugh at the look on her face as she mentally measured the distance between them. Not more than two meters. He'd already calculated it.

"Cozy," she finally said.

He stood up and walked toward the back, mostly to keep from laughing. "I hope you like expedition rations. That's what we are eating for the next few days."

Tru peered out of the tiny lav into the dim, quiet cabin. She looked down at the shirt she'd borrowed from Rayce to sleep in. It came only to her thighs. Why hadn't she planned for this? Nightclothes had never been a problem for her—she never wore any. Why would she worry about sleeping clothes? She lived alone. Besides, she thought they'd have sep- arate, *private* sleeping quarters. She glared at him in the dark. Just another little detail he'd left out.

She took a deep breath and made her way to the front of the ship and the bunks. The lights were dimmed low to simulate night onboard ship.

She bumped into a metal cabinet. "Ouch." Then she glanced quickly at Rayce's bunk in panic. No movement. In the low light, she could make out his big body, half-covered by a blanket. He was lying on his stomach, his arms stretched out over his head. From the waist up, he was uncovered. And naked. Either he slept nude as she did or she was wearing his top.

She stood transfixed for a moment as her eyes adjusted and his back came into focus. She'd never seen a man's bare back before except the glimpse she'd gotten of him yesterday at the spaceport.

It was wide, strong, and powerful even in repose. Sculpted, smooth skin over hard muscle. Beautiful.

She shook her head. She was doing it again. Ob- sessing. A definite weakness she'd need to over- come soon. Tru moved carefully to her bunk and climbed in. It was surprisingly comfortable and warm. She pulled the blankets up and tucked them under her chin.

For the first five minutes, she just stared at the ceiling, stiff and rigid, waiting for sleep to arrive. It wasn't cooperating. And she knew why. Turning her head slowly, she glanced at Rayce. His hair hung over his face, his eyes closed.

She'd survived the first day alone with him and it hadn't been all bad. He seemed more urbane now that she'd shown him the plate. They'd had a few meals, discussed some noncontroversial topics and kept it civil. But there was still a deep dislike there, a hard, cold stare she'd catch out of the corner of her eye. She'd sure like to know why.

At least he didn't snore. Not that she'd ever heard a man snore before. She frowned. For some bizarre reason, that bothered her. In fact, this was the closest she'd ever come to spending the night with a man. That bothered her even more. Never slept with a man, never woke up with a man, never had morning meal with a man . . . The list went on, getting increasingly depressing.

She shook her head and stared back at the ceiling. Life didn't revolve around men. She had priorities, a career, a promising future at the Institute. She'd worked hard to gain the respect of her colleagues, always fighting the whisper of birthright over merit. Being born on the Institute made her job even harder, having to prove she really belonged there with all the other brilliant minds harvested and collected from around the galaxy. Admission to the most prestigious academic center in the galaxy was strictly by invitation but she had earned her place.

She just needed to make it official and prove once and for all that she fit.

And a man wouldn't help her with that. Besides, any physical relationship would be doomed to disaster. She had no plans to relive the single, biggest, most humiliating failure of her life again.

Odell's words still lingered in her mind, even two years later. *You're frigid, Tru. You can't even do something as simple as have an orgasm.*

Frigid. She trembled. The memory of his penis limp and unresponsive between her legs, her fumbling apologies, his anger as he grabbed his clothes and left her apartment. During the previous private dates, she thought he really cared for her. But after that night the rumors had circulated, rumors only he could have started. And then, no man asked her out. Even worse, her professional image had been permanently tarnished.

Tru rolled over in her bunk to face the wall and stopped the tears before they had a chance to form. She'd failed and she wouldn't risk that again. She wasn't cut out for a physical encounter of any kind, that fact had already been proven.

Besides, she'd always felt that sex was highly overrated.

And that was, without a doubt, the most depressing thought of the evening.

"It's easier if I do you and you do me, that's why," Rayce muttered in a surly tone.

After a night of restless sleep, Tru was in no mood to be ordered around. "I can do myself."

"Well, I can't," he snapped back. "You'll have to do me, too."

She huffed and looked down at the face paint he'd dumped on the table. "Fine. I'll do both of us."

Now she was really riled. And he looked distinctly triumphant. She'd lost something somewhere and it was annoying her to no end.

"Sit down," she ordered him as she slid the makeup over to one side. "Computer, display stored composite image of male Curzon markings."

The holodeck rose and the face of a Curzon man appeared. Tru studied the paint lines. They flowed across the man's cheeks and around his eyes like a wave, the colors brilliant. Tru sat in her chair and picked up the first pen—black paint.

Concentrating on the image, she cupped Rayce's chin in one hand and began drawing a line around his eyes. The paint emphasized the blue-green in his eyes, making them even more striking. She felt the warmth of his skin, the smoothness of his morning shave, his steady breath on her face. The whole time, he stared into her eyes, a small smile playing on his face.

Tru pursed her lips and forged ahead, checking the holo image and then drawing. He was doing it to her again. She was not going to let him rattle her. This was *her* mission.

"So why do the Curzons have the face markings?" he asked, watching her intently.

She concentrated on her research, trying hard to ignore all the other distractions. "They have an archaic and rigid caste system. In order to maintain that system on a planetary level, they permanently tattoo the face of each family member to mark the family's place. It's not the kindest of societies," she said as she drew another line. "It's also not the worst. I did some research and selected an upper-middle caste family from the other side of the planet."

Black, then blue, yellow and finally green. Twenty minutes later, she sat back and squinted at his makeup. Not bad. Very close. This might actually work.

"You're done," she said with a nod. Then she studied the holo image again, committing the markings to memory in a matter of seconds—a gift she had been born with. She looked over to find a painted Rayce grinning at her.

"I can try to do you," he offered, a smirk coming through all that makeup.

"No, thank you," she replied quickly. She gathered the pens and headed toward the back before he could say anything. "I'll paint myself in the lav."

As she exited to the rear, Rayce watched her walk. Just walk. Could be a full-time job. He shook his head. What kind of power did she have over him to tempt him to forget so much? Without thinking, he glanced at the bunks tucked back into the walls.

It had been a long night, especially after she'd announced that she had no sleeping clothes. He growled. There was one visual he didn't need. So, like a gentleman, he'd given her one of his shirts.

It hadn't been easy but he'd managed to catch a glimpse of her in it. Long legs, nice high breasts and all that heavy blonde hair. It was enough to keep a grown man awake at night wondering how his shirt was faring.

He rubbed his neck and turned the seats around to the console. With a few entries, he approved the program sequence to drop the transport out of hyperspace. Right over Curzon. They'd be on the surface by mid-day.

He wished he'd had more time to prepare for this mission. A language interface would have made him more comfortable. He didn't have much of a chance to memorize Jabe Ku's layout but he'd marked a few escape routes. Getting to the pyramid was going to be a challenge. In the process of giving clients what they wanted, he'd been in plenty of places he shouldn't have been. Except this time, he had Tru along. Twice the danger. As long as she followed orders, they'd be fine. They would blend in and remain inconspicuous.

He turned to the sound behind him and forgot all about Curzon. Tru stood tall, face painted brilliantly, wearing a narrow column dress typical of Curzon women. Her hair was pulled back into a long braid, cheekbones high, eyes bright. She looked like a damn goddess. How the hell was he supposed to make *that* inconspicuous?

"It fits," she said simply.

He nodded and returned to his controls with a scowl. It certainly did fit. Perfectly over breasts, hips, and legs. This job was getting tougher all time. He'd thought he would have the upper hand here on his own ship. He'd be able to push her, intimidate her, and get whatever she was hiding out in the open. Instead, he found himself aroused and miserable. And so far, he hadn't even made a dent in that cool, calm armor of hers.

"Take your seat," he told her roughly. "We're dropping out of hyperspace in thirty seconds."

Silently, she slipped into her seat next to him,

brushing her hip against his shoulder, and strapped herself in. He glanced over to make sure she was secure. Bad idea. The straps caught her under the breasts just enough to pull the fabric tight over her nipples. There was no way he was yanking on her harness this time.

Instead, he stared out the viewport as the gray-blue nothingness of hyperspace transformed to a star-streaked view, and then star-studded black, with dizzying speed.

Curzon loomed large and green in the viewport. And busy. For a planet that discouraged outsiders, they sure had a thriving commerce network. Only problem was, most outsiders never got past the landing bays.

Of course, Tru sized it up instantly. "I didn't realize Curzon was such a popular place. Do you think we'll have any trouble gaining entry?"

"We'll find out in a minute." Rayce hailed the Curzon authorities, sending the authorization numbers. Long minutes passed before an affirmative was returned and a landing schedule transmitted.

"Entry authorized. Looks like your mission is a go."

She turned to him, scanning his Curzon outfit with a frown. "So why are we all dressed up as Curzons if we are just visiting?"

"The pass only gets us entry to the landing area, not into Greater Jabe Ku. The Curzons don't like foreigners tainting their soil."

Her frown deepened. "How do we access the pyramid then?"

He grinned at her. "We sneak out of the landing area and into the city."

"Sneak out?" she croaked. Then her eyes rolled to the ceiling. "That's your professional master plan?"

Rayce was smiling widely now. He loved shaking her up. "That's what you're paying the big credits for."

"Sneaking," she repeated fatalistically. "The Curzon authorities don't carry weapons, but do you have any idea how horrible their prisons are?"

He reached for the ship's controls and began their descent. "Trust me. Sneaking around is one of my specialties."

Chapter Five

Curzon buzzed by her in a blur of silver and gray plaster walls and roadways, broken by a smattering of color, courtesy of an occasional, brave citizen. Tru pulled the deep hood lower over her head so it wouldn't catch the wind as their rented speeder whizzed through the streets.

"Are you sure this thing is safe?" she yelled in Rayce's ear.

He turned his head just enough so she could see his big smile but he didn't say a word. She gritted her teeth, hating him. Besides the fact that he was driving entirely too fast, probably had no idea where he was going and had nearly run over several pedestrians, she had her arms wrapped tightly around an incredibly hard waist.

Physical. Definitely physical.

Even at Rayce's breakneck speed, she could see Jabe Ku for the city it was now and what it must have been at one time. Dry and gray, stripped of any and all embellishment, like a hunk of stone before the sculptor's chisel. Except that this world no longer had any sculptures. Sometime in the last 5,000 years, art and artifacts had became trivial and the systematic cultural destruction of Curzon had begun. The Curzons decided that they didn't need art. It didn't serve a purpose. They also discovered that their unwanted art was valuable and the galaxy lined up to buy it.

Even the planet's famous ancient fire pyres had long since died. On every street corner, their once-brilliant flames were doused, leaving behind empty, useless pylons.

Now the only art form the Curzons approved of were the permanent facial tattoos, used to shackle every person to his proper place in society. She caught glimpses of small, branded faces—scarred for life, their fates sealed even before they understood what the marks meant. These would be the lowest of Curzon society, the Inferiors. Most doors were filthy, damaged, the windows covered with rags, balconies used as laundry facilities. The stench filling the air could only be human waste. Every street looked identical, littered and neglected.

The speeder slowed suddenly, took a hard right turn into a long, narrow alley. Then they stopped dead, sending her sliding into Rayce's back with a grunt. She peered quickly over his shoulder, down the length of the dark alley. Through the other end, the pyramid shown bright in the mid-day sun. But between them and the pyramid swarmed hundreds of Curzons.

"Landwehr Square looks very busy. Is this good?" she asked.

He shrugged. "The more people there are, the easier it will be for us to blend in."

Tru nodded. She was all for blending in and avoiding the authorities. Sneaking out of the ship, through the transportation center and into the city had been more nerve-wracking than anything she'd ever experienced before. But Rayce was right about one thing: He was very good at sneaking around. Obviously, he did it a lot.

He reached forward and shut off the hover speeder. It lowered until their feet touched the ground.

She fidgeted in her seat. "I didn't realize how economically disadvantaged Jabe Ku is."

Rayce shook his head in front of her. "Poor."

"What?"

He turned slightly. "The people living here are poor. *Economically disadvantaged* is a term used by people who've never been. Haven't you ever seen poverty before?"

She bristled at his condescending tone. "Everyone at the Institute is at the same economic level."

His entire body tensed under her hands. "Well, take a good look around. This is how the other half lives."

She frowned, trying to comprehend how people survived in the conditions she'd seen so far. Children, elders. Thin and drawn. Did they laugh? Could they be happy? Did anyone care about them?

"Tru?"

"Hmm?" she responded, her thoughts whirling around hardship she was only beginning to imagine.

Rayce turned his head, his lips only inches from

hers. Tru pulled back quickly. His eyes narrowed.

"What?" she whispered.

"You have to let go of me."

Her eyes widened and she released her death grip on his waist. "Sorry," she sputtered as she struggled to disengage herself from the hovering speeder. The dress wasn't cooperating and she made a less than graceful dismount.

She stood back and watched Rayce swing a leg easily over the speeder seat. She wrinkled her nose. *Show off*.

He pulled a laser pistol from beneath his robe, checked the setting and slipped it into a back holster. Tru trembled. For the first time in her life, she was on a hostile planet, really and truly in danger. Already the adrenalin was pumping through her. She's planned this adventure for over a year and she was ready for anything, even sneaking.

Rayce looked at her. "Stay here. I'm going to do some reconnaissance."

Tru frowned, suddenly deflated. "I can come with you."

"No."

She put her hands on her hips. "I know how to speak Curzon, you don't."

He flicked on his datapad, completely ignoring her. "No."

She crossed her arms. "So what are you going to do if a guard stops you?"

"No." He turned off the datapad and slipped it into an inner pocket. "Stay here, Tru. Or we go home."

They stared each other down for a few long moments in a silent battle.

"Fine," she relented.

He grinned. "Now see? That wasn't so hard."

She speared him with a lethal glare. He laughed aloud and turned down the long alley. She watched as he disappeared into the crowd. Damn him.

She sighed and leaned against the speeder. Sooner or later, she'd have to tell him the whole mission. But not yet, not until she was sure of her theory, of the ultimate goal—the Curzon Collection.

A smile touched her lips as she allowed herself to dream just a little. The find of the millennium. An archeological discovery of galactic proportions. The history, the records of thousands of alien cultures buried for 5,000 years. It would keep her and the Institute's historians busy for their lifetimes and more. If the Collection was even half as extensive as she'd researched, the historical value would be immeasurable.

It would be a discovery worthy of a Van Dye.

"Ready?"

Tru jumped at the hand on her shoulder, the word murmured in her ear. She glowered at Rayce. "*Must* you do that?"

"I told you that sneaking around is one of my specialties," he said. "That's why you hired me, isn't it?"

She narrowed her eyes at him, his question more accusation than statement. "I hired you because you are supposed to be the best."

The smile started slow, built speed, flashing bright against his paint job. "I'm the best there is, lady. Let's go."

He led her down the alley. "Remember, no unnecessary talking, no eye contact, keep your hood down and stick close to me. Curzon women adore their men." He gave her a killer smile. "So act like you can't breathe without me."

Tru muttered, "I can't believe I'm paying for this."

The sunlight nearly blinded her and she shielded her eyes as Rayce's hand slipped inside her robe and pressed against her back. The combination was enough to set her senses on fire. His hand felt hot— driving and burning her as they made their way through the throng en route to the pyramid. It sat in the center of a vast public square surrounded by two- and three-story gray buildings. Brilliant and white in the direct sun, it commanded center stage—a man-made star.

"It's beautiful," she breathed toward Rayce.

"No talking," he whispered back. She raised an eyebrow at his serious tone and glanced up. His eyes scoured the area like a hunter, taking in everything, everyone. The man was working. It was about time he earned his pay.

They wound their way through the crowd of Curzons. Some were looking up at the pyramid, but most just passed through oblivious to the precious treasure in their midst.

But as they drew closer to the pyramid, Tru slowed. Graffiti lined the base of the pyramid and trash littered the ground around it. The white stone showed every mark, chip, and stain it had endured as target practice for the masses.

Her stomach lurched. How could they mistreat such a rare treasure? They couldn't destroy the great pyramid, couldn't hide that fact it was art. So instead, they defiled it and stole its dignity.

A flash of color caught her eye. A solitary flower, struggling for survival, lay pressed up against the stone. As they passed by, she wanted to reach down and scoop it up, save it from this indifferent planet. Then an errant foot trampled it, smearing a red streak against the pyramid, and it was gone.

Tru followed Rayce to the end of a short line waiting to visit the pyramid's summit.

She leaned into Rayce. "So how does this work?"

He turned slightly and whispered, "We get in line."

"And?" she prompted.

"When it moves . . . we move, too." He grinned widely.

She fought back the urge to smack him. "You don't get many repeat clients, do you?"

They stepped up, next to ascend the stairs. As Rayce slipped a card into the console to pay their admission to the top, a Curzon guard scrutinized them. Tru felt Rayce's hand against her back urging her quickly to the stairs.

Moments later, they reached the platform at the top. The city sprawled out around them, row upon row of plain gray buildings.

Tru walked to the exposed peak of the pyramid, laid her palm against the warm, smooth stone. History. She was touching a 5,000-year-old treasure. Incredible.

Her gaze slid upward along the slope. The pyramid apex was four meters above her, far out of reach. The polished stone casing would be impossible to climb. So how was she going to get the plate up there?

She looked over her shoulder at Rayce, who was

studying the other twenty or so Curzons circling the platform. "Now what?"

He moved up behind her, pressing his chest to her back. Tru tensed, her hand against the pyramid for support. His voice was low in her ear. "I'm going to lie against the pyramid wall. You climb up me and I'll push you up. You should be able to reach the peak. We won't have long, maybe ten seconds, so be quick. Do you have the plate ready?"

Her mouth dropped. "You want me to climb over you? Don't you think someone will notice that?"

Rayce whispered, "Hopefully they will be busy looking at the diversion."

She frowned. "What diversion?"

Suddenly, a loud bang reverberated through the square, followed by a chorus of screams. Tru twisted around to where smoke billowed from a far, vacant corner. Curzons scattered and stampeded out of the way.

Then Rayce's hands were around her as he fell back against the slanted pyramid wall. She landed on top of him—chest to chest.

"Go!" he said, pulling her up his body. Tru scrambled, fighting with the dress and trying to gain purchase wherever she could. He grunted as she stuck a foot in his ribs, then a knee on his shoulder.

She was too busy trying to keep her balance to be mad. But damn it, when she had more time, she was going to let him have it. Next time, she wanted his stupid plan up front.

She shimmied up the pyramid surface, her belly flat against the warm stone and her feet anchored more or less on Rayce's shoulders. Heaven only knew where her dress was. Amid the chaos in the square around her, she dragged the plate from her pocket and placed it blindly, delicately on the apex half a meter above her. As soon as she settled it on top, she felt a surge. Energy buzzed her fingers, up her arms and through every cell of her body. She groaned as a pure sexual current rolled through her, awaking and settling in the parts that made her a woman. It swamped her senses, dragging her under its power. She'd never felt such carnal freedom. She wanted it to last forever.

"Time's up, Tru. Grab the plate, you're coming down." Rayce's bark startled her.

Rudely yanked from ecstasy, she snatched the plate off the top and fumbled it back into a pocket, just as Rayce's shoulders fell out from under her. The wall slid hot beneath her stomach as she dropped abruptly before Rayce's hands caught her.

He planted her feet on the platform and promptly yanked her around the other side. Tru flattened against the wall beside him and surveyed the mayhem in the square. It had cleared out considerably except for the guards who swarmed the far corner. Lots of guards. So much for avoiding the authorities.

"Would you like to fill me in on the rest of this plan sometime *before* we get arrested?" she whispered.

Rayce ignored her, his full attention on the stairs. That was when she noticed the laser pistol in his hand. The breath froze in her lungs. Guards, trouble, incarceration and certain death all became distinct possibilities.

He tensed noticeably. Tru stilled. "What is it?"

"The guards are coming up. They must have spotted you on the pyramid," he said quietly.

"You have a plan, right?" she asked, terror creeping around her.

"Sure do. We run like hell."

Then she heard the stern shouts, the heavy steps on the stairs, then on the platform. Rayce grabbed her hand and pulled her with him around the corner of the pyramid and down the stairs as the guards circled the platform in the other direction. She glimpsed one guard pointing at them.

Rayce never slowed, dragging her down the stairs and across the now empty square. The guards on the platform were already descending the stairs and chasing after them.

Tru nearly tripped over her dress as they ran through the dark alley.

"Get on," he yelled, mounting their speeder first and starting the engine. Tru hopped on and looked up to see four Curzon guards running toward them, shouting.

The speeder surged straight ahead into the team of guards. Tru gripped Rayce's waist and screamed as bodies bounced off the front of the speeder and fell away.

Out into the sunlight they exploded, scattering guards before twisting, sliding and shooting down a side street. Rayce leaned forward, pulling her with him, and gunned the engines. Her hood flew off, air whistled past her ears.

"I hate to break this to you, but we are no longer blending in," she yelled.

She twisted around enough to see if anyone was following them.

Bad news. The guards on Curzon had speeders, too. At least, three of them did.

"Rayce, we are being followed."

He shot a quick look behind, his face lined with concern. Damn, she knew it. No plan. She wanted a refund.

"Hold on," he gritted. A second later, they took an impossible turn into a narrow alley, the rear end of the speeder scraping the wall with a spray of sparks. Tru watched as one of the speeders chasing them slammed squarely into the wall, crashed to the ground and the guard crumpled in a heap. The other two speeders negotiated the tight turn and zoomed after them. Their warning lights were now flashing and sirens echoed between the alley walls.

"Oh, good lord," Tru groaned. Noa was not going to be happy if news of this got back to the Institute.

Then they shot back out into a busy street. Rayce pulled the speeder up short and steered crazily through the maze of an outdoor produce market. In front of them, Curzons dove for safety, carts overturned and animals scattered. Barrels and boxes crunched and bounced off the speeder's bumper before a barrel of ripe fruit splattered on the speeder's shield and exploded, most of it landing in her hair. Then she sucked something small and furry into her mouth and nearly choked trying to spit it out.

They cleared the market and she turned around. The two speeders followed in their wake of pandemonium. Tru breathed a sigh of relief when one fell behind amid the cartons in the market and was immediately surrounded by an angry mob of

Curzon vendors waving damaged fruit and trying to calm scared livestock.

"One left," she yelled to Rayce. He nodded and cleared the market limits, accelerating down the quiet street at breakneck speed.

"Do you know where you're going?" Tru hollered.

"Don't worry. I know this city like the back of my hand."

She gripped his waist like a vice. "You've never been here before!"

Even from behind him, she could see his devilish grin. Then they were speeding through a too-narrow alley, the sound of the engine reverberating between the walls. They shot out, across a street, narrowly missing another speeder and scaring the driver half to death before diving through another alley.

She nearly fell off as the speeder careened out of the alley and took a hard right. At this rate, he was going to get them killed. If she wasn't so terrified, she'd free one of her hands and strangle him with it.

Then she looked up and forgot everything else. The transportation center where their ship was docked loomed large and was packed to the brim with travelers. Maybe he did know where he was going after all. But as they drew closer, he didn't slow down.

"Too fast," she screamed as the speeder veered left at the very last minute, down a ramp, through a tunnel, past a throng of surprised Curzons. They shot through open space next, then over a narrow bridge, finally skidding to a stop at end of a row of a hundred identical rental speeders.

"Come on," Rayce said, wrenching her off the speeder. He shot a quick look behind them before pulling her up a nearby ramp and onto a crowded moving walkway. The Curzon pedestrians stared at them with acute curiosity. And no wonder, Tru thought, looking down at her dress covered with a gummy residue and bits of produce.

The roar of a speeder engine brought her head up. Hidden behind a big male Curzon, Tru caught sight of the last speeder careening into the transportation bay. The guard stepped off his vehicle and stood, hands on hips, staring at the hundreds of rental speeders lined up. Then the walkway bent around a corner and he was out of sight.

She turned slowly and glared at Rayce with every bit of rage she'd stored up in the past fifteen minutes.

He grinned back. "I think that went well."

Tru stepped onboard *Miranda* behind Rayce, dragging her sodden, sticky dress around her.

The hatch closed. She stood just inside the door, her heart pounding in her chest, her fists clenched, trying like hell to control the wild rage flooding her senses. She'd never been this angry—ever. She'd never been in this much trouble, never even been close. She'd hired a madman.

"Hold onto something, Tru," Rayce called from the cockpit. "I'm beginning the liftoff sequence."

She turned the corner and held him in her sights.

"You are *insane*." Her voice shook with rage, much like the rest of her.

Rayce turned his head in her direction. "Would you rather be sitting in a Curzon prison?"

A piece of fruit fell off the dress as she raised her arm and pointed toward the city. "You nearly killed us."

"Not even close," he said with annoying calmness and looking far too happy for a man about to die.

"Tell me," she said, her teeth clenched tight. "Do you do anything quietly?"

He grinned. "A few things. Care for a list?"

She shook her head. Well, it was more like a tremble. "No, even though I'm sure it's a *very* short list."

He shot her a wide grin, which did nothing to defuse her rolling rage.

She closed her eyes, ticking off all the reasons why she couldn't murder him. Unfortunately, she needed this insane, trust-me-lady, seat-of-your-pants guide she'd hired. Maybe she'd kill him later. After she was through with him.

"I'm taking a shower," she said, suddenly too exhausted to fight anymore.

Rayce watched her limp to the back. Then he turned around and maneuvered the ship off the landing pad, spun it toward space and exited Jabe Ku's air space. Traffic was light and the course easy.

He broke into a slow, satisfied grin. Damn, that was fun. More fun than he'd had in a long time. So it was a little close, he'd had closer calls before. Terrifying Tru was becoming a new hobby. No doubt, she'd never experienced anything like today. It gave him some perverse satisfaction to be the one to break her in.

He rubbed his stomach where she'd latched on to him during the speeder ride. He'd enjoyed that, too. Then he shook his head. He was definitely developing a masochistic streak.

The ship pulled out of Curzon's atmosphere fifteen minutes later. He checked his scanners. Looked like they were clear, no one following them. A miracle, considering how much trouble they'd stirred up.

"Going to hyperspace in two minutes, Tru," he called out.

Moments later, she dropped into the seat next to him, looking sleek in her Majj uniform. Rayce could smell the shower she'd just taken.

The stars streaked by as the ship jumped to hyperspace. They were away.

He sat there wondering when she was going to light into him. Probably demand some kind of plan, some guarantee that there would be no more chases through city streets. Too bad. As far as he was concerned, this mission was over the minute he dumped her back at the spaceport.

He turned to Tru and met her smiling face. Now there was a surprise. She held the plate in the palm of her hand.

With great pleasure, she said, "The test was a success."

Rayce took the plate from her hand and felt it vibrate through his fingers. One triangular side had grown up from the bottom plate—completing one quarter of a miniature pyramid.

"What the hell?" he murmured. He glanced at Tru. There was a lot more to this mission than she'd told him. "Explain."

She took the plate back, admiring it in the cabin lights. "Ever heard of the Curzon collectors?"

Rayce narrowed his eyes. "Our Curzons?"

She nodded. "Five thousand years ago they were a much different society—the Old Order. Curators of the arts. Collectors. Self-appointed historians. They traveled throughout the galaxy collecting history, art and artifacts from nearly every inhabited world. Over hundreds of years, they managed to amass a huge archive of unparalleled treasure."

Rayce crossed his arms. Now this was getting interesting. "Doesn't sound like the Curzons we know and love. So what happened?"

"Economics," she replied simply. "The Curzons also had become great consumers, importing more than they exported and more than they could pay for. The planet's economy crashed. A movement began to sell off the Collection to save the society. The result was a deep division among the people and the government over the fate of the Collection."

Rayce tapped the console with his fingers. "I'm not surprised. That's a lot of wealth just sitting there."

She turned to him, anger easing into her voice. "The value is in the history. Do you realize how many of those civilizations they documented have disappeared in the past 5,000 years or changed beyond all recognition?"

He watched in fascination as her whole being vibrated with passion. Who would have thought it lay buried beneath that silver armor?

She continued, "In some cases, the artifacts in that Collection represent all that's left of those lost civilizations. You can't put a price on that. It's not about the wealth."

He studied her, almost believing her. Maybe she did genuinely care about the historical value but then again, she'd helped shape the Majj policies over the past years. There was no denying that. He'd believe his own eyes before he'd trust what she said.

"So what does the Collection have to do with the plate?"

"There is a rumor that the Curzon governing body decided to hide the Collection, somewhere so remote and so secure that no one would be able to locate it without the key. They originally believed that the civil infighting would eventually end."

Her expression saddened. "But it never did. Even worse, the Curzons turned their backs on their own culture, tossing aside history as nothing but trouble. They stripped their homes and cities of all art, selling it off to the whoever was interested. And the Collection eventually was abandoned after the key was lost."

Rayce considered that. "Didn't anyone look for the Collection?"

She laughed lightly. "Oh yes, for years. However, it was impossible to locate without the key. And eventually the few people who knew its location died with their secret."

Now he could see where she was heading. And he didn't like it. "So the plate is the key?"

"It's part of the puzzle." She swiveled her seat to the rear and called up the holodeck table. Rayce spun his chair to match hers.

"Starmap. Sector 142," she ordered. The holodeck

rose and displayed a smattering of stars.

"Denote Curzon," she told the computer. One star in the multitude lit up brightly.

"Curzon is one corner."

Rayce squinted at the starmap. "One corner of what?"

"Of this." She held up the metal plate and turned it slowly so it glowed blue in the holodeck light. "Here's my theory. I think there are three other pyramids on star systems in this sector that are markers. All identical to the one on Curzon, all missing a capstone. Each one marks a corner of the pyramid base, scaled to a galactic level, of course."

"Of course."

Ignoring his comment, she continued. "I believe that if we place the plate on each pyramid apex, another side will appear."

He growled at the "we" part.

"Once all four sides are completed, we can locate the final, fifth planet based on the positions of the other stars and the angle of the sides to complete a galactic pyramid in the stars."

"Why?"

She looked at him. "Why what?"

"Why bother? If you have two pyramids' locations, you can calculate the other two sides' lengths, locate the other planets housing pyramids using the holodeck capabilities and find the apex without having to visit them all."

She looked momentarily stunned. Apparently, she wasn't expecting him to have a brain.

"That's true. But I don't think you can access the Collection without the completed key." She held up the plate.

He stared at it and then back at her. *Damn*. She was going for the Collection. All that treasure, all those riches. To hell with whatever game she was playing, the whole historical business. He didn't buy it for a minute. What it came down to was more wealth to add to the Majj coffers. Over his dead body.

"Interesting theory," he said flatly.

Her expression clouded over. "You don't believe me."

"I believe you. I'm just not going to help you."

Her eyes widened and she shot out of her seat into the narrow aisle, facing him in obvious disbelief. "Didn't you understand what I said? The historical value of this find is beyond imagination. How can you not help me?"

"For one thing, you don't have enough credits in your account to hire me for the amount of time it's going to take to visit all these planets."

She set her jaw. "I can come up with more credits."

"And for another, I'm not helping you line the Majj's treasury."

The ship became quiet save for the hyperdrive engines and steady hum of equipment.

Her mouth dropped open. Then a strange look came over her face. He could almost see a light come on.

"So that's it," she said softly. "That's why you hate me. The Majj."

He set his teeth, the game up. "Nothing personal."

She gave a short, hard laugh. "Now why would I take that personally? I'm born and raised a Majj."

He didn't reply.

She tossed the plate carelessly on the table in front of him with a loud thump. He looked at it, then up at her. Her eyes drilled into him with an almost equal amount of anger and determination. Passion. Who would have thought?

"I've got a deal for you," she said with cool, crisp clarity.

"Not interested," he replied. There wasn't a thing she could offer him to make him change his mind.

"Partners," she uttered the single word with absolute conviction. "We split the Collection fifty-fifty."

Every muscle in his body tensed at the thought. "No."

She folded her arms over her chest and gave him a cold stare. "If you don't help me, I'll find someone else who will. It's only a matter of time before I claim the entire Collection for the Institute. And their treasury."

His fists clenched. She was bluffing and he wasn't biting. "Not interested."

For a brief moment, he thought she'd given up when she leaned against the counters and stared at the floor.

"And don't forget your spaceport," she added quietly. "I'm sure your investors won't be too happy if you go belly up. Selling off even a portion of your fifty percent could get the spaceport finished in your promised two-month deadline."

Rage stole over him as the realization sunk in. She knew everything, knew his financial position, his weakness. It all fell into place. She'd used him, manipulated him all along. Every step had been planned out, executed to perfection. He should have listened to his instincts.

And the final blow: a thinly veiled threat. It wouldn't take much to spook his investors at this point. They'd pull out in a flash if they even suspected problems and he'd lose everything. All the work he'd done for the past ten years would be for nothing. He'd never recover from the damage to his reputation.

"What's to stop me from getting rid of you, taking the plate and finding the treasure myself?" he asked in a soft growl.

Her eyes met his for a brief moment and then she pursed her lips. "Someone at the Institute knows my mission. If he doesn't hear from me at regular intervals, he'll call in the authorities and launch a full-scale investigation."

Rayce tapped his fingers lightly on the table. Everything. She'd planned for everything and backed him into a corner.

He pulled himself up from his seat, slowly and deliberately, with absolute menace. Her eyes widened marginally but she didn't back down even as he bore down on her. He moved within centimeters of her face.

His voice was low, hard. "Then I guess you've got a deal, *partner.*"

"One stipulation." She licked her lips. "I get to catalog your half before you sell it off."

He couldn't believe her audacity. "What?"

"I want to record the historical information before the pieces are divided up and scattered around the galaxy."

His eyes narrowed. He couldn't figure her out.

First, she'd threatened to ruin him, then she wanted more. The woman had no fear. Then a thought struck him.

Maybe she did have a weakness.

"On one condition."

She frowned. "What's that?"

"A kiss a day. Every day for as long as this mission takes. When I say, where I say," he said, blatantly perusing her body.

She bumped into the console behind her. Oh, yes. There it was. Panic in her eyes. Good. He wanted her to know fear, to know what it meant to threaten a man like him.

"Forget it," she rasped, shaking her head.

"Then no inventory." He said it in a way that left no doubt he meant it. Then he crossed his arms and enjoyed watching her squirm like she'd just done to him.

Her gray eyes clouded over like a storm. He could almost see her mind running through her limited options. *Come on, Tru. Give it up.* Her eyes turned icy.

"Deal," she said with a tight-lipped hiss.

He grinned. Time to keep her off balance. "Now."

She blinked at him. "What?"

"Now," he repeated as he moved in close, pinning her rigid body between himself and the console.

All the color drained out of her face. Her eyes grew huge and glassy. He leaned in until he could feel her heat and knew she could feel his. One little kiss, barely there, that's all he'd need. Enough to shake her, make her worry every day from now on until this damn mission was done, and a small moment of vindication for him.

That's what he'd intended when he bent and skimmed her lips with his, caught the smell of her, heard the quick little gasp she gave. Then heat ignited like a wildfire in his belly. Something snapped in his brain, probably his sanity.

He captured her mouth with his in one bold move, bearing down on her with all the frustration he'd stored up in the past two days. Her lips were soft and pliable under his siege. His tongue invaded her mouth—sweet and warm—there for the taking. She trembled under his hands like a captured animal.

Her hands pushed against his chest but he didn't budge his position. He had her trapped, just the way she'd trapped him. It was then that his body responded. He felt himself harden, felt the urge to push his hips into her soft body. It surprised him both in its force and its speed. But more than that, it angered him into sanity.

He broke off the kiss abruptly. For a few long minutes, he stared at her pale face, her red lips. He pushed back from the console and turned away. Without looking back at her, he took his seat and spun it around to check the ship's console.

He heard her flee into the lav.

His eyes skimmed the console.

How could he feel *anything* for her? Anger burned hot and fast, mostly at himself. He gazed blindly at his readings, his fists clenched. She'd lied to him. And he never saw it coming.

His mother was going to be very disappointed when she found out she had raised a fool.

Chapter Six

Tru splashed water over her face and stared at her red eyes in the mirror. *The bastard.* She grabbed a towel and patted her face, hands shaking. Then she collapsed against the wall behind her. What had she done?

It had all happened so fast. She didn't expect him to turn down the rest of her mission, didn't expect the fury. She hadn't planned to use the spaceport to coerce him to help her, but all she could think of was losing the Collection and seeing her life crumble away from her. It was an idle threat, of course, but he didn't know that. Not even a threat, really. She simply stated the obvious: that he could use the credits to help finance his spaceport.

She groaned. Who was she kidding? It was blackmail, pure and simple. How could she have stooped to that? Panic was her only excuse. And now she'd have to live with the consequences.

Maybe she should apologize. The idea faded in a flash. She shook her head. It was too late. He'd chew her up and spit her out. The mission would be over.

He was furious, dangerously furious. And he hated the Majj—deeply, genuinely and completely. Why? How could he hate her people when they rarely even left the planet? When they had contributed so much to so many?

She wondered if it was safe to sleep at night next to him.

Noa was right. Nothing about Coburne was predictable. She tossed the towel in the bin. Damn him for making this so difficult. Giving up half the Collection was not what she'd planned on but it was better than nothing.

The worst part was that he didn't give a damn about it. He'd sell it off piecemeal; irreplaceable history doled out to the highest bidder and placed in private collections, never to be seen again. There was no way she could bear that.

She rubbed her forehead where a crushing headache throbbed. And the kiss, hard and cruel, so unlike the heat of the VirtuWav exercises. He'd plundered her mouth ruthlessly, using his size and strength to his advantage. There was no doubt he wanted to rattle her. It was as if he knew her weakness.

Well, she decided, it was only a weakness if she let it be. A strange calmness flowed over her. If he wanted to kiss her, then fine. She could be as warm and inviting as a dead fish. After all, she was an expert at sexual failure.

She took one last look in the mirror. There was no way she would fall apart in front of him again. This mission was going to be a success. Even only half the Collection would be worth whatever hell she had to endure to get to it.

That included Rayce Coburne's kisses.

"How long will this take?" Tru asked coolly.

Rayce pursed his lips. There wasn't even a hint of warmth in her voice as she sat in the chair next to him watching the holodeck flash starmap after starmap at blinding speed. The holodeck's blue light and her silver suit made her look frozen solid. Frosty.

"A few minutes to check for pyramids built around 5,000 years ago in this sector. I've tied into every archive I can find. If we don't hit anything, then I'll open up the range, but that will take longer."

She nodded, her eyes glued to the images blinking away and her arms folded squarely over her breasts.

He shrugged off the cold and forced himself to relax. Although he would never admit it to her, thinking about what he could do with immeasurable wealth had a way of calming a man down considerably. If she was right, he'd have no financial worries by the end of this mission. If she was wrong, which he doubted, now that he'd seen her in action, he'd drop her back at the Institute and to hell with whatever damage she thought she could do to him. Majj or not, it was worth the risk to save his spaceport.

Rayce glanced at her sidelong. Still and cold as an ice statue. Amazing, considering how hot she'd felt under his hands. And her lips were about as soft and sweet as any he'd tasted. He'd bet his ship that somewhere under all that ice lay an untapped reservoir of heat. So how had she built such a thick wall around herself?

He shook his head. What the hell was he doing? She'd just coerced him into a partnership. She'd lied from the moment she had stepped into his life. As far as he cared, she could remain frozen solid. Besides, it would take too much effort to thaw her out. The corner of his mouth kicked up. But he wouldn't mind putting a few cracks in her.

The holodeck slowed its frantic pace. Tru leaned forward. "It's found something."

A pinpoint flashed up and the surrounding star system filled in—planets, moons, dust—around a soft yellow star.

Rayce started reciting the statistics. "Twelfth Quadrant. The Kira star system. The pyramid is located on the second planet, called Rostron. Inhabited planet. Minimum population. Atmosphere is hot and humid but tolerable."

"Minimum population," Tru repeated. "Enough to build a pyramid?"

Rayce shook his head. "I don't think so. Not even 5,000 years ago, according to the computer. Besides, they aren't humans. Sleewl."

Tru wrinkled her nose. "The Sleewl are not capable of such a project. The Curzons must have built this one also," Tru said.

"It appears the pyramid dimensions are almost exactly the same as the one on Curzon," Rayce added, sorting through the statistics and information scrolling up the holodeck. "Congratulations. Looks like your theory might actually fly."

"How soon can we get there?" Tru asked, ignoring his remark as if she already knew that.

Rayce glanced at her. She still hadn't spared him a look. "In a hurry?"

She turned and glared at him. Rayce grinned. Hoo-boy. A look like that could kill a mere mortal man.

"No hurry. I just want to get my share and go home."

His expression sobered. "You'll get your share, don't worry. Afraid I'll steal it from you?"

Tru raised an eyebrow. "Not really. But then again, your reputation precedes you."

Rayce leaned toward her and watched her pull back. "So does yours."

She frowned. "What are you talking about?"

Rayce laughed bitterly and shook his head. "Unbelievable. Loyal to the end. That Institute must pay you real well."

He addressed the holodeck before she could make some venomous retort. "Computer, calculate distance between Curzon and Rostron. Triangulate a perfect square and sweep for additional pyramids matching criteria."

The holodeck began flashing images again.

Tru asked, "So you hate the Majj because you think we are rich? Is that it?"

Rayce stared into the blinking holodeck. "No, I don't hate you for being rich. I know a lot of rich people."

"I'm not one of them. You've seen my account, remember?"

He paused for a second and then shrugged. "You could have a lot of accounts."

"Well, I don't. If I did—"

The holodeck went blank, another pinpoint appeared and a solar system exploded.

Rayce recognized the system and the marked planet. "Earth. There's the third corner."

"You know it?" Tru said in amazement.

He grinned and nodded. "I have an acquaintance from Earth."

Rayce said, "Computer, flag Earth and continue search."

The holodeck started and stopped abruptly. The computer announced. "No other locations match specified criteria."

"Damn," Rayce said.

Tru shook her head. "Why can't it find the last one? It should be easy enough with the other three markers."

"The pyramid probably hasn't been discovered. Or it may not be there anymore."

"That wouldn't be good," Tru said quietly.

Rayce said, "Computer, based on criteria, calculate the solar system that completes the fourth corner."

A star appeared in the holodeck along with one lone planet.

"That makes it easier," he said. "We are looking at Arête. Cold, icy, inhospitable." He glanced at Tru. "Sounds like your kind of place." And he grinned wide.

Tru glared at him. "And your kind of planet would be crawling with easy women."

He grinned wider but she pretended to ignore him. She leaned forward. "Computer, show all solar systems selected and link them together."

The starmaps reduced and merged until all four

corners fit within the confines of the holodeck. A fine line started from one to the next, connecting them and forming a perfect square.

Tru smiled slightly. "Now calculate the remaining pyramid shape above the square using a fifty-one-degree angle."

Four lines streamed out of the four corners and formed a perfect pyramid.

"A pyramid in the stars," Tru said reverently. "I was right."

Rayce marveled at the puzzle, at the fact that Tru had even figured it out. Hell, that she'd even come up with the theory at all. He addressed the computer, "Identify star system at the pinnacle."

The top point zoomed in to show a small solar system called simply AR-3346A. A red sun, one large planet with dozens of moons.

"Excellent," murmured Tru.

Rayce added, "It's the planet or one of the moons. We'll have to do a manual search when we get there."

Tru nodded, a smile still on her lips. "Good work, Rayce."

Her eyes widened and she looked at him as if she'd surprised herself. For a few long moments, their gaze met. He knew she'd slipped and she was regretting it already. He could pounce but for some reason, he wasn't in the mood for blood.

He manually shut down the holodeck. "You, too."

She exhaled quietly and rubbed her hands on her thighs. "Well, we have a direction now. Which planet is next?"

Rayce stood up and rolled his shoulders. "Let's

get Rostron over with. We'll leave right after we restock back at the spaceport."

She tapped a fingernail on the dark holodeck table. "Do we have to return after every leg?"

He glanced at her and knew what she was doing—trying to figure out long she'd be stuck with him, how many kisses it would cost her. Well, it wouldn't cost her half as much as it was costing him. Let her squirm.

"Probably. Depends how supplies and fuel hold up."

She gave him a skeptical look. "Can't you get supplies and fuel anywhere?"

He folded his arms and regarded her. "Maybe, maybe not. It also depends on how long we can stand each other."

Her eyes widened and then narrowed. She stood up, almost as tall as him. "I'm in this mission until the end. No matter how bad it gets. And no matter what kind of suffering I have to endure." Then she raised her chin slightly and headed to the back of the ship.

He smirked. "Maybe I'm the one suffering."

She spun around, her eyes cold. "I didn't make the rules, you did. So whatever anguish you endure, it's of your own doing."

He stared at her for a moment. Tall, sleek, beautiful. But more than that, she wasn't intimidated by him. A woman on a mission. For some reason, he found that extremely stimulating.

So he grinned. Wide. Just to disarm her. "I'll survive the torment. But will you?"

Tru didn't flinch. "I'll manage. By the way, it's my turn to cook." She turned and looked at him over her shoulder. "I hope you have a metal stomach."

He watched her disappear in the galley and wondered if she was past poisoning him.

He woke to gentle sobbing. Rayce turned his head to find Tru sitting up in her bunk, her head buried in her hands. In the dim light, her hair lay snarled and damp and her shoulders shook with each shuddering gulp of air.

"Are you all right, Tru?"

Her head came up in a flash, and eyes, swollen and wide with surprise, stared back at him. She straightened her shoulders and pulled her covers up to her chin.

"I'm fine. Just a dream."

Rayce squinted at her. Must have been one lousy dream.

"You want to talk about it?"

"No." Succinct and clear.

Rayce shrugged. Fine with him. "Whatever you want." And he rolled over with his back to her.

He lay there, staring at the gray metal wall, wondering what kind of nightmare a Majj could have. It's not as if they had *real* problems, like suffering and poverty.

He heard her stir, then her feet hit the floor and she softly padded to the lav. Then the shower went on.

He shifted on the bed. What kind of nightmares could she have that would be bad enough to make her cry like that? Even when he'd dragged her through Curzon, she'd gotten mad but there were no tears.

After a few minutes, the shower stopped. Then he heard her talking. He stilled. What was she doing?

He rolled out of the bed and walked quietly to the door. She was talking all right, rattling away. He knew it. A crazy client. He shook his head and went back to stretch out on his bunk.

Staring at the ship's ceiling, he wondered what he'd gotten himself into. How could a woman who was so beautiful and so brilliant be a total lunatic? Okay, so she talked to herself. He talked to himself occasionally, just not full conversations.

He covered his eyes with his forearm. It wouldn't bother him so much if it weren't for the fact that he was escorting her across the galaxy. And she was leading the way.

"Greetings, Noa. Did I wake you?" Tru said into her comm unit when his face appeared. She glanced at the lav door, not wanting to wake Rayce.

Noa shook his head quickly. "Evening here. Are you feeling okay?"

She gave a small smile and brushed her hair aside. "Fine. Just . . . couldn't sleep. I wanted to fill you in on my progress."

"Progress? That sounds good. When will you be back?"

Tru laughed. "Not for a while." Then she smiled triumphantly into the tiny comm unit. "It worked, Noa. My theory, the plate, the pyramid in the stars, the Collection. It's all there. We even know the rest of the planets and where the Collection is housed. Well, almost where. But down to a solar system, at least."

"No kidding?" Noa's eyes widened with excitement. "That Collection is the find of millennium, Tru."

Tru bit her lip. "Well, actually. I'm only getting half."

"Half? Why only half?"

She blew out a breath. "I had to give Coburne the other half. He's my partner now."

On the tiny screen, Noa's eyes rolled to the sky. "I knew it. You can't trust him, Tru. If he takes half, he'll take it all. Why did you have to give him any of it?"

She leaned back against the wall. "It was the only way I could get him to continue the mission."

"He'll sell it off, you realize that," Noa spat.

"He promised to let me inventory his half before he sells it off."

Noa humphed. "And what did that cost you?"

Tru touched her lips. "Nothing I can't afford to give up." She changed subjects. "Noa, he seems convinced that the Majj are . . . unscrupulous or worse."

"Unscrupulous?" Noa laughed. "That's pretty hypocritical, coming from him."

Tru nodded. "I know. Forget it. I don't give a damn what he thinks of me or the Majj as long as I complete my mission."

Suddenly Noa turned his head and froze, staring at some distant object.

"Noa? Is something wrong?"

He ran a hand through his mass of white hair but it quickly resumed its chaotic arrangement. "No. I'm not sure. Maybe. I think I'm being watched."

Tru frowned. "Watched? By whom?"

"Odell came to visit me today," Noa said with a disgusted look. "I really hate that arrogant bastard. I still can't figure out what you ever saw in him."

She muttered, "A weak moment that I will pay for for the rest of my life. What did he want?"

"He was looking for you. Everyone is. Just so you know, your ex-playmate, Odell, is leading the administrators' investigation into your, uh, disappearance. He's in a big hurry to prove he'd be a perfect *head* administrator and he's using you as an example."

"What did you tell him?"

Noa shrugged. "Nothing. I can't very well tell the administrators that I forged an off-planet pass for you. But sooner or later, they will find out. And Odell also spent most of yesterday grilling me on your latest project."

Tru laughed. "I'll bet. He'd love to see me fall on my face and I'm not giving him that chance. When I come back, it'll be with the Collection. That should get him off my back for good."

Noa looked at her for a moment, then added quietly. "There's more. I think someone has been in my computer files."

Tru stilled. "No one can access any of our files. The security is absolute."

"The administrators can," Noa said grimly.

A shiver went through her. The administrators protected the Majj, ran the Institute but stayed out of their research. "Why would they want to get into your files?"

Noa shrugged. "I don't know. Maybe I'm just getting paranoid in my old age but I've been seeing a lot of Milliman and Odell together lately. Milliman is anxious to prove he's a better head administrator than your father ever was, more hands-on, and Odell is ready to stab him in the back to get there first. I'd rather they both leave us alone and let us work. But I was thinking, if they could get into mine"—he winced—"they can get into yours."

Tru held the communicator for a few seconds in silence. She'd never considered cleaning out her files. All her theories, her research, her plans were in there.

"Let's hope they don't," she finally said, trying to convince herself. "Even if they did, I doubt they would come after me."

"No. But they might go after the Collection," Noa said. "Odell might."

She pursed her lips. She was beginning to think that Odell was on a mission, too.

"He's not getting close without the plate," Tru replied firmly. "And the only way anyone is taking this plate from me is off my dead body."

Noa shuddered visibly. "Don't say that, Tru. A lot of people would consider that a small price to pay."

Rayce heard her exit the lav. Maybe she'd run out of things to talk to herself about. He waited for her to get back into bed, but instead, he recognized the gentle hum of his data computer. Interesting. Since he was pretending to be asleep but actually spying on her, he couldn't very well turn around and see what she was doing in his computer.

Then he gave a mental shrug. Knowing her, she was probably running calculations on how long it would take to complete this crazy mission and get rid of him. Fine with him. A man could only take a gorgeous, intelligent, sexy woman for so long.

He stared at the wall while she began to whisper instructions to the computer. He tried to make out her commands but got nothing. After a while, he stopped caring and fell asleep.

A soft rustle behind him woke him. He had rolled onto his back in his sleep in time to catch Tru slipping back into her bunk out of the corner of his eye—a flash of long, bare legs just before she pulled the covers over them. He checked the time. She'd been up for four hours and it was almost morning on-board ship.

"You didn't get much sleep," he said casually.

There was a pause and then a quiet, "No."

He rolled over on his side facing her. "Do you always play games on the computer when you can't sleep?"

She turned her head to look at him with tired eyes. "I never play games."

His smirked a little. "Never? So what do you do for fun?"

She blinked as if she didn't know what he was talking about. Then she frowned in thought. "When I have free time, I usually undergo a neural language interface."

He laughed, shaking his head. She had a sense of humor after all. She slowly closed her eyes and turned back to the ceiling. That's when he realized that she was serious.

A disturbing thought nagged at him. "So how many interfaces have you had, Tru?"

Her eyes opened, stared far away. "Around eighty-eight, including Curzon."

He shot up in bed and looked at her in disbelief. "Eighty-eight? Don't you know that the maximum for humans is twenty?"

She shrugged wearily. "I needed to know them."

He leaned forward. "But it's not safe."

Her gray eyes rounded on him, slowly energizing. "Alien cultures are my specialty. I wouldn't be much of an expert if I didn't know their verbal and written language."

"It can do permanent damage to your brain," he said deliberately.

She yanked her cover off, sat up and swung her legs off the bed to face him. "I've had no ill effects. What do you care?"

"No?" He pointed to the lav. "What do you call talking to yourself for an hour?"

Her mouth dropped open. "You eavesdropped?" She huffed loudly. "How typical. For your information, I was talking to someone else."

He put a hand up. "I don't want to hear about all your imaginary friends. In fact, I'd really appreciate it if you could send them home until this mission is complete."

Her eyes widened. "I am *not* crazy."

"I sure as hell hope not, since you are the one leading this little adventure."

She dropped off the bunk to the floor and stood in front of him vibrating with anger, her face flush, eyes blazing. Passion. He knew it. So it *was* under there after all. He dropped down in front of her, close enough so he could feel her fervor.

Her eyes drilled into him. "This is still *my* mission. *I* did all the research, *I* came up with the theory, *I* found the plate."

He leaned in. "But don't forget, I'm your partner."

"So?"

He stepped toward her and she jumped as if she'd been shocked and backed against her bunk. He moved in closer, trapping her with his body and an arm on each side.

"We had a deal," he said softly.

All he could hear was her sudden gasp and the ship's smooth hum. Everything else disappeared as he lowered his head for the kiss that was owed him.

Her breath caught as he leaned in and brushed her full lips. He heard her faint, "Don't." He paused and looked into her eyes where tears welled up. Why? For a little kiss? Was she that disgusted with him? Anger flashed through him. To hell with it. He wasn't a monster. Not like her.

He skimmed her lips again firmly with great control, absorbed her heat, smelled her night scent. She didn't protest this time so he kissed her deeper, wanting a taste. And again, nibbling, sampling, testing her. His body responded to her little sighs, to the way she felt warm and soft against him.

Then, to his utter surprise, she melted into his body. Heat roared through him, hot and fast and more potent than he could handle. Recklessly, he captured her mouth. Her cheek was cool and moist next to his, her palms hot against his chest. She felt good, tasted even better, hotter than any woman he'd ever had. And just under the surface, he sensed a simmering pool of passion and the tenuous control she held over it as she leaned in and kissed him back for the very first time. He sucked in a breath when her arms went around his neck, pulled him closer to her . . . desperately. That was all he needed—to feel her desire for him.

"Damn," he muttered against her mouth, yanking her against him hard.

Their mouths fought for purchase, both hungry for more. Breath, hot and fast, fanned the flames. His hands went to her waist and up to her breasts. He thumbed a hard nipple through his own shirt and she moaned his name. It was enough to remind him who she was. He froze.

What the hell was he doing? *He wanted a Majj.* It wasn't supposed to be this way. *She* wasn't supposed to enjoy this. This was her punishment. He broke off the kiss and held her at arms length. Her eyes were closed tight, lips swollen, open and ready.

Suddenly her eyes opened and she stared back at him, innocent desire turning quickly to shock. She pushed him away and glared at him for a moment. He watched her expression harden and her eyes turn cool as she remembered who he was.

"Looks like you survived another day of torture," she said curtly and she headed to the lav.

Just before she reached it, he said, "No more language interfaces on this mission, Tru."

She stopped dead in her tracks but didn't turn around. "I'll do whatever I have to."

Chapter Seven

Tru watched the blue wash of hyperspace shift to star lines and then into pinpoints of light that dotted deep space. Rayce's spaceport sat directly ahead of them. Its silver-tiered layers looked stunning and precious against the black backdrop. She'd have never guessed Rayce could have envisioned such a project. But then again, many things were not as they appeared.

"Are you always so quiet when you don't sleep?" Rayce's voice cut through her thoughts.

She turned to him sitting in the seat beside her. "You wish."

He laughed. "Yes, I do actually. I'll have to find a way to keep you up at night."

Her eyebrows went up at his innuendo, but he didn't pursue it. She watched his hands move over the controls, guiding the small ship into a shuttle bay.

"I ran the calculations last night," she said casually.

113

He looked at her. "And how long will it take?"

"Each leg is around one point five days, a bit longer to the pinnacle. That does not take into account actually locating each pyramid, if they still exist, and placing the plate. Probably another day for each location. Since we don't know which planet or moon in the final solar system contains the last pyramid, I estimated two more days and another day to figure out how the Collection is released."

He nodded. "So twelve days at best."

"Unfortunately, yes," she muttered.

He grinned in response. She *hated* it when he did that. It always took a while for her brain to jump-start again afterward. Twelve more kisses like the one earlier this morning. She wasn't sure she could handle the way they scrambled her senses. Her brain could sustain permanent damage in twelve days. And he certainly was enjoying himself by making a fool of her. She tapped her fingernail against the seat arm. There had to be a way to defuse his little ploy.

"So can we do the whole twelve days without having to come back to the spaceport?" she asked.

He maneuvered the ship through the shuttle bay entrance. "We'll have to refuel at least twice."

The ship touched down gently.

Rayce powered down and turned to face her. "We'll do Rostron next and then Arête. Refuel back here. That should be enough for the last two legs. How's that sound?"

She gaped at him in shock. "Is this like an actual plan you are letting me in on? Beforehand?"

He narrowed his eyes and leaned forward. "Take it or leave it. I don't get in these moods very often."

"Then I'll take it," she said, failing to hide a smile.

They exited their seats. She was out of the ship first and Gil greeted her in the shuttle bay. "Welcome home."

"Greetings, Gil."

Rayce exited behind her and gave Gil a slap on the back. Tru heard the click of nails on the floor like a small army advancing even before Elvis bounded through the shuttle bay door and headed for Rayce. In a flurry of yipping and tail-wagging and pawing, the dog skidded to a halt and licked Rayce's outstretched hand. Then he ran around Rayce a few times, sniffing and nuzzling his legs.

"Is he always so . . . enthusiastic?" Tru asked Gil as she watched the strange rebonding ceremony incredulously.

"Daily. I'm told he'll calm down in a year or two but I have my doubts." Then Gil brightened. "So, it looks like we have an interesting mission."

Tru fell in step beside Gil with Rayce behind them and Elvis underfoot, running happy circles around them.

She raised a quizzical brow. "Did Rayce fill you in on the plan?"

Gil laughed and threw a glance back at Rayce. "There's a plan? With Rayce? Not likely. More like random inspiration."

Rayce muttered, "I'm getting pretty sick of you two knocking my organizational skills."

Tru grinned as Gil let out a howl. "Is that what you call those?"

"How are renovations coming along, Gil?" Rayce asked tersely.

Gil recovered from his own joke and answered,

"Great. I did, however, have an investor who insisted on seeing the place first-hand."

Rayce frowned, "Really. Who?"

They stopped in front of Rayce's office. The door opened and a tall, stunning woman stood up from the table. She floated to Rayce, her violet eyes on him, effectively ignoring the other two people in the room. A woman of obvious wealth, Tru realized, taking note of the delicately crafted jewelry against copper-colored skin, the slinky violet shimmer dress and alluring makeup. She was exquisite in every detail, breath-taking, seductive and regal. From her clothing and features, Tru would guess that she was from Freelynd, a wealthy and genteel planet famous for its generous philanthropists.

The woman wound her arms around Rayce and he reached around her waist. "Kasha. What a nice surprise."

Tru's stomach knotted uncomfortably as she watched him smile roguishly and kiss Kasha. Then he bent his head lower and whispered something in her ear. Kasha threw her head back and laughed, a throaty, sexy laugh that made Tru grind her teeth. So Coburne *could* be charming. Just not with her.

She felt Elvis next to her leg and glanced down at him. He was surprisingly subdued and serious. *Now* he decides to become civilized.

Then Rayce turned to her suddenly and said, "Kasha, this is Tru Van Dye. One of my clients."

Kasha stepped forward and gave her a formal Freelynd bow of greeting and a practiced smile. "Very nice to meet you."

"A pleasure," Tru responded, bowing similarly.

Kasha gave her a cursory glance and then slipped

her arm through Rayce's. "So how about a tour of your beautiful place? I've been waiting patiently for you."

He grinned. "I happen to be free."

"Perfect," Kasha purred. She turned to Tru. "I hope you don't mind if I steal him for a short time. We have much to catch up on."

Tru looked at Rayce. His eyes were on her intently. For some reason, she could feel the heat rise in her face and hated him for it. "I don't mind at all. If you will excuse me, I have plans to make." She accentuated the word *plans* and grinned at Rayce. His eyes narrowed. Good, she thought. Let him worry.

Then she bowed politely to Kasha, exited his office and was surprised to find Elvis by her side. She shrugged. As long as he didn't try to bond with her, he could tag along.

She walked down the corridors to her assigned room, wondering why she was so irritated. It occurred to her that she'd never been as frustrated, flustered, and unstable in her life as she'd been on this mission. And she could blame it all on one man.

Her room door opened and Tru walked in and directly to the giant window with a view of the stars. Billions of stars blanketed deep space but she barely noticed.

"So what that he has other women?" she said to the dog as he planted himself in the center of her room. "I know that. I knew that coming in." The dog's head followed her while she paced in a tight circle.

"He's probably had every woman in the sector."

Which would explain why he kissed so well, she added silently. What a fool she'd been, giving in to a simple kiss so quickly, so easily. It hadn't meant a thing to him.

He'd humiliated her again, breaking it off suddenly like that, toying with her. She had to get a grip on her runaway hormones. He was just a man, a guide, a forced partner. Oh, and a womanizer. She couldn't forget that.

She stopped and turned to Elvis. "How much do you want to bet that he called his ship *Miranda* after some past lover? It's a wonder he doesn't have a whole fleet of ships by now. Kasha, no doubt, would be a big, flashy one."

It was obvious that he'd had some kind of relationship with Kasha in the past. She wore the smug, superior look of a woman who knows she's been there first. And she oozed sexuality from her graceful walk to her body-clinging dress. Tru glanced down at her silver bodysuit and winced. It didn't ooze anything, least of all anything sexy.

Tru crossed her arms. "It shouldn't matter, Elvis. I'm on a mission. Period. Besides, it's not like *I* want him." She glanced at the dog. "The man is impossible. He's coerced me into a damn kiss every day. Can you believe that?"

The dog whined softly in sympathy. Then he cocked his head and his tongue lolled out.

Tru shook her head. She was talking to a creature with a brain the size of her fingernail.

She glanced out the viewport and saw her own reflection. And it wasn't a pretty sight. Her eyes focused in on the icy image of herself.

Her hair lay tight and knotted on her head, her

eyes cold, her posture rigid and stiff. She didn't
even have laugh lines around her mouth. Odell was
right. She was frigid, frozen. No wonder she
couldn't arouse a man.

Why was sex so easy for other women and so
difficult for her? The woman in the glass didn't answer. She couldn't. She didn't know why. At the
Institute, she had acquired so much education, how
could she know nothing of what it was to be a
woman?

Other women had sex and babies. All around her,
the universe was procreating. And she'd never even
come close. Sexuality wasn't a hot topic at the Institute. Odell's one attempt to bring her to orgasm
had proved a dismal failure. She'd been too embar-
rassed to research sex and if other women at the
Institute knew anything, they weren't talking.

All her accomplishments, the research she'd
helped her father with, the gains for humankind,
hadn't made her a woman.

She'd failed womanhood. Was that even possible?

She pursed her lips. A Van Dye didn't give up,
wouldn't be outdone by anyone. This was just another mission to conquer, another goal. She'd approach it as she would any genuine project.

But she'd need a research assistant, someone with
some experience with women. Someone whose reputation was well known. Someone . . . like Rayce
Coburne.

She groaned at the insanity of it all. Why did it
always have to be Coburne? Weren't there any other
men in the galaxy to choose from?

Besides, asking him was out of the question. She

could only imagine his response after she practically threw herself on him in the ship this morning.

Coburne, would you mind teaching me about sex? It'll only take a minute. Of course, we can wait until after you stop laughing hysterically.

No, she couldn't use Coburne. Ever. However . . . One side of her mouth lifted. Why have harsh, cold reality when you can be whoever you want to be in virtual reality?

Tru walked over to her desk and rifled through her bag until she found the VirtuWav cylinder containing Noa's program. It felt cool and smooth in her hand. Success was only a virtual step away.

She looked up at her reflection in the window, smiling like sin. Women everywhere have sex. A certified genius should be able to figure it out.

"Did you settle Kasha in a room?" Gil asked as Rayce entered his office.

He nodded. "She's suitably impressed with the place."

Gil grinned. "Really? I thought she was suitably impressed with you."

Rayce dropped into the chair next to Gil and sighed. "She's already mated. It doesn't matter what she thinks of me. I have no intention of standing between her and true love."

Gil laughed and shook his head. "I don't think true love is what she's after."

"You're right about that," Rayce agreed with a grimace, recalling how difficult it had been to extract himself from her grip. "But she's not getting anything else. I need her credits. And I don't need some crazed mate coming after me."

"Who would know?" Gil offered with a shrug.

"I would. Besides—"

The center comm link rang softly.

Rayce turned to the comm screen and answered. "Yes?"

A male face filled the screen. Dark eyes and full lips set off perfectly styled hair and a square jaw.

"Are you Rayce Coburne?"

Rayce frowned. He hated when a conversation started like this. "I am. And who are you?"

"Odell Horge. From the Koameron Institute. I'm the assistant to the head administrator."

Rayce clenched his teeth. *A Majj.* "And?"

"I have proof that you know the location of a Majj named Tru Van Dye. She left the Institute without proper authorization and is considered missing." Odell paused for a moment, then added. "We are concerned for her safety. Especially if she is indeed with you."

Rayce grinned. "Is that right? Well, that makes my day."

Odell frowned deeply, obviously not amused, and Rayce grinned wider.

"Her safety is of paramount importance. We would like her returned to the Institute as soon as possible. Is she there?"

Rayce studied Odell for a moment. What was going on? She was certainly here of her own free will. So why was the Institute looking for her? Improper authorization? Did she sneak out? He found that almost impossible to believe but then again, she'd coerced him into this damn mission. He wouldn't have thought her capable of that, either.

"Why would you think she was here?" Rayce asked.

Odell paused. "That is classified information, I'm afraid. *Is she there?*" he repeated again, more insistent this time.

Rayce crossed his arms over his chest. Obviously, she was in some kind of trouble with the Institute. They didn't want her loose. It occurred to him that he could turn Tru in and be free of her, her crazy mission and probably the Collection, as well.

But something wasn't right, he could hear his danger bells ringing. And he trusted this Odell less than he trusted Tru.

"I have no idea who this woman is. Never heard of her before, never met her."

Gil slapped the table and whispered "yes" but Rayce pretended not to notice.

Odell's permanent smile froze on his face. "If you are having trouble identifying her, I can describe her in detail."

Rayce narrowed his eyes as Odell smirked. A smirk of a man who'd just made a private joke. "So you know this woman personally?"

The Majj smiled crookedly. "Yes. We are . . . acquaintances."

Rayce didn't need a manual to tell him exactly what Odell was saying. His dislike for Odell doubled.

"No description necessary. I can spot a Majj a kilometer away. I haven't seen her," he said firmly.

Odell's expression went from barely pleasant to harsh in a flash. "I know she is there. You are hiding her."

Rayce leaned forward, so his face would appear

bigger in Odell's screen. "She's not here. I'm not hiding her. And I don't give a damn if you believe me or not. Have a lousy day."

He cut the comm link and the screen went blank.

Gil said, "What do you think that was all about?"

Rayce stared at the blank screen. "I don't know but I am *not* happy about it."

"No kidding. You think she snuck off that planet? Why? I mean, I thought she was here for a legitimate mission. You think she hasn't told us everything?" Gil asked in disbelief.

Rayce stood up and rolled his shoulders. "This may come as a shock to you, but she's been deceiving us from the beginning."

Gil shrugged. "Well maybe, but I'm sure she had her reasons."

"You think so?" Rayce asked him mockingly. "And here I thought she was just using us to get what she wanted."

Gil changed subjects. "That guy was pretty mad. Do you think he'll come looking for her?"

"I don't know," Rayce said. "Odell doesn't strike me as the adventurous type." He paused. "But I do think he knows why she's here."

"How would he know about that? If Tru slipped off the planet, she obviously didn't want anyone to discover what she was up to."

"That . . . is an excellent question. One I plan to get a lengthy, detailed answer to."

Gil looked at him warily. "So what are you going to do?"

Rayce grinned. "Don't worry. I won't hurt her."

"Well, I hope not," Gil sputtered. "Leaving her planet illegally isn't a crime, at least to us."

Rayce turned and headed to the door. "No. But bringing more Majj here will definitely annoy me for the rest of my life."

Rayce entered the VirtuWav bank and stepped next to Hencke at the console. The crewman dwarfed the small display. If it weren't for the fact that the man was as gentle as a lormux, he'd actually scare people.

Tru floated in the VirtuWav tube in front of him looking positively ethereal in the blue light. What was she doing in his VirtuWav?

"How long as she been in there?" Rayce asked.

Hencke blinked rapidly as he always did when speaking, "She just went in." He grinned. "Nice lady. I like her."

"Right," Rayce muttered. And a hell of an actress, too. "What program is she in?"

Hencke shrugged his massive shoulders. "I don't know. She brought her own."

Rayce paused. "Did she? Now that's interesting," Rayce said, as he stepped into the VirtuWav circle next to hers. "Enter me in her program."

Hencke frowned. "I don't think she's expecting you."

"It's an emergency."

The giant man's eyebrows went up and his blinking became furious. "Is she okay?"

"She's fine," Rayce said, becoming annoyed at Hencke's obvious loyalty to a woman he didn't even know. "Just put me in there, Hencke."

"Sure, boss."

The blue tube rose up around him, the gas making him buoyant while the VirtuWav's fingers tickled his brain and took over his senses.

In a flash, he was standing in the middle of a loud, seedy saloon. For a moment, all he could do was gape. Of all the places he could picture Tru in, this was the last one on the list. What the hell kind of program was she running?

Then he heard a familiar voice and spun around to find himself sitting on a stool at the bar. He stared at the virtual Rayce Coburne in complete amazement. She had him in a program.

Him.

In her program.

And what was he supposed to be *doing* in her program? He closed his hanging jaw and decided to find out. Besides, the virtual universe wasn't big enough for two Rayce Coburnes.

"Computer, cancel virtual Coburne character."

His virtual counterpart dissolved. Rayce sat down in the vacated stool and waited. This should be enlightening.

Around him, the saloon chatter ebbed and flowed. It could have been any saloon in any bad part of any town in the sector. He took a swallow of the drink in front of him. Safin. It burned down his throat and he coughed. One thing about the VirtuWav—everything felt acutely real.

He spun around and propped his elbows on the bar. Apparently, Tru had some kind of secret life he was only beginning to discover. He should have figured. Those brainy types were wound too tightly. All work and no play. He couldn't wait to see what she had in mind for him.

He took another swallow and caught a flash of red at the door.

The Safin nearly lodged in his throat. There stood Tru wearing a short, tight red dress and very little underwear beneath it. At least it looked like Tru. Her hair was down, cascading around her shoulders, lips red and full, and sultry gray eyes that zeroed in on him, alone.

The saloon got suddenly very quiet as her heels clicked across the floor toward him.

"Holy shit," he mumbled under his breath. She was hot. It was a wonder the floor didn't sizzle in her wake.

She stopped in front of him. "Mind if I join you?"

He almost didn't recognize her sultry, low voice. It took him a moment to realize he was supposed to answer her. "Not at all."

Her long body slipped onto the stool next to him, the short skirt creeping higher over creamy thighs.

"Can I buy you a drink?" she asked him, her eyes slightly hooded.

Okay, fantasy date program, he thought. Apparently, they weren't supposed to know each other. "Sure."

She leaned over the bar, her breasts settled on the metal surface, her nipples hard as bullets.

Rayce downed his entire drink in one swallow and tried to focus his eyes on something less distracting. That was when he noticed the other male patrons in the saloon ogling Tru and gave them a warning look. Virtual or not, no one was getting near her until he figured out what was going on. Two new drinks appeared and Tru handed one to Rayce.

"I understand you are a man for hire, an acquisitions specialist," she said as she sipped her drink.

He eyed her warily. This was getting downright weird, but he'd play along. "That's right. Can I help you with something?"

She smiled slyly. "It must be dangerous what you do." His eyes followed her long throat down to her breasts pushing against the thin fabric, her narrow waist, and the endless legs.

"Sometimes," he said slowly. "I have a feeling it's less dangerous than you are."

"You think I'm dangerous?" she said, genuinely surprised and pleased.

He watched her smile blossom. Damn, she was gorgeous. His body was wide awake and fully attentive. It finally dawned on him. She was trying to pick him up. And it was working.

"What are you doing in a saloon?" he growled.

Her eyebrows rose and she glanced around. "I like it here." Her head swung back to him. "Don't you?"

"No, I don't." He shot down his drink and slammed it on the bar. "Look, we need to talk about a few things ..."

Suddenly Tru stood up and sauntered toward the door. She turned and looked at him over her shoulder. "Coming?"

He shook his head. She wanted to play games with him. Fine. He shoved off the stool and walked behind her, watching her sway gently beneath the slinky red dress.

He stepped outside into a dark, empty street and was about to set this whole matter straight when

Tru turned, slid her arms around his neck and pulled him down for a lethal kiss.

Instinctively, his hands went to her waist. She leaned into him, pressing all those curves against him while she kissed him with a vengeance, unleashing that underlying passion, just for him. He didn't stand a chance. All he felt was heat, instant and overwhelming, as desire consumed his every cell.

Her hands ripped at his shirt, snapping the front releases until she could slip inside. He groaned as her warm hands skimmed over his skin, found his nipples and gently scratched at them.

"What are you doing?" he croaked.

"Do you want me?" she whispered.

He should have thought about it, should have let reason into play, but it was too late for his brain to chime in now. Besides, there was no way to deny it with his erection pressed against her soft belly.

"I want you," he mumbled, telling his brain to go to hell. This was virtual reality. She didn't know *he* was real. He could be whoever he wanted.

"Computer," she said softly. "Bed chamber."

The saloon and street were immediately replaced by a dimly lit room and a large bed. Rayce's head came up as he looked around. The room was lined with flowers, their scent sweet and heady. Damn, she meant did he want her *now*. She was seducing him. Actually, she was seducing his virtual twin. But they were the same . . . weren't they?

"Listen, I think you should know something," he started, his voice sounding a little strangled as her lips made their way down his bare chest. She found his nipple and tongued it.

He swallowed hard. "I'm not who you think I am."

"I know exactly who you are. I need you to teach me," she said as she turned her head up and looked into his eyes. "Show me what it's supposed to be like. You said you wanted me. Do you?"

He gazed at her eyes, full of fear and determination. He realized that she did need him. And for some reason he couldn't fathom, she'd picked him of all men to show her . . . sex? She was a grown woman. Didn't she already know?

She didn't wait for his answer, instead stepped back and peeled the dress up and over her head, and stood naked before him. He almost couldn't breathe, had never seen such a perfect body or skin so smooth. Dusty-rose nipples tightened before his eyes. He reached out his hand and skimmed one with his thumb. Her body shuddered.

He wanted her, all right. More than any woman he could remember in a very long time. His body was screaming, drowning out any valid excuses he tried to conjure up.

Besides, it was only sex. It didn't mean anything.

He yanked his shirt off, left his pants on for some semblance of control. He was hard as a rock, ready to burst already and they hadn't even started yet.

"I have to warn you," she said quietly as he pulled her down on the bed on top of him. "I'm not very good at this."

"You could have fooled me." He chuckled low, caressing her back, buttocks, legs with his hands while his mouth covered hers. Then he felt hot tears on his face.

He pulled back and frowned up at gray eyes crying. "Why?"

She tried to pull away but he held her tight. He'd seen this look before. On the ship when he kissed her, every time he got too close. She wasn't escaping until he started getting some answers.

Her body trembled under his hands and she shook her head. "Maybe this isn't a good idea. It probably won't work."

"Why would you think that?" he asked, wiping the tears from her face and hair. They felt real enough.

"This isn't really me. I'm not sexy, I'm not seductive," she took a deep breath. "I'm not what men want."

His hand paused. "Who told you that?"

She pursed her lips. "Someone at the Institute."

Rayce narrowed his eyes. "Let me take a wild guess. Odell?"

She blinked at him. "You know Odell?"

"I've heard of him," he said, evading the slipup. "He's a friend?"

She bit her lip. "Not really. More of a failed lover. He couldn't . . ." She looked away as another tear rolled down her face. "I didn't excite him."

A quiet anger filled Rayce. "Odell's a prick." He snagged her hand and pressed it over his pants and erection. Her eyes widened as she traced the outline and stroked the length.

Rayce groaned and struggled to talk coherently. "Happy? Let me tell you with absolute certainty that you are a very sexy woman."

She slid her palm over him. "I never realized . . ."

Rayce moaned and pulled her hand off him.

"You'd better stop or I'm not going to be able to finish what I started."

He rolled them both over so he was on top and in control. Well, in as much control as was possible under the circumstances. She watched him, waiting for him to teach her.

"We lost momentum," he murmured against her lips.

She laughed softly, rubbing her thigh against his crotch. "You don't feel like you lost anything."

He kissed her jaw and throat. "You created me, remember? I can do whatever you want." At least, he hoped so.

"You're different than before," she whispered, frowning a little.

He stilled. *Before?*

So, she'd been here before with his virtual self. Was this some kind of seduction fantasy program? No. This was new for her, he could tell. So what had they done *before?*

"You are different, too," he whispered back, took her head in his hands and kissed her hard enough to make her forget all her questions. She responded in kind, their tongues tangling and untangling. He ran his tongue along her lips, she nipped his. Heat, reckless and wild, returned just like that. Rayce felt raw desire overtake him.

He clamped down on it, forcing his body to obey, bent his head and kissed the hollow of her throat. She sighed. He kissed her again and she arched up, subverting his self-control with her passion.

Little peaks demanded his attention. He wrapped his lips around one nipple as Tru's breath caught and exhaled in a quiver. Was it virtual reality that made her feel so perfect?

His hands moved over impossibly soft skin and well-toned muscle, from waist to hip to thigh. Physically, she was perfection, everything he'd ever wanted in a woman. His erection was becoming painful, demanding attention, or at least, liberation.

"Undress me," he murmured against her skin.

"What?" she mumbled, her eyes blinking open.

He rose up over her and nibbled the corners of her mouth.

"Take off my pants," he clarified. He wanted her to do it, to see how hard he was for her.

He felt her hands fumble over his body, fingers find and work the fasteners on the pants, every move torturous to a man in his condition.

Then his erection dropped heavily, freed. Tru shoved the pants down his legs as far as she could and he kicked them off the rest of the way.

"Better," he said. Then he felt her hands wrap around him and squeeze. He growled low. "Much better."

Skin to skin, he knew he didn't have much time. Not with her warm hands on him and her soft body beneath him. He reached down, skimmed the blonde curls between her legs. Then lower.

His fingers grazed her soft folds and felt every muscle in Tru's entire body freeze in unison.

"Easy," he said in her ear.

"Don't. I can't—" she said haltingly. "I'm frigid."

Rayce banked his rising anger and continued his gentle ministrations. "Odell."

She nodded, but didn't seem all too upset about it this time. Instead her eyes were closed tightly, a slight frown on her face as she concentrated on the new sensations he was unleashing.

"He hurt you," Rayce said softly. "I'm not Odell. You know that, right?"

She nodded again, distracted, lost in sensation. "Yes. Don't stop."

He smiled. "I won't. Not yet."

He stroked her gently, watching her reaction to each minute move he made. His fingers found the tiny bud and rubbed it gently. She moaned and writhed beneath him. As he worked, he stroked her body, kissed her lips, the line of her jaw, behind her ear. Minutes passed and she relaxed, in tune to his every move.

"Oh," she moaned finally. He could feel her body heat rise, steam from within. The passion he'd sensed and tasted so briefly in her kisses blossomed like a delicate flower. He looked down at her flushed face, her parted lips, felt her quick breaths against his skin and knew that she was close.

"Too hot," she gasped and tried to escape. "No . . ."

"Relax, Tru," he whispered.

Her head rolled back and forth, her fingernails dug into his shoulders. She coiled, grimaced, sucked in a breath. Then she stiffened and cried out and a great shudder wracked her body. He watched her orgasm swallow her in waves. He'd never seen anything more beautiful.

As the flood subsided, she struggled to catch her breath, moaning softly. "Oh lord," she whispered between shaky breathes. "No wonder people love sex."

Rayce noticed her glowing face, the look of surprise and discovery. "Was that your first orgasm?"

She nodded, swallowed hard and wet her lips. Her gray eyes opened to his—soft and heavy. She reached up and stroked his cheek, seemed fascinated by it. "It was wonderful," she said, hushed and then smiled. "But, I'm pretty sure there's more." She rubbed her thigh against him, taking all thoughts from his mind. "Show me the rest."

He was her first. Emotion surged through him, stronger than lust, more than desire. Possession. Even a virtual man could take only so much. He parted her thighs with his and positioned himself. She felt wet, ready and more relaxed than he'd ever seen her.

Control. Control was in short supply at the moment but he wrestled with it anyway. He gritted his teeth, drew a deep breath and surged steadily into her. No resistance, but tight.

She cried out, her nails piercing his skin.

"I'm sorry," he rasped.

"Oh . . ." she moaned. "That feels so good," and she wrapped her legs around him so that their bodies fit together.

He exhaled in relief. He hadn't hurt her.

"Just hold on," he said in her ear. And he proceeded to roll into her, pulling her into his rhythm. Her soft whimpers of pleasure fed him like fuel.

She murmured little words to him in his ear, her breath hot. He was losing the battle with control, her heat subverting his best intentions. She kissed his face, her fingers exploring his body while her own body enveloped him. And then there was only driving, merciless lust, an urgency and need so great, he never knew he had it. He pumped faster, bringing her along with him. He felt her tighten around him, watched her head loll back and then blinding release ripped through him. He grunted at the intense pain and equally powerful pleasure—both welcome.

Minutes ticked by before he finally opened his eyes. She smiled at him, sexy and sweet. Lazy satisfaction.

"So now you know," he said with great effort, his body sprawled over hers on a soaked bed.

Her voice was hoarse. "Odell's a prick."

"You learn fast," he replied with a chuckle, rolling off her and onto his back.

She curled up next to him. "Us cerebral types don't miss a thing. Ask me anything."

He thought about that for a moment, his fingers running idly through her thick hair splayed across his chest. *Ask me anything*. Why did she sneak off the Institute? Why was Odell the Prick tracking her down? Why hadn't she said she was hiding? Why was this mission so secret?

He had questions for her all right, but they would have to wait. So instead, he asked her the obvious. "Why me?"

He felt her still, and then she replied softly, "I don't know. I suppose there were a few reasons. You have experience. You are physically compatible. But mostly because I trust you."

His hand and heart stopped at the same time. "Maybe you shouldn't."

She yawned. "I know you are a decent man, even if you don't like who I am."

A decent man. Right. A decent man would have

told her that he was real and not a virtual simulation. If she ever found out, he'd be a dead decent man.

It suddenly occurred to him that he had to get out of there. If she came out of the program first, she'd see him floating in the VirtuWav next to her. That would be a hell of a coincidence for him to explain his way out of.

Her steady breath told him she'd dozed off. A lucky break for him. He slipped carefully out from under her. She looked like an angel sleeping on the bed. A trusting angel.

He frowned grimly. "Computer, exit."

Blue filled his eyes and reality flashed back. The gas lowered him gently to the floor and the tube slid away.

Hencke gave him a curious look. "Is everything all right, boss?"

"Fine," Rayce replied. He stepped up to the giant and looked Hencke in the eye. "But when Tru comes out, it's important that you don't tell her I was in her program."

Hencke's mouth dropped open slightly in confusion. "Didn't you go in there to find her?"

"Yes, I did but things didn't work out like I planned. Just don't tell her."

Hencke blinked several times. "If that's what you want, but I don't understand."

"Trust me. It's a matter of life or death," Rayce muttered as he watched Tru float in the VirtuWav tube.

Another thought occurred to him. *Before.* There was a virtual Rayce in that program that he knew nothing about. She built him based on what she could find on the "real" Rayce Coburne. However, there had been times in his life that he wasn't particularly proud of.

He turned to Hencke. "And one more thing. If she comes in here again with that program, let me know immediately."

The giant looked at him with growing skepticism. Hencke may be slow but he wasn't stupid. Rayce sighed. "Let's just say that she might get hurt if I'm not there."

Hencke shrugged his massive shoulders. "If you say so."

Chapter Eight

Sex. No wonder everyone did it.

Tru smiled smugly as she strolled slowly down the corridor back to her quarters, humming a nonsense tune. Not just sex, but great sex. The kind that ruins you for the rest of your life.

She wanted to commit each sensation, each caress to memory, replay it over and over in her mind until it was real. There was so much more to it than she'd imagined. So much . . . touching.

She hadn't been touched in a very long time, not since she was six, not since her mother died. Her father had never hugged her, never laid a hand on her. Public physical contact on the Institute was simply forbidden and private contact discouraged.

She shook her head. Stupid rule.

And the heat. She could still feel it smoldering in her belly. Not like the empty, horrible pit she'd suffered after Odell stripped her of everything with his cold hands and colder heart.

At least this time, she'd picked the right man. It

was as if Rayce knew exactly what she needed, moving slow enough to make her want more, fast enough to keep her on the edge. He knew how to touch and where; his hands were firm yet gentle; his body hard and strong. Her ideal lover.

Too bad he was impossible in real life. If she could only keep him virtual and naked, he'd be perfect.

She entered her quarters and stopped short. Kasha stood at her viewport, silhouetted by black space. Covered from neck to ankle in gold fabric, the woman turned around, her expression hard.

Tru frowned. Where was Elvis when she needed him? "Can I help you?"

Kasha raised her chin. "How well do you know Coburne?"

Interesting opening line. Tru countered, "Why?"

Kasha folded her arms and regarded Tru coolly. "Because he turned me down."

"Turned you down?" Tru repeated slowly. For a moment, she drew a blank and then realization set in. This stunning, alluring woman had propositioned him and he'd turned her down. If she hadn't heard it from Kasha's lips, she wouldn't have believed it. Maybe there was hope for him after all.

"I'm sorry, I don't know him well. I hired him as a guide."

Kasha narrowed her eyes, skeptical, although Tru couldn't figure out why. It couldn't be too difficult to see that there was nothing between her and Rayce. At least in this dimension.

Kasha walked over to a tall vase brimming with fresh flowers from the gardens and removed a perfect stem. She took a deep sniff of the delicate flower and then proceeded to pluck out a petal, tossing it on the floor. Another followed.

"I knew your father," Kasha said casually. "We had—" she glanced up from mutilating the flower and finished, "dealings."

Tru's blood ran cold. "He's dead."

Another petal floated away. "Yes, I heard. A pity. He was most cooperative. I admired his way with credits." Kasha smiled at Tru. "Among other things."

"Why are you telling me this?"

"Because I gave your father Rayce's name. And that's why you are here, isn't it? It must be important if you are finishing your father's work."

So that's how Coburne's name came to be in her father's belongings. Had her father planned on going after the Collection himself?

"What is your point, Kasha?"

"Perhaps you need a backer. My mate and I are always looking for a new project." Kasha gave her a pasted smile.

"I don't need your credits. And I thought you were already backing Rayce."

Kasha shrugged. "I'm not so sure this spaceport is such a good investment anymore."

"How can you say that? I'm sure you've seen the plans. It's going to be magnificent."

"I'm losing interest."

Anger welled up in Tru as she watched the once lovely flower float to the floor, bit by bit. So maybe she didn't like Coburne all that much, but Tru knew a good idea when she saw it. And she knew trouble when she saw it. Kasha was definitely trouble. Tru didn't know how many credits Kasha had invested, but she'd bet it would be enough to ruin the project if it was withdrawn.

"There is nothing like this spaceport in the sector. It's a certain success."

Kasha tossed the wasted stem aside and brushed her fingertips clean. "Perhaps. I just don't feel . . . enthusiastic about the project anymore."

Tru crossed her arms. "You seemed enthusiastic enough when you arrived. Perhaps your mate would like to know why you had a sudden change of heart."

The other woman glared at her. "I'll tell him the spaceport won't open on time. And he will believe me."

Tru took a step toward Kasha, using her height to intimidate. A little trick she'd learned from Rayce. "And when it does finish on time, who will your mate believe?"

"It's obviously behind schedule," Kasha snapped.

Tru's anger trembled within her. "Oh, it will be finished on time. I guarantee it."

Kasha glanced at Tru's Majj crest. "Really? And how can a Majj *guarantee* it? Do you have your coffers behind you?"

"No," Tru growled.

Kasha crossed her arms. "So how *will* you guarantee that Rayce will make this metal bucket work?"

Tru looked past Kasha at the stripped stem and clenched her teeth. "Let's just say I have a plan."

It was night on the spaceport. Although space didn't need day and night, humans did. Rayce walked the corridors of Level Six, noting work that still needed to be completed. He shoved his hands in his pants pockets. From the beginning, he'd believed he could pull this off and expressed his absolute confidence to every investor he could find. They had all trusted him. And now, he wasn't so sure.

A long time ago, he'd dragged himself out of poverty with gambling, stealing, illegal jobs, whatever it took to eat and help his family survive. His entire life he'd overcome one obstacle after another, worked jobs no other man wanted, taken risks that no sane man would have taken. All to reach this point and the biggest gamble of his life.

He needed that Collection and he didn't want to need it. Didn't want anything remotely involved with the Majj near his dream. Blood credits. And every time he'd walk these halls, he'd know that the Majj were here.

He turned into the shuttle bay where *Miranda* was docked and walked over to the front of the small ship. He placed his palm against the black hull. He'd named the ship after Miranda the minute he'd seen it. She was fast, agile and tough. Just like his sister before the Sykes Fever stole her energy and destroyed her body.

Rayce closed his eyes and heard again her cries as the disease ate away at her. Twenty years and he could still hear it. He'd have sold his soul if it would have helped ease her pain those long, final days and nights. He had laid in his bed, fists clenched, listening to each labored breath she took, the pain it cost her, his mother's constant soothing words. For days, she lingered, suffered and fought a war she would not win.

Worthless and unsuccessful treatments sapped her energy, leaving just a skeleton of the girl he'd loved and grown up with, and put his parents into a debt they could never repay in a lifetime.

Until one day, silence. No more pain, only weeping. And anger. Lots of anger. Rage so strong he'd wanted to tear at the walls, rip away everything that reminded him of his desperate life.

She shouldn't have died, not so young, not so horribly. Her innocence and generosity were no match for a killer disease and a senseless death. There was no reason for it. No reason except that the Majj needed credits before they would distribute the only effective treatment. So there *was* a price for a human life and the Majj had set it. No apologizes, no sympathy. No one cared that a poor girl from an impoverished, plebeian planet had died with her small family watching. Her only crime was being born poor and, therefore, invisible to the Majj.

He'd vowed to never forget her, never to forget the injustice, never to let her disappear without a trace. He would remember and honor her if only with his own passion. And that's what he'd done all these years.

Now he'd just made love to a Majj. Given into his own selfishness and betrayed his own blood. Disgraced Miranda's memory for both credits and sex. So who was more immoral—the Majj or the man who helped them?

He hung his head and whispered, "I'm sorry, Miranda."

Tru sat next to Rayce, who hadn't said a word since they boarded *Miranda* this morning. She cast him a sidelong look. His profile was rigid and unforgiving. She crossed her arms and stared out into the blank hyperspace viewport. She shouldn't expect anything from him but somehow she felt vaguely rejected. All that heat, all that passion and kindness, gone.

A steady panting in her ear caught her attention and she turned to find Elvis seated on the floor next to her.

"Why is he here?" she asked Rayce.

He reached out and ruffled the dog's head. "Gil threatened to quit if I didn't take him with me."

Elvis turned and licked her cheek. She pushed him away. "I can't imagine why."

Rayce didn't respond, turning his attention once more to the scanners. Back to brooding.

Tru shook her head lightly. And to think she'd guaranteed the completion of his spaceport in front of Kasha. Some gratitude.

She had to stop thinking that he'd change into the same wonderful man she'd made love to in the VirtuWav. That man only existed in a digital program on a cartridge. Amazing how the real man could be so different. Noa would be very disappointed.

"Odell contacted me yesterday," Rayce said, interrupting her self-pity session.

Her heart seized up. She turned her head slowly toward him.

"Odell?"

Rayce's blue-green eyes swung around to her. His gaze was steady. "Odell. From the Institute. He was looking for you."

Looking for her? Tru blinked at him. Oh, lord.

How would Odell know where she was? Had Noa told him? She shook off the thought. No, Noa would never betray her. Had she left a trail? Had she . . . Then she remembered her files. Noa was right. The administrators had infiltrated her files, read them, and traced her to Coburne.

She barely got the words out, "What did you tell him?"

Rayce paused and said, "I told him I didn't know who or where you were."

"You did?" she asked in disbelief. "Why? I mean, you don't even like me."

He shrugged. "I didn't like Odell more. Why did you lie to them?"

Tru took a deep breath and rubbed her hands along the tops of her thighs. "I had to get off the Institute in order to find the Curzon Collection."

"So, what's wrong with that?"

She glanced at him in surprise. "Because no one leaves the Institute. Not unless they aren't coming back."

Rayce stared at her for a moment. "You mean you can't leave? Why not?"

"That's the way it is," she replied. "Admission to the Institute is by invitation or by birthright. But no one can leave unless there is special deviation. It's not allowed."

He narrowed his eyes. "You're prisoners?"

"Why, no," she said, appalled by the term. "We live there. We work there. We have no reason to leave."

"So you can't leave and if you do, they come looking for you. And that doesn't sound like imprisonment to you?" Rayce pressed.

Tru clenched her teeth. "I wouldn't expect you to understand the way the Institute works. The isolation makes us more productive."

He gave her a lop-sided grin. "Really? And is productivity why Odell wants you back?"

Tru stared down at her hands. "No. Odell wants me back so he can ruin me."

"Why would he want to do that? I got the impression that he was more than just a casual colleague."

Heat rose in her face. She really didn't want to have this conversation . . . again. "Odell and I are mutually incompatible."

Rayce started laughing, lightly at first and then out loud. When he stopped, he said, "That's a hell of a way to put it, Tru. I doubt mutual incompatibility is the reason he wants to ruin you."

"No, that's not why. Odell is one of the youngest administrators with his sights set on the head administrator position. I think he sees me as some sort of threat."

"Because of your father?"

Tru glanced at him. "Yes, but I'm not sure why. It's not my goal to become an administrator. It would cut into my work."

"I thought you Majj were all the same. How is an administrator different?" Rayce asked, suddenly serious.

"The administrators take care of the Institute, us, secure sponsors, distribute our ideas and discoveries. In short, they are our link to the outside world. It leaves us free to work. Rarely, as in my father's case, the administrators will accept a Majj. He continued his work even after he became head administrator, although I did the bulk of his research."

Next to her, Rayce stilled. Tru frowned at him. "Is something wrong?"

His gaze met hers. "So the Majj have no contact with the outside?"

She shook her head. "None."

"Just the administrators do," he prompted.

"Yes," she replied slowly. "Why are you asking?"

He stared at the console for a long time before answering her.

"So how did you find me?" he asked, a look of accusation on his face. "And how did Odell track you to me?"

"Is this an interrogation?" she asked. "I'm not putting you in any danger, if that's what you are worried about."

His expression hardened even more. "I figure you owe me some answers since I've got Majj calling me now and I'm not too happy about it. One is more than enough."

She felt the anger creep over her. She hated the fact that he could do that to her, but what the hell? She might as well use it. "What is your problem with the Majj? What could we have possibly done to you?"

He swung around so fast, she gasped. Even Elvis clawed the floor in a panic and skittered away. Rayce yanked her seat around to face him, his face stoic and harsh, his eyes dangerous.

"Do me a favor," he said in a low voice. "Don't ever ask me that again. You really don't want the answer."

She leaned forward, into his space. She was not going to pay for something he wouldn't even talk about. "Fine. Then you don't get any more answers from me, either."

His jaw muscles worked hard, she could tell he was fighting to maintain control. Then she watched his eyes fall to her lips and her heart sank. Oh no, not after the VirtuWav, not after the way he'd loved her so well. If he kissed her with all this anger, she'd . . .

Suddenly, he backed off, stood up and walked to the back of the ship, leaving her to exhale in silence.

She closed her eyes. Why hadn't he done it? It would have been so typical of him to try to intimidate and crush her. His anger was real and directed at the Majj and her by association. Whatever happened between him and the Majj was personal, but that didn't make any sense. The Majj didn't even have outside contact.

An uneasy feeling settled in her belly. The feeling that she was missing something significant.

Rayce woke to her cry, childlike and terrified.

"Don't go. Don't leave me."

At the foot of his bunk, Elvis was alert, watching Tru, his head cocked to one side.

Rayce rolled over and glanced toward her in the dim light. "Tru?"

She sobbed, shaking her head back and forth. "No . . . no . . ."

"Damn," he said as he rolled off his bunk and crossed to hers. Her face was contorted in grief.

"Tru?" He shook her shoulders. "Tru, wake up."

Her eyes flew open and stared into his, unfocused and terrified. For a few moments, she didn't register anything and then drew a shuddering inhale as her eyes settled on him.

"I'm fine," she blurted, clumsily brushing his hands aside and sitting up. Her hands shook as she fought with her wet and tangled hair. The shirt she was wearing—his shirt—clung in bunches around her, soaked.

"Are you all right?" he asked.

She nodded adamantly but didn't say a word, shaking hard now, from the cold wet shirt and residual anxiety.

She licked her dry lips. "I'm sorry I woke you," she said quietly. "I'm fine. Just a dream."

Long seconds passed before the intelligence returned to her eyes, when coherent thought replaced the ghost of nightmare. Her wounded eyes met his. "You can go to sleep now. It won't happen again."

He just stared at her. "A dream? It better not have been about that bastard Odell."

Tru adjusted the shirt around her legs. "I don't dream about Odell."

Rayce leaned back against his bunk, assessing her. "So how often do you have this particular dream?"

She winced. "Occasionally."

"Twice in four days. That's more than occasionally. How long?"

"It's really none of your concern, Rayce," she said, hugging her knees.

"How long?"

She glared at him. "Since I was six. Are you happy? Can you just go back to sleep and pretend you don't care about me again?"

"That's young. What did your parents say?"

Silence.

Rayce took a deep breath. "You did tell them, didn't you?"

"Dreams aren't real, Rayce. They have no factual basis or practical value."

"Don't go technical on me, Tru. You never told them."

"My father wouldn't understand," she said with a hitch in her voice.

"What about your mother?" he pushed.

A tear rolled down her cheek as she stared straight ahead. "She was dead."

For a minute, he couldn't think of a thing to say. Then he walked over to a cabinet and withdrew one of his clean shirts. He handed it to her. "Change."

She glared at him half-heartedly but he could tell there was no fight in her. She took the shirt, slid off the bunk and disappeared into the lav. He heard the shower run as he yanked off the wet sheets and threw on new ones. So the dream must be about her mother's death. That's why she sounded so small and sobbed like a child.

For some reason, he thought all Majj lived in a sort of sustained bliss. No worries, no debtors to pay, no pressure, no bad dreams, no going hungry. Now he was beginning to wonder just what kind of society this Institute had.

"Elvis," he said, glancing at the dog on his bunk, watching him intently. "Stay."

The dog yawned and lay his head down on his paws.

The lav door slid open and Rayce turned to Tru. In his shirt, she looked small and pale.

"Thank you," she said quietly as her eyes rested

on the clean bedding. "I apologize for waking you. Good night."

Her eyes widened in alarm as Rayce smiled wolfishly. "No problem."

She eyed him warily and climbed into the bunk, laid down and pulled the covers up to her neck.

"Good night," she repeated.

He grinned. "Move over."

"What?"

Rayce tried to lift the cover, but she clenched it tighter. He leaned over her and said each word deliberately. "Move. Over."

"No," she shot back. "Sleep in your own bunk."

He smiled. "I'm stronger than you."

She raised her chin. "I'm smarter."

"Then you should know your hard head is no match for my hard muscle."

"Why are you doing this?" she asked testily.

He pulled the covers from her hands and slid into the bunk beside her. "Because you'll spend the rest of the night on the computer if I don't."

He slipped his hands around her waist and held her tight, trapping her between him and the wall. Her back was pressed against his stomach and he could feel her heart beating wildly.

"It was only a dream. You don't have to hold me like a child."

He inhaled her fresh scent, felt her cool, damp hair against his cheek. "I'm not. I'm holding you like a woman."

He could feel the tension radiate from her body like a tightly wound spring. The problem with tightly wound springs was that they could do some serious damage if they went off in your hands.

She took a deep breath. "How long do you plan on staying?"

"Longer than you want me to, I'm sure," he said with a smile.

"Why?" she demanded quietly.

"Damned if I know." It was the truth.

For an hour, he stared at the wall over her head knowing that if he fell asleep before she did, she would escape to the computer for the rest of the night. He wasn't about to let that happen, even if it did shut her up for a while. She needed to be rested for Rostron.

And it had absolutely nothing to do with the fact that she felt damn good in his hands. Smelled good. Warm. Real. It beat virtual reality any day.

She relaxed one tiny, torturous, stubborn increment at a time. Finally, her last muscle relented, her breathing grew steady and shallow as sleep took her. The battle was over.

She sighed softly and snuggled closer to his warmth. He stifled a groan. She felt the same as she had in the VirtuWav. Her skin was as soft, her body as perfect. He wanted to explore her again, kiss her lips, and bring her to sweet release as no other man had done. Bury himself in her until she surrendered her body and soul to him.

He shook his head. The best sex he'd ever had had been virtual. His ego would never recover.

Tru woke up staring into a man's face. *Rayce.* In her bed. She lay sprawled over his chest and legs, her arm wrapped around his neck, her body nestled comfortably against his as if she belonged there.

She froze as his hands flexed on her waist and

his blue-green eyes opened to hers, near and sleep-laden. The shadow of a beard, the lazy gaze gave him a rogue's countenance.

Not a single thought came her to mind. Probably a first in her entire existence.

"Morning," he murmured low. And sexy. Just like he had in the VirtuWav. Her stomach clenched.

His eyes narrowed, intensified, the flame stealing any fledgling thoughts she was trying to gather. She could feel her nipples tighten against his chest. How did he do that?

Then he leaned forward and skimmed her lips against his, like a whisper. He pulled back and looked into her eyes. No anger. No punishment. Sweet, gentle. She wanted more. She just didn't know how to ask him for it.

He released her, stretching his big body with a long, male groan.

Tru watched in fascination as he swung his feet off the bed and stood up. Muscles flexed and cut across his back and broad shoulders. Thick thighs stuck out from under the thin shorts that did little to hide an impressive set of buttocks. He rubbed his neck with one hand and walked toward the lav without a word.

Tru stared after him, her heartbeat pounding in her ears, her body thrumming with tension. Desire. Sexual desire. She wanted him.

She closed her eyes. And not in some virtual world, either. She wanted him in this one. Wanted to feel his heat, his power, his skill. But more than that, she wanted what he'd given her last night. Compassion.

All night he'd held her. Just held her. Nothing

more. Didn't ask anything from her. Didn't try to analyze her. Didn't expect her to take care of herself. Didn't expect anything in return. And she'd had the best night's sleep of her life, feeling safe and cared for.

Vulnerable. Indebted. Dependent. She frowned. What a terrifying thought.

Chapter Nine

"So this is Rostron. Lovely. I can't wait to get to the surface."

Rayce eyed Tru as she gazed out the viewport. She turned quickly, caught him staring and smiled. A simple, soft half-smile, but potent. He shifted in his seat. It was becoming downright uncomfortable to be around her. Last night didn't help, only confirming that the VirtuWav was very accurate. A realization not easily shaken, especially by the rest of his body.

Somehow she'd changed since the VirtuWav, become more alluring, more touchable. Physically, she was the same except that she'd unknotted all that hair on her head and now it cascaded loose around her shoulders. Every time he looked at it, he wanted to reach out, slip his fingers through its heavy weight, bury his face in it, drag her beneath him and take her, make her his again . . .

He realized he was clutching the ship's controls white-knuckled, his body rigid and his pants even tighter. He took a deep breath, let it out and forced his taut muscles to relax. Where did that come from?

Beside him, she was concentrating on the planet's surface. "The atmosphere is tolerable for humans, a little on the warm and steamy side. The terrain is largely bogs, marshes and mud. Level of intelligence in the Sleewl species is unknown, as is their lifestyle, but I'm pretty sure they aren't the brightest species around. The Sleewl are rarely seen and their habitats have never been located. They have no perceptible commerce, industry, formal government, technology, communications capabilities or extraterrestrial contact."

Listening to her, Rayce shook his head in wonder. It was like having a walking, talking computer.

"So how do you study civilizations when you are stuck on that Institute all your life?"

"Our archives are the most comprehensive and complete anywhere," she replied, a note of pride in her voice.

He thought about that for a minute. "Would you know if they weren't?"

Her eyebrows rose. "Why wouldn't they be?"

He shrugged. "Your knowledge is only as good as your information."

She frowned deeply at him. "My information is the best. What are you getting at, Rayce?"

He didn't know exactly what he was getting at. But something didn't feel right. How could she be so knowledgeable about some things and clueless about others? Like how disliked the Majj were. Like the truth of poverty. Like sex.

"There's one thing you missed about the Sleewl. They can be very violent."

Tru bristled. "I've never read that. In fact, they are a mostly peaceful people, simply territorial."

"Uh-huh. Especially with their women," Rayce added.

"Their women?"

He grinned. "Don't they mention that in your archives? Apparently, good women are hard to find on Rostron. Better watch your step."

She narrowed her eyes. "Don't get any ideas."

He chuckled. "Just do everything I say."

"That'll be the day. There it is," she said, pointing to the left.

Rayce maneuvered the ship toward the pyramid, an exact replica of the one on Curzon except for its green tint. Circling the pyramid slowly, he scanned the surrounding terrain—black streaks scarred an otherwise non-descript surface of grays, greens and browns. Finding a solid place to put down was going to be a challenge.

He chose a dark spot about one hundred meters from the base of the pyramid, settled the ship onto it and hoped she didn't sink into the mud forever. Before the engines had even stopped, steam had already collected over the viewport.

He turned to Tru. "Ready to play in the mud?"

She looked distinctly repulsed. "Not particularly, but let's get this over with." She climbed out of her seat and stepped to the back where Elvis sat waiting patiently.

Rayce followed, smiling at how good she looked in the green flight suit he'd given her. It was identical to his own but she filled it out better.

Elvis nudged his hand excitedly and Rayce gave him a rub. "I have a feeling you are going to be one disgusting dog by the time we get back."

The dog barked and wagged his tail.

"Does he understand anything you tell him?" Tru asked.

"Probably not," Rayce conceded with a laugh, looking into the dog's grinning face.

Tru leaned against her bunk. "So have you figured out how I'll reach the top of the pyramid?"

"We," he said, off-handedly as he pulled two packs from the cabinet.

"Excuse me?"

"*We* reach the top."

Tru crossed her arms. "That's really not necessary. I'm perfectly capable of doing this alone."

"Look, partner," he started, shoving gear into one of the backpacks, "I'm going to make sure you and that plate stay safe. I don't need you breaking your neck."

"Ha!" she laughed. "And you think I'm safer with you?"

He sealed the pack and shoved it at her. "You are here. Know how to use a weapon?"

She took the pack and hooked it over her back. "We don't need weapons, Rayce. I told you the Sleewl are peaceful."

Rayce pursed his lips. "Regardless, I'm taking certain precautions. I'll handle the protection." He slipped a laser pistol into his side holster and pulled on his backpack. They headed to the back cargo bay.

"Open hatch," Rayce told the on-board computer.

The wide hatch door slid open smoothly. The first blast of humid air was the worst.

"That's repulsive," she said, waving her hand in front of her face. "Do you think something died nearby?"

"I think we landed on it."

Elvis jumped out first, his paws sinking into the soft ground. Rayce surveyed the immediate area. Through the low mist, mud mounds and skeletons of trees dotted the swampy landscape between small tufts of reeds and grasses struggling for purchase in the spongy soil.

Although it was mid-day, the sun's rays barely penetrated the dense fog that rose from the bog. Through the waves of mist, he could just make out the outline of the pyramid.

And it was quiet except for a strange, undulating buzz that he didn't like at all. Even Elvis was still, ears up, concentrating on the sound.

Pistol ready, Rayce took a step out of the ship and immediately sank to mid-calf. Within seconds, a steamy film covered his body, his gear and his weapon. It was going to be a long, miserable, filthy day.

He heard Tru step out behind him. He glanced back. She stood looking at her feet sunk in the muck and then up at the pyramid.

"You couldn't have landed any closer?"

He shrugged. "Feel free to drive next time. Just remember where we parked."

He pulled out a datapad, set their current location and pocketed it. Then he gripped the pistol and pulled Tru toward the pyramid. He became aware of the stillness all around them and how much noise two sets of feet made sloshing through the swamp. Walking was difficult; the soil formed a suction underneath every footstep. Elvis proved to be fairly quiet, his webbed paws negotiating the mud easily.

Beside him, Tru was keeping up, concentrating on her footing, her suit already covered in mud and humidity.

"Rayce, don't step on the flowers," she said in a firm tone.

"What?" he said, looking down. Next to his foot was a pathetic-looking plant with a few equally pathetic gray clusters sticking out from its stem.

She pointed toward it. "That's a flower."

He kept walking. "I doubt anyone on this disgusting planet cares if we crush a few flowers."

"I do," he heard her say behind him.

Well, hell. They were on an alien planet with unpredictable life forms and she was worried about the damn flowers. He shook his head and did his best not to step on them all.

It wasn't easy. The fog kept moving around them, clearing and then filling in again. It was the longest 100-meter walk of his life. Ahead, the pyramid rose up out of the swamp, a perfect shape in an otherwise lawless landscape, glowing pale green like a beacon.

As they drew closer, he could see the smooth stone that covered the giant structure; closer yet and the green tinge became algae clinging to the surface.

He stepped up onto the stone platform that formed the massive pyramid's foundation. Solid ground felt good.

Elvis leaped up to a walkway around the base, shook himself and immediately trotted around the perimeter.

Rayce helped Tru up onto the stone platform and gave her a cursory look. Thick mud encased her legs and boots and was spattered across her suit, which was plastered against her skin. He didn't need any imagination to see what was underneath.

He scanned the swamp behind them as Tru examined the pyramid wall.

"How did they make this?" she whispered reverently. "Where did they get the stone from?"

He shook his head. "We'll probably never know."

He reached out and slid his hand along the smooth, seamless surface. It came back covered with green, just as he'd figured it would. "This is one slippery pyramid."

Tru gazed up the side and pursed her lips. "I hate to even ask, but you realize this requires a plan?"

"I happen to have one," he said, reaching into his bag.

Next to him, she gasped. "You do?"

"Yes, and if you're really nice to me, I may even let you in on it."

He pulled out a compact cleaning unit and examined the underside, programmed some settings and attached the little machine to the side of the pyramid. It whirred and stuck hard with no sliding or movement.

"A servo-unit?" Tru asked. "What is a cleaning machine going to do for us?"

"Trust me," he said with a grin. Then he retrieved a grapple pistol and attached the grapple end to the servo-unit. With a quick flick of his hand, the entire length of cable shot out into a pile at his feet.

Rayce pulled out his datapad, entered a few commands and the servo-unit began to climb slowly up the side of the pyramid, cleaning a path as it went, its powerful suction holding it tight to the surface.

He said, "I figured if it can climb walls and ceilings, scaling a pyramid would be easy."

Tru looked at Rayce. "Where is it going?"

He watched the servo-unit disappear into the fog. "To the top, hopefully. I used the datapad to program it to stop when it detected a change in footing. If you hear a crash, it miscalculated and shot off the side."

While the cabling advanced at a steady rate, Rayce glanced around. No sign of Elvis. He whistled and within seconds, Elvis came bounding around a corner.

"Where have you been?" he asked the dog. Elvis rubbed his hand and then snapped his head around toward the swamp. A low growl emanated from his throat.

"Is something wrong?" Tru asked.

Rayce looked out across the swamp and shook his head. "I don't know. But Elvis generally hears better than humans. Keep an eye on things, pal." He patted the dog's head.

Suddenly, the cable attached to the servo-unit stopped dead.

Rayce picked up the pistol and attached it to the integrated harness on his flight suit, then reached out and pulled Tru to him, harness-to-harness and attached them together with a resounding click.

She looked down at the setup. "What are you doing?"

He grinned. "Protecting my partner."

Then he took her with him as he fell back against the hard stone of the pyramid. She landed on his body, her arms against his chest and froze.

"Rayce, I don't like this plan. I think we should discuss it first," she said, her gaze moving from his face to the cable and back.

"Too late," he said as he wrapped one of his arms around her tightly and triggered the grapple pistol with the other hand. They shot up the side of the pyramid, both of them riding on his back. Tru buried her head in his chest and held on for dear life.

The ascent was slow but steady. He became acutely aware of Tru's heat against his front and the cool slime against his back. Their ascent slowed to a halt with the back-end of the servo-unit just above his head. Tru finally looked around and then glared at him.

"This is the best solution you could come up with?"

"No, but it's the most interesting. Comfortable?"

"Now that you've got us up here, what do we do?"

"The apex should be on the other end of the servo-unit. Can you reach it?"

Tru stretched as far as she could. "I don't think so. Let me move up a little."

He groaned as she levered her body higher, pulling the harnesses as far apart as they would go, her breasts now pressed into his face. She had no idea what she was doing to him. He could feel her groping around above the servo-unit.

"I can reach," she said finally.

"Got the plate?" he asked, semi-muffled against her breast.

"Yes, but it's in my pocket. I don't think I can get to it."

Not that he was complaining, but they were dangling from a servo-unit far above the ground on a hostile planet. So he asked, "Which pocket?"

"Right hip."

He slid his hand along her waist and buttocks. Damn, she felt good. It took him a while to locate the plate and hand it up to her.

"About time," she muttered and stretched up. A second later, he heard her give a little moan. Not in pain; it sounded more like pleasure. Much like one he'd heard from her in the VirtuWav. Then her body rolled against his. Hot. Sexual. He groaned. She had lousy timing.

Then she slid back down with a strange look on her face.

"What happened?" he asked.

She showed him the plate. It now had two sides completed. Then she shoved it back into her pocket and he grunted at the move.

Tru's eyes widened. "Did I hurt you?"

He chuckled and dropped his head back against the hard pyramid wall. "Not quite. Now comes the fun part."

Tru frowned. "Fun part? What fun part?"

He released the grapple and they dropped—fast. She clutched his shirt and gave a small scream.

As the bottom drew near, the descent slowed and finally stopped and below them, solid ground. Rayce planted his feet and took a quick look around. Elvis didn't even acknowledge their return and stood facing the swamp, the hair on his back raised.

Tru was already fumbling to release her harness but the clips wouldn't cooperate. His hands closed over hers.

She looked at him with a jolt. He gazed back as he deftly released her clips.

"Like the ride?" he asked, detaching his own harness.

"Not particularly, no. You have a real sadistic streak in you," she said, annoyed. Then she glanced at the top. "What about the servo-unit?"

Was she worried about a little, brainless robot? He shrugged. "I don't feel like lugging it back to the ship so I guess it can spend the rest of its useful life cleaning this pyramid."

She stared up at the pyramid wistfully. "I bet it was stunning when it was first built."

"Too bad there isn't anyone around to appreciate it." He pushed off the pyramid wall. "Let's get back to the ship before the locals show up. Come on, Elvis."

He drew his pistol and jumped off the platform, Tru and Elvis right behind him. Using his datapad for direction, they trudged through the muck. About halfway back, the buzzing swelled and Elvis's growling with it. It didn't seem to be coming from one place, it was more like a chorus around them.

Suddenly, a giant shape lunged up out of the mud in front of Rayce. Beside him, Elvis barked and bared his teeth.

"Oh, no," Tru gasped.

The Sleewl blinked at them, his outer eyelids sliding over the inner ones and the whites of his bulging eyes. The rest of him was covered in a slimy mud but the shape was unmistakable. A hooded head, wide mouth, barrel chest, long arms with four-fingered, webbed hands. He towered above them, the muscles stretched and bulging in his powerful legs. His mouth split open, revealing jagged teeth and a thick tongue. The tongue slid out, wiping a swath of mud from the creature's face and eyes, then drew back in slowly.

That tongue was a weapon, long, fast, muscular—capable of wrapping around a human neck and crushing it in seconds. Rayce gripped his pistol.

The Sleewl hissed loudly and a choir of buzzing answered. Elvis stepped up between the Sleewl and Tru, barking and growling.

"Easy, Elvis," Rayce said firmly. He whispered to Tru, "I don't suppose you had a language interface for Sleewl."

She answered, "Are you kidding? If they have a language, no one knows it. Smile at him."

Rayce muttered, "I don't think he's going to be swayed by our good graces."

The Sleewl gave a massive bellow and the buzzing rose to a fever pitch.

Rayce took a step around the swamp beast. It didn't move. He took another and motioned to Tru to follow him. The Sleewl simply watched them. Rayce waded past the beast, dragging Tru along. Elvis brought up the rear, snarling at the Sleewl.

"Come around in front of me," Rayce told Tru as he shot a glance over his shoulder. The Sleewl was gone, leaving Elvis to bark at the mud where the beast had stood. "And get back to the ship as fast as you can."

166

She struggled in the mud but made good progress. All around them, the swamp droned. Rayce could have sworn he saw waves in the muck, ripples just under the surface. The fog surged like an ocean, making it difficult to see clearly. Elvis followed behind, stopping to bark at every shadow.

They were fifty meters from *Miranda* when Rayce felt the prickle in the back of his neck that told him trouble was close by. He spun around to find the Sleewl looming behind him, looking far more menacing than before. It screamed and, behind him, another Sleewl rose up out of the swamp. Then another.

"Tru, move!" he yelled and took off with her. All around them, Sleewl were appearing. "Elvis, come!"

He heard the dog's four paws splashing through the muck.

"They are surrounding us," she called back.

"Don't stop for anything. I'll make sure we reach the ship."

He looked ahead. The good news was that *Miranda* appeared unscathed. The bad news was that a hulking Sleewl was waiting for them. And Rayce had a feeling it wasn't going to move out of their way without a little encouragement.

He raised the pistol and shot past Tru and into the mud at the Sleewl's legs. The beast gave a great bellow but didn't budge.

They were almost to the ship now, not more than twenty meters. Rayce aimed at the Sleewl's head and fired. There was a sizzle as the laser hit between his bulging eyes and he crumpled to the ground.

Around them, the rest of the Sleewl began closing in. Rayce charged ahead of Tru and activated the cargo door. It gaped open and he leaped inside, sliding in mud, and then turned and fired at the closest one. Tru reached the door seconds later and he grabbed her outstretched hand.

Her eyes widened just as he tried to pull her into the ship. Halfway into the ship, she stopped. He looked up and saw a slimy, mud-encrusted hand latched onto her left arm.

"Rayce," she cried out, terror filling her eyes as she was stretched between him and the Sleewl. Her hand started slipping from his. He heard a loud pop in her shoulder and her scream of pain. Then a black flash as Elvis leapt up and latched onto the Sleewl's arm, snarling and growling and holding fast. The Sleewl shrieked and released Tru. She tumbled into the cargo bay on top of Rayce.

"Elvis, come!"

The dog bounded through the hatch, skidding across the floor beside them.

"Computer, close hatch," Rayce called out. The door sealed immediately, followed by a series of hard thumps. The Sleewl were trying to get in.

Tru moaned, her face twisted in agony. The entire ship rocked as Elvis barked at the cargo bay ceiling. The beasts were climbing on top and *Miranda* was sinking.

Rayce slid Tru flat on her back across the floor to the wall and secured her harness to wall straps. She moaned loudly, holding her right arm, tears streaking down. Elvis had moved beside her and licked the mud off her face.

GET TWO FREE* BOOKS!

SIGN UP FOR THE LOVE SPELL ROMANCE BOOK CLUB TODAY.

LOWEST PRICES EVER!

Every month, you will receive two of the newest Love Spell titles for the low price of $8.50,* **a $4.50 savings!**

As a book club member, not only do you save **35% off the retail price**, you will receive the following special benefits:

- **30% off** all orders through our website and telecenter (plus, you still get 1 book FREE for every 5 books you buy!)

- Exclusive access to dollar sales, special discounts, and offers you won't be able to find anywhere else.

- Information about contests, author signings, and more!

- Convenient home delivery of your favorite books every month.

- A 10-day examination period. If you aren't satisfied, just return any books you don't want to keep.

There is no minimum number of books to buy, and you may cancel membership at any time.

* Please include $2.00 for shipping and handling.

NAME: _____

ADDRESS: _____

_____

_____

TELEPHONE: _____

E-MAIL: _____

_____ I want to pay by credit card.

__ Visa   __ MasterCard   __ Discover

Account Number: _____

Expiration date: _____

SIGNATURE: _____

Send this form, along with $2.00 shipping and handling for your FREE books, to:

Love Spell Romance Book Club
20 Academy Street
Norwalk, CT 06850-4032

Or fax (must include credit card information!) to: 610.995.9274. You can also sign up on the Web at www.dorchesterpub.com.

Offer open to residents of the U.S. and Canada only. Canadian residents, please call 1.800.481.9191 for pricing information.

If under 18, a parent or guardian must sign. Terms, prices and conditions subject to change. Subscription subject to acceptance. Dorchester Publishing reserves the right to reject any order or cancel any subscription.

"Hold on, Tru. We have to get out of here. I'll be back in a minute, I promise."

He stood up and raced into the cockpit, yelling orders to the computer as he went. By the time he sat down, the engines were running and the liftoff sequence had begun. The banging outside grew louder and harder. Sticks probably. Tools. It appeared the Sleewl were moving up the evolutionary ladder.

Miranda shuddered hard, her engines whining. He increased thrust and the ship bucked right, then left, then lifted free.

Rayce grinned as he gunned the engines and Rostron fell away, leaving the Sleewl staring up at him.

He swung the ship around hard to the right and saw a black body roll off the ship and plummet to the ground below.

"That was for Tru," he growled. He laid in a course to take them out of Rostron's atmosphere, jumped out of his seat and grabbed the medical kit on his way back to Tru. Elvis whimpered to him. She hadn't moved. Her face was pale and cool, her breathing shallow. She was going into shock.

"Talk to me, Tru," he said quietly as he kneeled down next to her, trying to calm his breathing and his rattled nerves.

Her eyes fluttered open and she looked back at him, pain clouding her gray eyes. "I hate Rostron."

He smiled. "That's unanimous. Hold still." He stretched the med-vid film across her right shoulder. Bones, ligaments, blood vessels appeared and statistics scrolled up from the bottom. Diagnosis: dislocated shoulder. The med-vid displayed the recommended manipulation to relocate the joint.

He exhaled. That shoulder wouldn't wait two days until they arrived back at the spaceport. He set the film aside and pulled out an Aritrox injection. He gave it to her and said, "I'm going to have to relocate your shoulder. The Aritrox will help heal the damage in a day or two."

With pain-filled eyes, she watched him pull off his muddy shirt and toss it aside.

She whispered, "Tell me you've done this hundreds of times and it won't hurt a bit."

He swallowed as he laid her right arm out flat and felt around her shoulder, mentally practicing the necessary manipulation. "I've done this hundreds of times and it won't hurt a bit."

She nodded stiffly and her eyes began to glaze over, the Aritrox taking hold. "Then do it."

Rayce took a deep breath and gripped her arm with one hand and placed his other hand over her shoulder, his face close to hers. Tears rolled from her eyes in silent pain and cruel anticipation.

He gritted his teeth and pulled her arm straight out firmly, then slid it back up into the socket with a dull pop. Tru threw her head back and screamed, long and hard. His stomach did a tight pitch and roll as Tru's head lolled back and forth, her eyes glassy from pain and Aritrox. Elvis whined and nudged her hair.

A quick scan with the med-vid showed the socket to be normal again, aside from ancillary swelling.

"We're done, Tru," he said. "I need to get you out of this flight suit and into your bunk. Try to support your arm for me."

She mumbled something unintelligible, the Aritrox swamping her ability to speak.

He released her suit's fasteners from the neck to the waist and pulled the flaps back. Creamy skin and breasts greeted him. He sucked in a breath. She hadn't worn anything beneath it. Damn. And he thought the shoulder was tough.

His hands shook slightly as he gently tugged the suit over her shoulders and maneuvered it out from under her, pulling the mud-caked outfit down her legs and off.

Eyes closed, she hugged her right arm across her chest to support it, just like he'd asked.

"Good girl. I'm going to carry you into the cockpit," he whispered to her, slipping his hands beneath her body and lifting her up. She curled up against his chest as he made his way to her bunk and carefully laid her down on it.

"Rayce?" she murmured as he pulled covers over her.

"Yes?"

She licked her dry lips. "Thank you."

He leaned against her bunk and hung his head. "Don't thank me. I lied to you."

"About what?"

"I never did that before and it hurts like hell."

She gave a pained laugh. "I kind of figured that out myself." Then her eyes opened, focused on him for a second and closed. "You didn't get your kiss today."

He traced the tears down her face with his fingers. "I'll make up for it tomorrow."

"Now would be okay with me," she said with a

tremble in her voice. Gray eyes struggled open, defenseless.

He fought back the overwhelming guilt. Those kisses were supposed to be punishment, and somehow, for some reason, she wanted one now. From him. After all she'd just been through. She wanted him to kiss her.

He lowered his head and skimmed her lips with his. Her hand came up around his neck and held him in place while she kissed him back softly. Then she gave a great sigh and slipped into a Aritrox healing sleep.

He watched her for a while and faced something he didn't want, didn't need. He cared about a Majj.

She swam through a haze of scrambled thoughts, connecting and disconnecting. With great effort, she opened her eyes and looked around. *Miranda*, her bunk, safe. Not a Sleewl in sight. The memories flashed back—mud, black figures everywhere, the horrible pain, Rayce's gentle treatment, and then nothing. Not even a nightmare.

She shivered under the covers and realized that she was naked. Funny, she didn't remember getting undressed. She touched her face that had been spattered with mud. Clean. Rayce must have . . .

A wet tongue licked her face. She turned her head away from where the dog sat next to her bunk.

"Elvis. You really need something for your breath." The dog gave a sharp bark in greeting.

Rayce appeared instantly from the galley, looking tired and a little ragged.

"Are you all right?" she asked.

He walked to her side, a weary smile crossing his face. "Fine. How's the shoulder?"

Shoulder. She rolled it and winced. "Feels great."

"Right." He pulled the covers down a little and she was acutely aware of his warm hands on her skin as he examined the area.

"It's a wonder that bastard didn't break your arm," he said bitterly.

She smirked a little. "I'm surprised you didn't let him have me."

Rayce's blue-green eyes met hers with a steamy intensity that went right to her belly. She felt the wave of desire roll through her, ignited by his hands on her bare shoulder.

"I would have gone back for you," he said seriously, and covered her shoulder again. "How's the pain?"

"Not bad," she murmured, preoccupied by the fact that he would have fought for her. He didn't even like her. He didn't care about her mission, he didn't . . .

Then lucid thought and sudden panic seized her and she shot up on the bunk, taking the cover with her. She rifled through the blankets. "Where's the plate? We didn't lose it, did we?"

She looked up to find Rayce staring at her, a look of annoyance on his face that she didn't understand. Then he reached into a nearby cabinet and set the plate in her hand. Half complete now, it hummed and vibrated, stronger than before. She looked up at Rayce. "Can you feel that?"

He nodded and crossed his arms. "It's getting more powerful."

"Almost as if it's collecting energy from the pyramids," she surmised.

"Damn," Rayce said, shaking his head. "That's exactly what it's doing. I felt the surge when you set it on the pyramid at Rostron."

Tru blinked at him. The same surge she felt? The same sexual current that almost incapacitated her? Did he know that the only reason she hadn't attacked him was because they were hanging off the side of a pyramid? Then another thought struck her: If this one was stronger than the first one, what was the next one going to feel like?

"Yes," she stammered. "There was definitely a surge. I wish I knew what all this stored energy is for."

"Maybe we'll find out at Arête," he said.

"So are we heading there now?"

He shook his head and ran a hand through his black hair. "Back to the spaceport. The Sleewl damaged the outer hull and one of the wings. Nothing serious, but I don't want to chance it. Shouldn't take my mechanics more than a day to repair but it'll put us behind schedule." His eyes met hers. "Your schedule. I hope you don't mind."

Mind? No, she didn't mind. She should but she didn't. Even if he hated her, even if he hated the Majj, she felt safe with him. Felt . . . special. He'd have gone back after her. No one had ever come close to that.

"No. What about you?"

A smile spread across his face. "Whatever it takes. We're past the point of no return, partner."

Chapter Ten

"I've been thinking."

Rayce eyed her sitting next to him at the helm. Thinking. Always a dangerous thing with Tru.

He entered the commands to bring the ship out of hyperspace. "About what?"

She rubbed her hands along the tops of her thighs and stared out through the viewport as the galaxy streaked to a halt around them. "I made a mistake on Rostron."

"How do you figure that?" he said, glancing up to find the spaceport directly in front of them. *Home.*

"I didn't know the Sleewl were violent. I should have done more research. I failed on my end of the bargain. I'm sorry."

He shrugged and checked the readings. "If you say so."

Then he noticed her hands were trembling on her lap and he looked at her serious expression.

She shook her head. "I'm supposed to be the

alien-cultures expert. I didn't do my job. I could have gotten us killed."

"You didn't, so don't worry about it. None of us is perfect, Tru. We all make mistakes." He grinned. "Even I, occasionally, screw up."

She frowned. "I don't."

He leaned back and crossed his arms. Huh. "Never?"

"Never."

"That's a lot of pressure, to be perfect all the time."

She stared at him for a moment before replying. "There's no excuse for mistakes."

"Does that apply to the rest of us mere mortals?"

"My rules apply only to me," she said steadily.

"Well, normal people screw up all the time. It's called *life* out here. Didn't you ever make a single mistake at the Institute?"

"Just one," she said sadly. "Odell."

Rayce humphed and entered the ship's landing procedure. "I wouldn't call him a mistake. More like a prick."

His hands froze for a second over the controls. Shit. He knew he'd erred the minute he said it. He also knew she wouldn't miss it.

She blinked. "Excuse me?"

"Don't beat yourself up over picking the wrong man." There, that should throw her off.

She stared out the viewport pensively. "My mistake was thinking that there was a right man."

Rayce laughed. "Tru, you are hell on a man's ego. Every man likes to think he's just right."

She said softly, "Right or not, it just wouldn't work."

"What about sex?"

Her gaze swung around to him. That got her attention. "Sex?"

"You know, sex. A man, a woman, lots of heavy breathing and grunting."

She opened her mouth to speak, closed it, and finally said, "Not every woman needs sex."

He grinned. She didn't sound at all convincing. "What about making love?"

A slight frown crossed her face. "Same as sex."

He shook his head. "No, not the same. Sex is the act. No attachments. No strings. Making love is a bond, a connection." He leaned toward her. "Risk."

She backed up a little. "I don't take risks."

"You hired me."

"My synapses misfired," she muttered.

He hummed. "So you are saying that if you really cared for a man that you wouldn't want to have sex with him?"

"I've never cared that much for a man," she said coolly. "Have you ever cared that much for a woman? To risk?"

"No." He gave her a wide grin. "But I still like sex."

"So you can have sex with a woman and just walk away and feel nothing?"

He scowled, wondering when he'd lost control of the conversation. "You make it sound like I have sex with every woman I meet."

An amused look crossed her face. "You have quite a reputation."

"Maybe so, but I'd sure like to have enjoyed it more."

Gil's voice interrupted. "Welcome home. Shuttle bay 13-A is open for you."

"Thanks, Gil. See you shortly," Rayce replied and cut the comm.

"Back to my mistake," Tru said with a great sigh. "I promise I'll be more thorough next time. I won't jeopardize the mission again."

Rayce stared at her. "Tru, it's all right to screw up."

"No, it's not," she said in a hushed voice.

He watched tears well up in her eyes. No, it was not all right to make a mistake. Someone had drilled that into her head. Some prick.

"Let's make a deal. When you screw up, I'll save your ass and when I screw up, you can save my ass."

Her mouth dropped open. "That doesn't seem to be much of a deal. You screw up all the time."

He laughed. "Hey, you don't hear me complaining."

Rayce guided the small ship into the cargo bay and touched down lightly. Tru had her harness unsnapped and was standing up when he caught her by the arm. She raised her eyebrows in question.

"Kiss," he said softly, looking into her eyes. And he waited. She didn't move for a long time and he wondered if she forgot what she had said under the influence of the Aritrox, if the drug had brought out the truth or the lies.

Then she leaned forward, her eyes staying open, watching him as she lightly kissed his lips. A tender, sweet, lingering kiss that set his blood boiling. It was all he could do to control himself, to keep from pulling her onto his lap and giving in to clamoring hormones.

Her eyes were steady on him as she walked to the back of the ship, leaving him alone with his imagination.

"So, how was it?" Gil asked as they exited the med center. Rayce glanced back over his shoulder to make sure the door was shut so Tru couldn't hear him.

"Bad," Rayce replied quietly. "Hopefully, I didn't do any damage resetting her shoulder."

Gil gave him a lop-sided smile. "Don't worry. The medics will take care of any damage." He shuddered. "But I still can't believe you did it."

They turned into an elevator.

"I had no choice. She couldn't stay like that for two days." The vision of her rolling in agony flashed back. It was an image he'd never be able to shake. Just like Miranda.

Rayce cleared his throat. "How are things here?"

"Not good, either," Gil answered, shaking his head. "The investors are getting restless, the subs want their pay, and our suppliers won't extend us any more credit until we give them an opening date. So if you could get your hands on a small fortune in next few days, it would help greatly."

Rayce eyed his partner's weary expression. "I'm working on it. Didn't expect to be back so soon. How long for repairs?"

"A day should do it," Gil said, running a hand through his thick hair. "We are running out of time, Rayce. It could all fall apart."

Rayce hated to call in his friends but that's what they were there for. "I'll contact Cohl. He should be able to float us some credits. Enough to get everyone off your back temporarily."

Gil brightened considerably. "That would help. If nothing else, so I can sleep at night."

The elevator doors opened and they exited.

"So," Gil said as they walked the corridor. "You and Tru seem to have reached a truce."

One corner of Rayce's mouth went up. "In a way. There's a lot more to her than I expected."

"No kidding. How long have you been blind, deaf and dumb?" Gil shook his head and laughed.

The office door opened in front of them and Rayce entered, ordering the computer on. "I still don't like the Majj."

"No one says you have to like the Majj. I'm talking about the woman," Gil said, taking a seat at the table.

Rayce sat down in front of the comm and shrugged. "She's okay."

Gil slapped his leg and laughed. "Right. She's gorgeous, brilliant, and she can go nose to nose with you on an hourly basis. That puts her in the goddess category for me."

Rayce said to the computer, "Get me Cohl on Yre Gault."

Then he turned to Gil. "Let me tell you one thing I've learned about Tru. She wants that Collection and nothing is going to stop her. Do you know after the shoulder dislocation, all she cared about was that damn plate?" He shook his head in disgust. "As if nothing else mattered."

Gil crossed his arms. "Maybe that's all she has. Maybe it's her one shot. Like this spaceport."

Rayce scowled at him. "This spaceport is different. When it opens, a lot of people will benefit—my parents, workers, families—not just a bunch of credit-hungry bastards who don't give a damn about anyone outside their little world."

"Like Kasha? Our investors get a big chunk, too," Gil interjected.

Rayce growled. "It's not the same, Gil. I'm not in this to get rich."

Gil shrugged. "I know I am."

The comm bleeped and a familiar friend appeared. At least Rayce knew Cohl was on his side.

"How's the life of a king?"

Cohl grinned, his golden gaze meeting Rayce's. "It has its moments. Greetings, Gil. You still with this madman?"

Gil leaned forward and waved. "Still alive. And yes, I realize that's quite an accomplishment. How's Tess?"

Cohl hitched his head back. "She's probably in the lav. She hasn't been feeling well for the past few weeks."

Rayce frowned. Tess was a tough lady. "Is she sick?"

Cohl shook his head. "Pregnant."

"Congratulations," Rayce said with a growing smile. "That didn't take long. Your people must be thrilled."

Cohl gave a great sigh. "The pressure to produce an heir was brutal."

"Don't even try for sympathy from me. I've seen Tess. You weren't suffering," Rayce said with a laugh.

"And she'll never forgive me if I don't ask about her dog."

Rayce shook his head. "He's big and goofy."

There was an amused laugh. "I'll tell Tess. Is he around?"

Rayce looked around and realized that Elvis hadn't followed him out of the med center. "No. I think he's dumped me for my client."

"Your client? I thought you were done with acquisitions?" Cohl asked with a little concern.

"I need the credits," Rayce conceded. "And she might have a big payoff."

"She," Cohl repeated. "Now why doesn't that surprise me?"

Rayce shook his head. "Forget it. Not even close. She's a Majj."

Cohl's eyebrows went up. "No kidding. What's the payoff?"

"The Curzon Collection."

Cohl's eyes widened and he nearly jumped through the comm. "Do you have any idea how much that Collection is worth?"

"More than any one person can spend in a lifetime," Rayce muttered.

Cohl ran a hand through his hair. "That's a hell of a find, Rayce. The discovery of the millennium. Does she have the key?"

Rayce nodded, always amazed at Cohl's artifact knowledge. But then again, legendary artifacts were Cohl's former life. "She has it and it works." He hoped. "We're halfway there but I'm running on empty until we find it. I was wondering if you could front me some credits. I'll give you whatever you want out of the Collection."

Cohl whistled long and low. "What's your cut?"

"Half."

Cohl gave a good-hearted chuckle. "How did you manage half?"

"It cost me more than you'll ever know. Are you interested?"

"Sure, I'm interested," Cohl said, still shaking his head. "Half. Damn. I wish I could be there when you find it."

"So do I. I have no idea what to expect," Rayce said with concern. "Don't suppose you have any information?"

"Not right now, but I'll send you what I can find. And let me know what you need for credits."

"Thanks, Cohl," Rayce replied. "Give Tess my best."

"Good luck," Cohl replied and the comm went black.

Rayce leaned back in his chair. "Looks like we bought some more time."

Gil nodded. "I hope it's enough, but you might want to move your schedule up a little, just in case." He glanced at Rayce. "And try to stay out of trouble this time."

"I always do. Unfortunately, trouble always seems to find me."

The magnificent vase of flowers was the first thing she noticed when she entered her room. Gil must have ordered fresh ones just for her. She walked up the eclectic assortment and inhaled deeply.

She looked over the vase out into the star-studded eternal night of space, feeling good even though she wasn't sure why. Maybe because everything was coming together. Maybe because she finally felt that her mission was moving along and that success was assured. Nothing came close to the victory of a job well done, of a goal realized.

She doubted Rayce felt the same way, though. He seemed so casual about the whole thing. Didn't even bother him that she screwed up. Didn't matter that those mistakes could slow them down. They weren't the end of the world to him. As if it was the most natural thing.

Nothing less than perfection, Tru. She trembled, even now, even though her father hadn't uttered those words in years. She had performed well for him and given the flawless research he demanded. There had been no mistakes. Nothing but perfection.

But she knew few moments were truly perfect. She wanted that one perfect moment for her own, the time when she would stand up in front of her peers with her own Charter and take her proper place. It would be a moment like no other, never to be repeated again. A formal Majj Induction was performed only once and she planned to savor every second of it. The rumors would be gone, the snickering, the wise side-glances. She would belong, as was her destiny.

She touched a single ivory petal, humbled at the creation of such splendor. Funny how a flower didn't need to be perfect to be beautiful.

Tru pulled the stem from the arrangement, holding it to her nose as she crossed the floor and retrieved her comm unit. Its heady scent filled her senses while she activated the unit and waited for Noa to appear.

It took longer than she expected before his face appeared, tired and worried.

"Tru, where have you been?" he said roughly.

"Getting the second piece of the plate. Are you feeling well, Noa?" she said with deep concern. It was very unlike Noa to be so blunt and discourteous.

He looked behind him and returned. "Don't tell me any more than that."

"What?" A chill stole over her. "Noa, what's wrong?"

He gave her a beaten look. "Odell has started the disassociation process on you."

"He can't do that yet," Tru bristled. "Disassociation takes several months to get underway. I should have plenty of time to find the Collection and get back before it begins."

Noa shook his head. "Well, Odell has pushed the process. He's ripping your reputation to shreds, Tru." The old man sniffed hard. "I've done what I can but he's getting more powerful by the day."

"Prick," Tru muttered, under her breath.

"If the disassociation process is completed before you find that Collection, it'll be too late," Noa said, his eyes misting over. "You'll never be able to come back, no matter how valuable that Collection is."

Tru closed her eyes. *No.* It wasn't fair.

Noa continued, "And I wouldn't put it past Odell to come after you, either. Just to prove his point to the administrators and put himself ahead of Milliman. I have to believe you are in real danger."

"I have one weapon that Odell can't beat. Coburne."

"Do you really think Coburne will protect you at all costs?" Noa asked with a frown.

"If not for me, than for the Collection. He needs it as much as I do. Why are the other administrators allowing this, Noa?"

The old man gave a great sigh. "I'm not sure. I always thought they worked for us, protecting us. But lately . . ." He paused and lowered his voice. "But lately I've been wondering if they really are on our side."

She stared at him. "Why wouldn't they be?"

"I'm not sure," Noa said, shaking his head. "I've been trying to do some research but I'm not getting much. I seem to run into walls."

Would you know if your information wasn't complete? Rayce's words haunted her.

"Perhaps I can do some research on my side and get back to you," Tru suggested.

"No." Noa's abrupt reply surprised her. "You aren't going to be able to contact me anymore after this communication."

"Why not? We're secure."

"I can't guarantee that anymore," the older man said sadly. "My files have been compromised and so have yours."

"Noa, don't cut me off. You're my only link," she said, holding her voice steady through the panic rising inside her.

The old man's expression broke. "I can't guarantee that they won't trace our communications. Every time you contact me, you put yourself at risk."

Tru pleaded, "I'm willing to take the chance."

"I'm not," Noa said, sadness twisting his face. "I'm sorry."

And the screen went black.

Tru stared into the empty viewer, her heart pounding painfully in her chest. She tried to reconnect, but there was no response. Noa was gone.

She laid the comm unit down and steadied herself on the bed. *Disassociation.* A fate worse than death. It only happened to failures, those who couldn't cut it at the Institute. Those who weren't good enough. But she was good enough. She *had* to be. There was no other place for her.

She rubbed her hands on her thighs until they burned, until the numbness no longer held her. For a long time, she sat very still, trying to sort through her emotions. It didn't help, didn't resolve the mix of panic and anger and fear clamoring inside her, undermining her usual logic. She couldn't stop her hands from shaking. She rubbed her arms, suddenly chilled.

What she really needed was comfort, human touch. Heat.

Her gaze fell upon the bag containing the VirtuWav exercise.

Rayce sprinted toward the VirtuWav bay. Although Hencke had followed orders, he looked less than pleased as Rayce entered the room and ran to the tube next to Tru's floating body.

"Thanks for calling me, Hencke. Put me in," Rayce said. Then he closed his eyes, shutting out Hencke's scowl of disapproval. This was his business. It was for Tru's own good, too. And that's what he told himself as he stood in the middle of the battered saloon and dismissed his virtual self for the second time.

He'd barely sat down on the stool when she appeared. With growing concern, he watched her walk toward him wearing her silver bodysuit, no pretenses, no sway, no games. Her eyes caught his attention next, filled with sorrow and shame.

She stopped in front of him and for a few moments, said nothing. Then she whispered, "I hope you don't mind, but I need you again."

He wanted to ask her what was wrong, why the pained expression, why the request. But a virtual man wouldn't care about such things. A virtual man wouldn't know that this was not to be a lesson on sex. A virtual man wouldn't see that she needed something more.

So without a word, he stood up and followed her out.

Chapter Eleven

The bedchamber filled in around her, cool against Rayce's heat. That's why she was here. That's why she wanted him—to banish the empty, unrelenting cold like he'd done on *Miranda*. Only his passion could restore her. She needed to touch his fire.

His body heat wrapped around her from behind, penetrating her thin suit, radiating into her. She stood still, afraid to turn around and ask him for what she needed, afraid to kiss the flame.

Fire seared her neck first. He kissed her gently and nuzzled the soft spot behind her ear. Hands like embers wrapped around her waist, holding her prisoner as he pressed against the length of her in a long, slow burn.

His mouth moved over her skin leaving trails of moist kisses so soft and sweet, she held her breath just to feel each one. His hands smoothed over the suit, lingered on her breasts, and up to the high neck. Then she felt cool air as he released the front fastener, freeing her from the stifling shell and baring her sensitive skin to the blaze.

His fingers slipped inside while his lips worked their way down the shoulder he'd just exposed. Her breasts were freed and unprotected, followed by her belly and hips.

She moaned, laid her head back against his shoulder. *Yes.* This was what she wanted, his burning body behind her, his hot hands on her body. Fire so intense, it consumed everything else until all that remained was just enough air to breath.

Fabric rolled down her body, every centimeter of skin coming alive under her lover's skilled fingers. Nipples hardened painfully as he skimmed them, squeezing each one gently. Fingertips explored the valley between her breasts to the hollow of her throat, tracing the line of her jaw.

"Tru," a sizzle in her ear.

Tell him what you want, she thought. But fire needs oxygen and there simply wasn't enough left for words.

Then his fingers skimmed down her sides, sliding over her small, round breasts, gliding along her waist and the flare of her hips.

She rolled her head back, seeking him. His lips met hers with desire and need. Their tongues danced and fed off each other as a flame licks its fuel.

She turned in his hands, pressed her body against his, and gasped at the overpowering contact. Bunching her hands in his shirt, she pulled at the fasteners until they relented. As he tugged the shirt off, she rifled her hands inside and ran them over every part of his chest. Her mouth opened to his, invading. A need so great, it bordered on fury, filled her. Passion ignited, uncontrolled and swift. She didn't care, didn't even try to harness it. No fear here. No rules. This was her refuge.

Her fingertips slipped into his waistband, pushing his pants down. He growled and pulled her back onto the bed with him, kicking off the rest of his clothes as they tumbled over the sheets.

Her skin felt too tight and too hot. Her mind was frenzied, merciless, and wild.

"Tru, slow down. I want to do this right." The words mumbled in her ear did nothing to soothe her. There was only one answer and *slow* was not it. She didn't come here for tenderness and sympathy. She came here to be burned alive.

She pushed him on his back and threw a leg over him, pinning him beneath her. He was hers, at least in this world. His eyes burned into hers—the fire she sought.

"I don't want slow," she said, seething, gripping his hard length in her hand.

"Tru," he rasped.

"I don't want pity," she said, pulling him up beneath her.

"I don't want to be perfect," she gasped, impaling herself on him until she swallowed him whole.

She leaned down and bit his lower lip. "I only want you."

His hands gripped her hips and he arched hard into her, lifting her knees off the bed. Then back down and up again. She caught on to the rhythm, taking over. Bodies pounded together, parting, then binding again as the steam rose between them. She threw her head back, closed her eyes and concentrated on the new, terrifying sensations taking control of her body. No thinking, no analyzing. Just raw, sexual desire, drowning out space and time and reason.

Then it seized her, that sweet ecstasy she knew from the first time. She gazed down at Rayce. His eyes were slitted, as lost and wild as her own. And she growled, from her gut, from her center where her own fire began to burn. Then she held her pace, waiting for that moment of sheer terror when her body was no longer her own.

She felt his fingers dig into her thighs as the first wall of flames burst forth. A scream rolled from her throat, ripped from her soul as another flashed through, gutting her. Her body lifted and vaguely she felt her lover arch up and pour his release into her with a rumbling groan.

Spent and shaking, she collapsed on him and closed her eyes. Ashes and smoldering embers. A wildfire subdued—nothing left but a whisper of smoke. If only. If only it could always be like this. This simple. And she dozed off, content in her own body.

She woke alone on a rumpled bed, cold without Rayce's passion. She wrapped the soaked sheets around her.

Heat had faded to dismay. Why was she here? Why was she doing this? Using Coburne? What kind of woman needed a virtual man to fulfill her?

Tears burned her eyes and she buried her head in the bedding. It didn't take a genius to figure that one out: the kind of woman who couldn't cut it in reality. A failure.

*   *   *

He was still hard when he reached his quarters. Rayce waited until the door slid shut behind him and exhaled the breath he'd be holding for the past couple minutes.

He hadn't expected that. Hadn't expected to be seduced so fast and fully. He hoped she was satisfied because he sure as hell wasn't. Virtual reality did nothing to relieve the flesh and blood man floating inside the blue tube, but tell that to his very real and very frustrated libido.

He walked over to the table with the Safin and poured himself a short drink. Never had any woman given herself to him like that. No holds barred, all-out, screaming sex. Passion so intense, it was all he could do to stay with her as long as he did. He ran a hand through his hair. So much for tenderness and slow, leisurely lovemaking. Bring on the fire.

He took a swallow of the Safin. Usually it burned down his throat but its heat was nothing compared to Tru's.

He'd been in dangerous situations more times than he cared to remember. They all paled in comparison to Tru's primal passion. She'd dragged him under, into her spell until he didn't know where he ended and she began. There was no escape, even if he'd wanted it, which he didn't. How could he turn down the chance to see her on fire like that? To know that she'd never done that with any other man, to have her all to himself? Real or not, she wanted him. She could have picked any man.

So you are saying that if you really cared for a man that you wouldn't want to have sex with him? His own words. He smiled. She'd lied. Maybe there wasn't a right man for her, but she'd decided he was close enough. At least in virtual reality.

And where did that leave him?

He closed his eyes, the realization that she only wanted his virtual twin beating at his ego. And if that wasn't bad enough, Hencke's surly scowl flashed back. The one he received as he'd exited his tube.

The truth was that he wanted her here, in reality. Wanted her to want him, too, and not just some digital image—the real man.

Even if she was a Majj.

That popped the rest of his fantasy. She only cared about one thing—the Collection.

So she was using him for sex. He'd be insulted, if it weren't for the fact that he was more a beneficiary than a victim. And she wasn't exactly using *him*, just his digital replica.

He shot down the rest of the Safin in one gulp, amazed at how heat had become relative.

I hope you don't mind, but I need you again. Her words haunted him, her wounded expression even more. Something had happened after they returned, crushing her. He'd sure like to know what. Getting it out of her would be the challenge of his life.

He set down the glass and flopped down in a chair. Well, he had time. He had opportunity. What was life without a few challenges?

The bigger problem, of course, was knowing what she was capable of and not being able to do a thing about it.

"You look a little tired. Sleep well?"

Tru looked at him across *Miranda*'s small table as

they ate, her eyebrows high. "I slept fine."

He gave her a sly, fleeting smile that worried her more than the lady-killer version did. A smile that meant something. She just didn't know what.

Halfway to Arête and he'd done that a handful of times. And every time he looked at her, her body trembled. As if he knew something she didn't. He couldn't possibly know about Noa, that channel was secure. Maybe she'd given something away about the VirtuWav. Could it be? Was she that transparent? She shifted in her chair and concentrated on her space rations.

"So are you worried about going to Arête?" he asked.

She stopped chewing and looked at him. "No. Should I be?"

He gazed back at her. "No more than usual."

"I hate it when you say things like that," she said, spearing another morsel. "Do you want the summary on Arête now or would you rather go in blind and be creative?"

"What have you got?"

She blinked at him in surprise and he shrugged, "I'm beginning to see the benefits of a concrete plan."

Her jaw dropped. "You are?"

His amused gaze met hers. "I know a good idea when I see it."

"Huh," she said, floored.

He pushed his tray away and leaned back in his chair, giving her his undivided attention. "However, in my experience I've found plans to be a general waste of time since they rarely end up the way you intended."

C. J. Barry

"Tell me about it," Tru muttered. She knew all about plans going to hell. "Let's give it a try, though, shall we?"

He grinned that grin in reply. She squinted at him. It was making her crazy.

"Arête will be more difficult to access than Rostron," she began. Idly, she rubbed her shoulder. "It is definitely uninhabited. Average temperature is minus forty with winds averaging over fifty klicks a standard hour. The surface consists of ice crystal formations, many of which are over 100 meters high."

She glanced at him, worried. "I don't even think we can land on the surface."

He nodded, deep in thought, his gaze settling on her breasts. She frowned. Then his eyes lifted and met hers, filled with heat.

"Did you hear anything I just said?" she asked, crossing her arms over her chest in protection.

"Formations, difficult to access."

She glared at him and he burst out laughing. "Sorry. I don't think we'll have to land at all."

"Then how do we place the plate?"

He eyed her seriously. "How do you feel about dangling out the cargo bay from a harness several hundred meters off the ground in freezing cold while I try to hold the ship steady in high winds?"

"Do you have a Plan B?" she asked, suddenly not so enthused.

"You're lucky I've got a Plan A," he replied with a scowl. "We don't have a lot of choices."

She blew out a breath. "I'll do whatever I have to."

"I figured you would."

196

She played with her food and asked as casually as possible, "Is there any way we can move up the schedule?"

His expression hardened. "Tired of my company already?"

"No," she replied hastily. "That's not why."

"Anxious to get back to the Institute with your prize?" he said softly.

She took a deep breath. She may as well tell him. What difference would it make? "Actually, that *is* part of it. I need my Charter."

"Charter," he repeated. "What is that?"

"My right to become a full Majj," she said, setting down her utensil. "The Curzon Collection would be my entitlement to a permanent position at the Institute."

He frowned. "So you aren't a Majj yet? You wear the uniform."

She felt the familiar heat of humiliation in her cheeks. She hated this. "Technically, no. I was born there, which gives me some right to stay. But every Majj candidate must make his or her own discovery, invention, whatever it may be, by the age of thirty."

"And what happens if you don't get it?"

She closed her eyes as she said the words, "I'd be forced to leave." *I'd lose everything.*

"Just like that? Even after all your work?"

She winced at his critical tone. "They must make room for newcomers. There is no place for candidates who can't produce."

He didn't say anything for a few minutes, just scrutinized her.

"And you are almost thirty."

She nodded. "Yes."

He regarded her seriously. "So why has it taken you so long to find your own Charter if you've been there your whole life?"

"I'd been doing work for my father up until he died last year. I've only just begun to work on my own projects."

He crossed his arms and asked, "Don't you get any credit for that?"

She shook her head. "They were his projects."

"Yes, but you worked on them. In fact, I'll bet you probably put in the majority of the effort."

She scowled. He was beginning to sound a lot like Noa.

"I did," she explained as patiently as she could. "But they were still *his* projects, under *his* credit."

Unrelenting, he asked, "Couldn't he give you some of that credit? He *was* the head administrator."

"That's not the way it's done," she said, testily.

"Sounds like a lousy deal to me."

Tru pushed her tray away. "It's not your worry. It's mine. And I need that Charter now. So the sooner we finish this mission, the faster I get my Charter and the faster you get rid of me."

She lifted her chin. "And that's the main objective, right? So, can we move up the schedule or not?"

He didn't answer her for a few long seconds. She expected him to say something smart or sarcastic but instead he spoke quietly, "Tru, are you happy at the Institute?"

Happy? She blinked at the sudden change of direction. "What does that have to do with any-thing?"

His blue-green eyes settled on her. "I get the impression that the Institute is not a nurturing, homey kind of place. Are you happy there?"

"Why wouldn't I be? It's my home."

"Do you have friends?"

"I'm not a social misfit, Rayce. Of course, I have friends." Okay, she had *one*, but he didn't need to know that.

"Will they still be your friends if you don't get your Charter?"

She pursed her lips. "It's a moot point. I'll have to leave so I won't be able to talk to them anyway."

He nodded as if vindicated in some way. "Lousy deal."

A silent anger welled up inside her. Why was he asking her all this? She stood up quickly and collected their trays. He hated the Majj so why would he care if she was happy or had friends or ever got her Charter? There was nothing wrong with the Institute. It had its rules and everyone knew them. She didn't need to be patronized or pitied by someone who knew nothing about life there. What she needed was a partner who didn't ask so many damn questions.

With a tray in each hand, she turned toward the galley and found him blocking her path.

The look on his face started her blood pumping wildly through her veins.

He placed his warm fingertips along her jawbone, spreading them wide enough to hold her captive. Then he leaned in and swept his lips across hers. She took a shuddering breath. His eyes intensified, locked onto hers, and he kissed her again. Deeper this time, still gentle, but more seductive and urgent. She forgot all about breathing, and to hell with the trays in each hand holding her prisoner. His lips returned again and again, each time different but the same, bringing her closer to the fire.

Then cool air. She opened her eyes to find him walking to the back of the ship. It occurred to her that her hands were empty. He'd taken the trays from her without her even noticing.

Her fingers touched her lips where they still throbbed along with the rest of her deprived body. Just kisses. How did he do that? How could he ignite such deep desire with just kisses?

Or was it pity? If it was, then she'd have to seriously reconsider her position on pity. She dropped her hand. No, it was more frightening than pity. He'd given her compassion and consideration. He'd given her part of himself.

It was almost like he cared about her.

Chapter Twelve

She should have held out for Plan B, she thought, fumbling with the space suit fasteners around her wrists. She'd never worn one of these things in all her life. Meant for space walks, it should be enough to keep her from freezing to death in three seconds or less while dangling over Arête. But damned if she could figure out what all these attachments were for.

It suddenly occurred to her that she'd had a lot of firsts with Rayce. Not all of them had been good, but at least it hadn't been boring. She smiled a little. The Institute would seem awfully quiet after this.

"Let me do that," Rayce said as he took over. She watched him work on the suit. He was close. Close enough so she could smell him. She loved his scent, clean and male. Did all men smell that good? Did he realize smell could arouse a woman, make her want to do things she'd never dreamed of before, like rip her clothes off and jump the nearest hot body? She stifled a little groan, the heat building in her belly. Funny how a body could react even before the mind put reason to it.

He raised his gaze to hers and their eyes locked. "Are you ready?" he asked, his voice low.

"Ready?" she whispered back.

A hint of amusement lit on his face. "To go outside."

She blinked. "Oh. Of course." Then she shook her head and rubbed her forehead. "No, not ready. Explain this to me again."

He checked the various fasteners and controls on the flimsy suit she was risking her life in. "I'm going to get us over the pyramid and hold the ship steady. I can't promise you much but I should at least be able to hover in place for a few minutes. You'll be attached to the ship with a main control cable. Once you are outside, you can manipulate your position with the controls. I'll be monitoring your main cable and the safety lines. I can watch you and you can talk to me through the suit's comm. Too much tension on the cables, too much wind, any problem whatsoever and I'm pulling you back in."

His eyes met hers. "Whether or not you have the plate completed."

She knew exactly what he meant but there was no way she was leaving Arête without that third side. He didn't understand. This wasn't just a Charter, it was her life. A silent battle of wills waged until she finally gave him what he asked for, even if she had no intention of honoring it, and replied, "I understand." And changed the subject. "This is the tough one, right?"

His expression darkened. "Can't be any worse than Rostron."

She nodded in complete agreement on that point, glancing over at the main viewer. "How long before we drop out of hyperspace?"

"Just a few minutes. Sorry to suit you up so early, but I won't be able to help you once we drop into Arête's atmosphere. Take a seat," Rayce said, walking toward the cockpit. "We still have to locate the pyramid."

"That shouldn't be too hard," Tru offered, following him. "The planet is small and uninhabited. The pyramid will stick out pretty well."

"Maybe," Rayce said, dropping into his seat.

"You don't think so?" she asked, sitting next to him.

"If it was easy to find," he looked over at her. "Someone would have found it by now."

Tru gave a groan. "I hate it when you say things like that."

Rayce grinned. "You just hate it when I'm right."

She wrinkled her nose. Right again.

He took the ship out of hyperspace. When Tru looked up, Arête filled the viewport. It was white, almost translucent, its sun gleaming off the frozen surface. She'd never tire of the beauty of space, how a mass as large as a planet could seem to be suspended in place as though a giant hand had placed it there for eternity. Of course, the planet was not stationary; it was traveling through space at a fraction of light speed, dragging its gravitational weight against the fabric of space and time.

Sometimes physics took all the fun out of things, she thought sadly.

"We're descending to scanning range," Rayce said as the ship drew closer to the planet's surface.

"Do you think the scanners will pick anything up?" she asked.

He shook his head. "Doubtful. I can try for solid mass and size sweeps, but that's about it. Visual is going to be our best bet."

Tru pulled the half-completed plate from her suit. It hummed in her hand.

"I wish I'd had the time to analyze this," she murmured to herself.

"How did your father get it?" Rayce asked, gazing through the viewport as Arête drew closer.

She shook her head. "I have no idea. He went off-planet many times but he never mentioned the plate to me."

"I doubt he found it himself," Rayce said.

"No, he wouldn't have found it himself," Tru agreed. "He must have gotten it from someone else."

"Payment."

She turned to Rayce. "Excuse me?"

He gave her a pointed look and then went back to his controls. "He probably received it from some government or group as payment for one of your inventions."

She stared at him for a moment. Payment. She had never thought about the fact that the Majj's inventions ultimately cost their beneficiaries something. She'd never bothered to ask about that part. Once the product was finished, the administrators took over.

"Yes, I suppose it would be payment," she agreed.

Rayce shook his head and muttered something that sounded like, "Majj."

She glared at him and vowed to do some research on one Rayce Coburne. Somewhere in his past was the explanation for his hatred of the Majj and she was going to find it. There had to be a reason for all that anger.

She tapped her fingernails on the armrest absently. Even if she found out why, what would she do about it? Would it be something she could resolve? Probably not. If it was fixable, Rayce would have fixed it by now. So what could be so bad that he'd carry around that degree of animosity?

It was all so simple in the VirtuWav. Just a man and a woman. No baggage, no disappointments, no anger, no communication problems.

"Start looking," Rayce ordered bluntly.

If this wasn't her mission, she'd tell him to go to hell. But she leaned forward and scanned the surface as so rudely commanded. Below her lay a land of ice crystals, jutting from the surface in an explosion of formations. They reminded her of fragile glass flowers, but she knew some of those crystals were several hundred meters tall and hardly fragile.

She shielded her eyes from the sunlight flashing off the crystal facets. The more she watched the terrain pass them by, the more she realized their predicament. It looked like a forest, a jungle of white and light and reflections. Rayce was right. Again.

"Can you get us any lower?"

He nodded. "Hold on. The wind will bump us around a little."

And it did, but at least she could make out individual clusters of crystals. But no pyramids. If the pyramid was like the others, it would be white as well. And finding it would be practically impossible.

For three hours, they flew low over Arête, the winds buffeting and jerking the ship. Absently, she rubbed the partially completed plate. It couldn't end like this, flying over a lifeless planet, unable to find one, single pyramid.

Then her fingers stopped, a soft buzz running through them and with it, a familiar surge of sexual energy. She groaned out loud.

Rayce looked at her. "Something wrong?"

She shook her head and swallowed back the sudden, urgent, visceral ache in her bones. "The plate. The vibration is getting stronger."

"Maybe we are getting closer to the pyramid," he offered and checked the scanners. "And it's acting like a beacon."

Made sense to her logical side. However, her sexual side was making too much noise for her to care much. Then the sensation faded.

"It just weakened," she said, lifting the miniature pyramid for inspection.

"Then we change direction," he said. He banked the ship and headed west.

"Better?"

"No."

"Hold on," he said and turned back.

In a few seconds, she felt the plate come alive. "Yes." This time she braced herself for the primal rush and forced her mind to pay attention. If there was one thing she'd learned in the past ten years, it was how to block out sexual urges.

The vibration grew stronger, so strong she could not only feel it, but see it as well.

"We're close," she said, a little strangled. Rayce eyed her but she ignored him. If he flashed that little smile, he'd get the surprise of his life. She was in no mood to play games and he happened to be prime male stock.

Luckily, he went back to checking the scanners. "I'm picking up something. A large mass straight ahead." He looked out the viewport. A few seconds later, he added, "And we have visual confirmation."

"Thank goodness," she muttered, stuffing the plate into an arm pocket and cutting off the sensations it was feeding her.

"That was easier than I expected," he said with a grin.

She narrowed her eyes at him. Easy for him to say. His libido wasn't working double-time. Her heart pounded in her chest and her body was overheating in the suit. What bothered her more was that this was only the third leg. Just how strong was the next one going to be?

She unharnessed herself and stood up.

"I'm going back," she told him as she pulled on her gloves. She wasn't touching that plate again without protection. A woman could only handle so much sexual frustration in one day.

"Don't forget what I said." His eyes met hers. "Any problems and you are coming back in."

She smiled and batted her eyelashes. "Yes, sir."

He stared hard at her for a moment and then nodded. "That's what I like to hear."

She headed to the back, shoving aside any misgivings about lying to him. Every side of the key meant she was closer to her goal. Regardless of what Rayce said, she was going to get this one.

Alone in the cargo bay, she attached the main cable and safety lines like Rayce had taught her. Then she switched off his override capabilities. Rayce wouldn't be pulling her in. She'd come in when she was good and ready. Nothing and no one was going to stop her mission.

She slipped the helmet over her head and it snapped into the suit with a suction click.

"Can you hear me?" she said.

"Clear. We are positioned over the pyramid. Are you secure?"

"All secure. I'm opening the hatch door." She touched the panel and the door disappeared. Wind beat against her body as she leaned out and looked down. The pyramid was below and behind them, Rayce compensating for the winds. But surprisingly the ship held steady.

"How long can you hold us here?" she yelled over the howling wind.

"Just make it quick," he replied. She could hear the tension in his voice. He was not having an easy time.

She took a deep breath. Do or die. And winced at her choice of words, even if they were appropriate. Her hands flexed on the doorway and she jumped out into thin air. She fell a short distance before the main line snapped, caught her, and the wind flung her beneath the hovering ship.

"Damn," she gasped, spinning haplessly.

"Tru?"

"I'm fine," she said, struggling to right herself in the high wind. She finally managed to flatten out, belly down, facing the wind by using her arms as stabilizers and staring down at the pyramid. It was as magnificent as the others, nestled in a forest of crystal flowers.

She gauged her position and reported back to Rayce, "Can you get me lower? Maybe twenty meters?"

"Affirmative."

The ship whined loudly above her as they dropped within ten meters of the pinnacle. She lengthened her cable, bringing her closer yet. Her hand reached for it, grabbed it, and slipped off.

"Drop another two meters," she shouted. The ship lowered a fraction and she gripped the top of the pyramid with both hands, wrapping her arms around it while her body was held horizontal in the raging wind.

"Forward two meters," she grunted. Rayce complied and she floated past the peak and planted her feet against the pyramid wall in a squat, her back to the wind. The main cable went lax.

"Tru?" Rayce said urgently in her comm.

"I'm fine. Perfect. Hold her steady."

She rested for a few seconds, the most she could hope for.

"I'm in position," she said, out of breath. She could feel the sweat running between her breasts and the tremble of overexertion in her muscles.

"Tru, look toward the base. I'm detecting movement below you."

She glanced down the pyramid wall and squinted. A dark line was moving up the pyramid,

209

but that was impossible. There was no life on Arête.

"I'm going to be really upset if I get another planet wrong," she muttered.

"It's advancing toward you, on your side," Rayce added. "I can't get a good reading but you better hurry."

She retrieved the plate with great care as she protected it from the wind howling around her.

"Tru, move it. I can see them now. Some kind of insects. Mechanical composition."

She looked down and saw thousands of tiny legs scaling the wall. Claws to be more precise. "Oh, damn," she uttered under her breath. They were racing toward her now, within twenty meters.

"You won't make it. I'm pulling you in," Rayce's bark came through the comm.

She didn't reply. It would take him a few seconds to realize she'd shut off his control over her cable. Long enough.

With both hands she placed the plate and caught sight of the first wave of creatures out of the corner of her eye. They were nearly to her feet.

"Hurry," she said to the plate, through clenched teeth. She couldn't even think, panic choking her. The wind whistled by her head, the tiny claws vibrated at her feet as the third side slide up from the base of the tiny pyramid.

"Damn it, Tru!" Rayce roared in her ear. He'd discovered her override. Just as the first creature latched onto her boot, there was a great roar of engines and she became airborne. She clutched the plate to her chest while the wind twisted her mercilessly. The creature held on also. She gave a little cry of panic and with as much strength as she had, she smacked her boots together again and again until the metal beast dislodged and fell to the surface now far below her.

The wind tore at her space suit, engines roared in her ear and cold permeated her foot, but she didn't care. She was too busy trying to calm her terror. That was close: heart-pounding, gut-wrenching, shaking-in-her-boots close.

"If you don't pull yourself in right now, I'm going to drag your ass through the atmosphere and things are going to get mighty hot."

She winced at Rayce's hard words and held the plate tighter. *Oh hell. Why did everything about this mission have to be so damn difficult?* With dread, she set the controls to take her back in.

Minutes later, she stood safely in the cargo bay, struggling out of her space suit. The boot looked severely chewed, nearly clean through. She shuddered, wondering what a few more of those little bastards could have done to her.

She felt the gentle pull of hyperspace and knew that Rayce had already laid in the course for Earth—the fourth leg. If she survived that long.

She'd just freed herself from the suit's grip when the door to the cockpit opened and Rayce stormed through.

"What the hell did you think you were doing?" he seethed, his words soft through clenched teeth. She'd seen him angry before, but not like this.

She stood tall. "I knew you'd pull me in too soon."

He reached down and snatched her suit off the floor. His gaze settled on the mangled boot and then he shoved it at her. "Is it worth this?"

She shoved the plate toward him. "I got the third piece," she snapped back and immediately regretted her poor choice of dialogue.

He looked ready to kill as he tossed the suit down and stepped toward her. She stepped back.

"Is that damn plate all that matters to you?" He wasn't even blinking.

She raised her chin. "Yes."

"Just so you can become a Majj?" He took another step toward her, the heat of his anger reaching her.

"Now you're getting it," she shot back.

"There's nothing else to you?"

"No."

"You're wrong," he charged, his voice steely.

She blinked at him in surprise. Then shook her head. "My work is my life, it's who I am. It's *all* that I am."

"Wrong," he repeated, taking another step and backing her to the wall.

"Ask anyone," she stammered. "If I lose my career, I lose everything I am. I lose myself."

"Wrong."

His mouth closed over hers and if she'd had anything else to say, it was quickly forgotten in the great rush of blood from her brain. He kissed her hard at first, anger ruling, his mouth plundering hers. But slowly the rage faded, leaving only fire. And she dove into it, wrapping her arms around his neck and welding him to her.

He groaned low, pressing his body against hers, pinning her to the wall. She ran her hands over hard muscle and warm skin, frantically trying to satisfy her own desire. It wouldn't be enough this time, just a kiss. It wouldn't give her what she needed.

So she reached down, slid her hand along his length and found him already hard. He froze, inhaled sharply and released a long growl. He placed his hand on hers.

"Tru," he whispered. Then he pulled her hand away, pinned it to the wall and ground his hips into hers. He felt as good as he had in the VirtuWav. Just as hot, just as solid. The next thing she knew she was being lifted off her feet and carried into the cockpit.

"Bunk down," Rayce ordered from the door and threw her on her own bunk even before it had fully descended. He yanked his shirt off, mounted the bunk and stretched his body over hers.

She didn't have time to speak, couldn't think of a thing to say, anyway, before his lips quelled thought itself. Her palms pressed flat against his chest. Her fingers found the tiny nipples and traced around them. He kissed her everywhere—her face, throat, shoulders—she lost track or didn't give a damn, or both.

Then she felt her suit being peeled back and his bare skin against hers.

"I hate this suit," he mumbled as he kneeled and tugged it down her body. She lifted her hips to help him, baring her body to him in increments until he was at her feet. The silver suit sailed through the air and she lay before him naked, with nowhere to hide.

Tru shivered under his scrutiny. It wasn't like the VirtuWav. She couldn't halt the program if he didn't like what he saw.

His gaze traveled over her. He never said a word but his eyes burned, she could see the fire within. Or was it her own reflection?

His hands slid warm along her feet, over her ankles, caressing as he went. They wrapped around her calves and massaged the thick muscle. He bent and his lips kissed the inside of her knees, his breath hot against her skin.

She let out a moan. His touch would be her downfall.

Up the inside of her thighs, he moved slowly, torturing her with kisses, nips, his face rough against her tender skin. His hands gently but firmly pushed her legs apart. She jumped when he reached her center.

"Rayce?"

"Relax," he said softly, nuzzling her. "I promise you'll like it."

She didn't doubt that. She just wasn't sure if she could handle what he was planning. He lowered his mouth to her and then there was only intense pleasure, an intimacy she'd never known, as he worshipped her.

She gasped as his tongue touched her, his lips circled, and he lightly sucked. Over and over he repeated his skilled ministrations until her hands were wild, buried in his hair, grasping the sheets, her body writhing in sweet agony. It was almost enough to wipe away the fear. What if she couldn't do this, what if she failed? What if . . .

Then the wave rose within her and crashed over with no warning except for her scream, which came too late to save her. She thrashed helplessly and only when she pushed him away—the sensation too intense—did he stop.

"Oh lord," she sobbed, aftershocks ravishing her body from the inside out. Did he have any idea what he'd just done for her?

She looked down to find him kneeling between her shaky legs, releasing his pants. His erection, thick and urgent, emerged. He shoved his pants down his legs and dropped over her, supported by his arms.

Then his lips grazed her abdomen and heat returned, just like that. He nipped at her hipbones while his fingers traced the underside of each breast. His lips followed the valley up the center of her ribcage and between her breasts, his cheek rubbing each mound.

She whimpered, wrapping her leg over his back and arched into his mouth as he tongued around the areola and tugged gently on her nipple. She felt it straight to her groin. He was nuzzling and nipping her breasts when she finally couldn't take it anymore and pulled his face to hers.

He kissed her fully and on his lips she could taste herself. Musky and a little sweet. He'd done that for her. Because he cared about her. Because he wanted to give her pleasure.

Tears burned her eyes. She couldn't tell if the tears were for him or her. She wanted more than anything to make it right for him, to make sure he knew that she cared enough to give as much as he had.

His full weight settled on her, her legs spread wide to accommodate him, ready. He linked their fingers together and pulled back enough to look into her watery eyes. She felt the pressure of his erection burn against her, but he didn't push.

"Have you done this before?" he asked softly.

Her fingers clenched his hands hard. What would he think? That she was nearly thirty and still a virgin? That no one else wanted her in all that time? Would he laugh at her inexperience?

No, he wasn't like that; he wasn't Odell. He didn't care if she was less than perfect.

So she spoke the dreaded word. "Never."

He nodded and closed his eyes, utter concentration and silent torture on his face. Then they opened and watched her as he surged forward, into her core with one movement.

She cried out at the pain and beauty of it all, at such pure pleasure.

"Stay with me," he ground out.

She did, savoring every stroke, each sensation, the delicate bond between them. They moved together, riding the same wave, reaching for the same crest. They were one force, one breath, closer than she'd ever been to another human being.

She sensed the change in his breathing, the heat of his muscles flexing and driving the new urgency in his rhythm. Instinctively, her nails dug into his back as she clenched her legs around him, knowing what he needed. Then a great roar built from his chest. His face twisted in pain as his body tightened, driving into her one more time, giving her everything. She held onto the most perfect moment of her life as long as she could.

He collapsed on top of her, both of them gasping for the same air. It took a while for her brain to surface.

A man, a woman, lots of heavy breathing and grunting.

She shook her head. No. No, this wasn't like that. This was more, terrifyingly more. This was risk.

"Did I hurt you?" he murmured in her ear.

She smiled. "No. Did I hurt you?"

"No, but you can try again later."

She laughed. Laughed in bed with her lover. What a delightful first.

"I'm still mad at you," he mumbled. "Don't think sex will save you."

She twirled his hair in her fingers, the way she'd always wanted to. "I screwed up. I didn't know there were any life forms on Arête. Thanks for saving my ass."

"You screwed up alright. You disobeyed me. If you ever cut me out and put yourself in danger like that again . . ." he stopped.

"You'll what?"

"I'll dump you back at the Institute and let them deal with you. With or without the Collection."

"What about the spaceport?"

"I'll get by."

He would, too. She knew that. He had his goals. It was the one thing they had in common. That and sex.

"Was it okay?" she whispered.

"Was what okay?"

"The sex." She waited.

"You're changing the subject."

"I need to know."

"You're going to make me move to answer this, aren't you?" he said, then groaned and pushed himself up on one elbow so he could see her face with his beautiful eyes. He looked utterly sexy and supremely satisfied. Because of her. She couldn't believe it.

His fingertips traced the dried river of tears. "The sex was great. Too great."

"How can it be too great?" she asked, not that she really cared. She was "too great" at sex. Nothing could be better than that.

He grinned wide as sin. "The ultimate distraction. We have two days to Earth. We may never leave this bunk."

Chapter Thirteen

He woke up sometime in the middle of the night in a place that had no day or night. Spooned against Tru's back, he noted *Miranda*'s lights faintly flickering as the ship functioned automatically.

Tru's heavy golden hair lay draped over his arm, his hand palmed one breast and the bed smelled like sex. He grinned. Great sex. And then more great sex. He may never be able to get enough of her.

It hadn't been like the VirtuWav. She wanted him—the man—not some virtual stimulation. He was going to find and destroy that program when they got back.

When they got back . . .

A familiar ache returned. Nothing had changed. She was still a Majj. Or close to it. And why, he couldn't understand. She didn't fit his greedy, merciless, uncaring image of a Majj. It didn't make sense. She didn't want him stepping on an ugly, worthless flower on a sinkhole like Rostron. How could she want to be a Majj?

Besides, there was so much more to her than just some Charter, some discovery. She could be whatever she wanted to be. Too bad she couldn't see that. That damn Institute had brainwashed her into thinking that if she couldn't make it there, she was worthless. It made him furious.

She gave a small sigh and nestled closer to him, torturing a fully advanced hard-on and reminding him that he wanted her again. But he'd let her sleep. He had a feeling that peaceful sleep was not easy for her. So he lay there, wide awake and aroused, and listened to her breathe.

A niggling thought surfaced. She wasn't a Majj yet. Maybe if he could prove to her that she could do more, be more than a Majj, she'd rethink her goal.

Now that would be a challenge—proving to Tru she was more than a Majj. Some prick had pounded into her head that she was nothing without that one Charter, even to the point of risking her life. She'd rather die than be seen as a failure. That wasn't going to be easy to correct.

He strummed the soft skin of her breast idly and smiled. What was life without a few challenges?

"How do you plan to penetrate Earth's atmosphere undetected?" she asked.

"There's that word again," he said, working the ship's controls from his seat next to her.

She crossed her arms and arched an eyebrow. "What? Penetrate?"

He smirked. "Plan."

"*That* word," she said, trying to keep a straight face, "would have been my last guess."

"Well, consider this your lucky day because I actually know what I'm going to do. Before I do it." He glanced at her and stole her breath away. His eyes narrowed and she knew exactly what he was thinking about: the last two days spent in bed. Two days of making love, kissing, long massages, of discovery and learning things she never could have imagined. Heat rushed to her cheeks. How could one man do that to her? It was like a flood had been unleashed and she'd completely lost control of her senses.

"And what is that?" she asked, hanging onto the conversation by a thread.

A sexy smile spread across his face slowly. "I'll mirage our ship and confuse their sensors."

She licked her dry lips. "Do you think that will work?"

He eyed her lips with deliberation. "It usually does. But landing on an inhabited planet is always risky."

It was becoming warmer in the ship, or at least, inside her clothes. Her eyes dropped to his crotch. She noticed he was aroused again. Was he always like that? She'd never noticed before.

"Something wrong?"

Her gaze shot back up to his. "No." Both his eyebrows went up and she gave a little sigh. *Oh, what the hell.*

"I've been wondering about a few things. About men."

He gave her an amused look. "I qualify. Shoot."

She rubbed her hands on her thighs and forced

C. J. Barry

herself to ask questions she may never get the nerve to ask another man.

"Does it hurt when it's hard?"

He grinned wide. "Depends how long it's been hard for."

"What does it feel like?"

He paused. "It feels full, achy. Hungry."

She nodded in curious understanding and glanced down at his crotch again. It was damn hot in this ship. "How fast can it get hard?"

He shrugged. "Depends on the woman. With you, about ten seconds. Faster when you talk about it."

"I can see that," she said with a nod, staring at the healthy bulge in his pants. "What does it feel like . . ." She licked her lips again and searched for the words. "When you reach . . . critical mass?"

He threw his head back and laughed, a deep, rumbling, heart-felt laugh that made her smile despite her own bumbling embarrassment.

He finally shook his head. "Critical mass. Damn, Tru. It probably feels the way you do when you reach critical mass."

"That good," she whispered.

His eyes narrowed at her and she could feel the heat. "That good."

Parts of her were feeling a little hungry, too, and she nearly lost her line of questioning. "So, how many times a day can you have sex?"

"Men in general, a few. More often when we are younger. Fewer as we get older, but we have more stamina."

Stamina. Yes, he had stamina. She blurted out, "And experience."

His eyes gleamed. "Not as much as I'd like. In fact, I'm beginning to see the advantages of a lengthy and thorough research plan."

"You are?" It came out as croak.

He turned back to the controls. "And if we weren't going to drop out of hyperspace in about thirty seconds, I'd show you my detailed plan first-hand."

"There's more?" she asked, thinking back to everything he'd already shown her. Her body was still reeling from sensual assault.

The ship whined and starlines filled the front viewport. She barely noticed the lovely blue and white jewel of a planet in front of them.

"There's more," he said with a slight smile. "We've just started." Then he leveled his gaze at her. "Speaking of research, you haven't launched into your Earth tour guide monologue yet."

She blinked at him. *Well, damn.* The conversation must have affected her brain. How could she have forgotten? With one look at Rayce and that sexy grin, she realized how.

"Are you even going to listen to it?" she asked, spinning her chair around.

He smirked. "Of course."

She rolled her eyes. That just meant he'd take it into general consideration when he was freewheeling through Giza. She ordered the holo table up and within minutes, she had located the area around the pyramid and began scrolling through the statistics one by one.

"Earth has a humanoid population of around six billion. The closest city is Cairo, with about seven million people."

"Lots of company," Rayce said grimly.

"Exactly," Tru added. "Hopefully, not so many around Giza, where the pyramids are located. The terrain is primarily desert, currently hot and dry. Earth's worldwide level of technology is moderate, communication mostly. They have not advanced a manned mission further into space than their satellite moon."

"Good news for us," Rayce interjected.

"However," she added. "They do have the capability to shoot an object out of the sky."

"That would be the bad news," Rayce amended. She glanced at him and he added, "Trust me, they won't even see us. We're going in miraged and we're going in at dusk. That should help."

"What about the ship once we land?" she asked, looking over her shoulder as the planet filled their viewport, stunning with its blue oceans and white swirling cloud cover.

"I'll mirage the ship on the ground, too. Should work perfectly in the desert. Unless someone runs directly into it."

Tru groaned. "Of course."

He shrugged. "Frankly, it ranks low on my worry list."

`Her jaw dropped. "You have a worry list?"

"Don't you?"

"Just one big one," she muttered. And he had black hair and blue eyes and could make her feel like the only woman alive. Even thinking around him was becoming a challenge.

There was a moment of silence before he asked, "Have you considered what you would do if you didn't get your Charter?"

She blinked at the sudden and unwelcome change of subject. He was serious despite the easy way he'd slipped that question in, but frankly she wasn't going to discuss the possibility. She wasn't going to think about it, consider it or even entertain it. There were no other options.

"I'll get my Charter," she said firmly. *Or die trying.* Then she concentrated on the holodeck again, ignoring his steady gaze. "The ancient civilization in place in Cairo 5,000 years ago would have provided the perfect conditions for the Curzons to build their pyramid marker: able bodies, enough raw material, little or no technology. In fact, I wouldn't be surprised if the Curzons used their own technological advancement to convince the locals that they were heaven-sent."

Rayce nodded. "And the locals would have given the Curzons anything if they thought it would help their crops grow."

"Yes, unfortunately. The Curzons were opportunists, if nothing else," Tru conceded. "There are three major pyramids built around that time along the Giza Plateau. The largest, Cheops, was the first and I believe it is the one we want. The construction differs from the others. It's more sophisticated and precise."

A visual of the pyramid region filled the holodeck and Tru noted the number of people surrounding the base. "And it would appear the pyramids are a major tourist attraction."

"Good," Rayce said. "We can *definitely* be considered tourists."

"Quiet tourists," Tru insisted, spearing him with a stern look.

He just turned and grinned at her, doing nothing to alleviate her worry list.

"We're going to *have* to be quiet because I don't know any Earth languages," she said with a sigh.

"I do."

She turned her head slowly and gaped at him. "Why?"

He smiled crookedly. "Elvis is from Earth. I figured if I learned the language, I'd be able to communicate with him better."

She started giggling. "Communicate with Elvis? So how's it going?"

He scowled. "Not well."

She burst out laughing. Well, it was more like a howl, and she couldn't ever remember howling before, but it felt awfully good. When she'd composed herself, she found Rayce watching her with a faint smile.

"Glad you think its funny," he said.

She waved a hand in front of her face and tried to stop the giggling, with little success. "Talk about a waste of a language interface."

"What else have you got?" he asked, sounding a bit irked.

She wiped the tears from her eyes and turned back to the holo display. Cheops filled the grid in detail. She squinted at the image, zoomed in further and frowned.

"At least, we'll have no trouble getting to the top," she told Rayce. "They stripped it of its smooth outer protective material so the stone blocks have been exposed like steps. There's a tremendous amount of damage, erosion. So much for preserving the past."

226

His eyes met hers. "You'll be able to complete your key, so why do you care?"

"Because someone has to," she replied. "These aren't just objects, Rayce. They're history and once destroyed, they can never be recreated. The hands and the skills and hearts are no longer there. You only get one shot at making history."

For a few long moments, their eyes stayed locked. Tru didn't blink. There was no way she was backing down. Why didn't he understand the enormous value and the great loss? Did he care nothing about the past?

Curiously, Rayce relented, turning back to his controls.

"Entering the atmosphere," he said. "We'll be on the ground in time to watch the sun set."

"If anyone asks, we're Americans," he whispered close to her ear.

Tru turned to him and nodded. Her hair shown golden in the waning Earth sunlight and he caught his breath. She looked so perfect at that moment—her classic features, those big, bright eyes, rich hair. A goddess in the monotonous desert. No wonder he was beating off the locals.

They walked along the side of a wide road toward a flashy light show that bounced off the pyramids and nearby relics in the distance, trying to mix in with the other tourists on foot. Tru wasn't making it easy.

She looked good in the Earth clothes he'd brought. Pants, shirts and jackets that Tess had recommended to make them look like American tourists. He approved of the way they hugged Tru, but damn, she was sure drawing a lot of attention, even in this rather quiet part of Giza. If one more man tried to rub up against her or grope her, he was going to knock him on his ass and to hell with the local authorities. Almost without thinking, he patted his jacket and the laser gun beneath it.

Besides the datapad for orientation, the only other items he'd brought were two small lightballs. The hovering balls of light would follow whomever they were assigned to, illuminating the way. But the moon had risen bold and bright in the night sky and he doubted he'd need them. Just as well. The problem with light was that everyone else could see you, too.

He waved off yet another persistent local dragging a giant, ugly beast in tow and looking for a fare. The walk from the ship had been long and hot but they'd had no choice. He didn't have any Earth currencies to pay for a ride on a beast. So they walked, drawing closer to mammoth pyramids and the lights and the throng milling in the night. Luckily, most people had their eyes on the trio of pyramids and not on them.

As they drew near, Rayce pulled Tru off the beaten path and out into the choppy desert plateau, away from the herd of people. The moon rose up above them, whole and bright and about as beautiful as any moon he could remember on any planet. He could feel the wind out here away from the masses and see Cairo's city lights across the river. The sand felt warm from the day's heat as they circled the pyramid in a wide arc.

"Is anyone following us?" Tru whispered.

"I don't think so. But I saw guards around the

pyramid. Let's camp out here until show is over and they turn out the lights. Maybe everyone will go home."

She nodded and they settled down on the soft sand, far enough away from the pyramid to avoid being seen.

Tru sat between his legs, her back against his chest with the view of the three mammoth pyramids directly in front of them. Night descended gracefully over the great ancient monuments as it had done for the thousands of years since men had created them, pulling stones from the earth and casting them into willful form.

He'd seen some amazing things in his travels around the galaxy, but the sheer determination of man never ceased to humble him.

For a long time Tru said nothing, but he could tell her brain was working by the subtle tension in her body.

Finally she asked, "I'd really like to study this ancient culture when I get back to the Institute. They have incredible artistry. I'm wondering how much of it was influenced by the Curzons."

His hands flexed when she mentioned the Institute, a reminder that he was just a temporary fixture in her life.

She added, "Do you think the locals had any idea that what they were building was going to be nothing more than a marker in a cosmic puzzle?"

"Doubtful. They probably never imagined life on any other planet but this one."

"They didn't have any construction technology at the time. The data I found indicates they built it literally by hand," she said softly. "I'll bet there's a

229

great deal of blood between those stones."

He squeezed his arms around her, fending off the quickly cooling temperature. "It's history. You can't change it now."

"Doesn't make it any less important," she said. He could hear the regret in her voice and wrestled with his own. She cared. She hurt. Why? How could she care about a dead civilization when people died all the time due to the Majj's greed?

She snuggled against him. "So. I suppose you've had a lot of relationships."

He smiled at her spontaneous question. The one she'd probably been running through her brilliant little brain for the past two days.

"A few."

Her head nodded against his cheek. "Anyone special?"

Oooo, dangerous territory. He thought about it. She didn't want to hear about all his adventures. She wanted something else.

"No." There. About as safe as a man can get.

"So you've had a lot of casual sex?"

Damn. He forgot who he was dealing with. There was no safe territory with Tru.

"I cared about all the women I reached critical mass with."

She laughed lightly. He loved the rare sound of it, surprised at how good it made him feel.

"But you haven't found the woman you want to spend forever with yet?" she asked.

He considered that question. The forever woman. Not something he'd given much thought to, not with his former lifestyle. Not many women could handle long trips on a small ship. Not many women he wanted to try it with. Funny that it didn't seem to be a problem with Tru.

"Guess not," he answered vaguely.

She nodded but said nothing more, for which he was eternally grateful. He didn't have any good answers, anyway.

Several hours passed and the site cleared out slowly. The night took over as the lights shut down, leaving the moon to its privilege. Rayce watched the occasional bobbing handlight of a guard circling the grounds and mentally calculated the timing of the rounds.

"Time to do a little night climbing," he whispered, helping Tru to her feet.

They made their way to Cheops from the quiet side, the moon lighting the way. Rayce watched the guard disappear out of sight and pulled Tru to the pyramid base.

"Up," he said in a hard, hushed voice as he gave her a boost over the first row of large steps. They had scaled the next four levels and flattened against the stone floor before another guard walked by.

The rest of the climb went much the same. The soft stone crumbled beneath his hands and feet. With each step, he knew he was destroying history. Until now, he'd never cared. Tru remained silent, climbing without a break, focused on the only goal in her life.

Several hours later, the summit was within reach and the moon gigantic in the star-studded sky above. They were tired, dusty and scraped up by the time they reached the tiny plateau where the top five meters or so of pyramid were missing.

Tru scrambled the final step, crawled to the center of the platform and collapsed on a low block of limestone.

"I had no idea this mission would be so physical," she said, out of breath. "I would have prepared myself better."

Rayce sidled up next to her and for the first time gazed out over Giza. A sea of tiny lights from homes and businesses stretched to the horizon in every direction, with the only break being the barren desert and the River Nile.

"How beautiful," Tru said, mirroring his thoughts. "I bet you can see forever during the day."

"Fortunately, we'll be long gone by then. Do you have the plate?"

She gave him a cavalier look, as if he were crazy to even suggest she'd forget it, and pulled out the nearly completed pyramid. It vibrated, and Tru's eyes closed. Then she shook her head and set it down roughly.

"The top of the pyramid is gone," Rayce said. "Will this work?"

"I hope so. The energy is still here. If I center the plate, it should pick it up."

Scanning the small area, she pushed the plate near the center where a makeshift stick tower had been erected.

In the moonlight, Rayce watched but nothing happened.

He heard her moan of disappointment. "It's humming but its not completing the side."

"Let me try."

He kneeled beside her and guided her hand and

the plate to the left half a meter, directly beneath the stick tower.

Then an overwhelming sensation rolled through him—urgent, consuming, intoxicating lust. He gave a long, deep groan. Vaguely, he was aware of Tru moaning his name. Blinded by lust, he grabbed for her, wanting nothing more than to relieve the crushing sexual energy surging through his veins. He was burning alive, obsession coursing through every nerve ending in his body.

He pulled her beneath him, barely noticing that she had ripped his shirt open. His hands wrestled her pants down, fumbled with her boots until he'd freed one pant leg and could spread her legs wide. With one hand, he opened his own pants, the chilly night air doing nothing to cool his excruciating erection and his fevered mind. There was only one cure and he found it as he lifted Tru's hips and drove into her.

She cried out softly, digging her fingers into his arms and wrapping her legs around his hips. He plunged into her time and again, stoking the fire, each thrust closer to relief. He felt hard as steel, beyond human, sheathing himself in her soft depths. His eyes opened just enough to see Tru, her hair fanned out around her head like a halo in the moonlight, her head back and her lips parted. She was climaxing, he could feel her squeeze around him until he could take no more and sweet ecstasy ripped through him, screaming its liberation. His heart pounded painfully in his chest, muscles taut and tortured, as he poured what was left of himself into Tru.

Then there was silence and peace and the luminous moon above.

He became aware first of Tru's soft body crushed beneath him, the cool, calm night, and his knees aching on ancient stone.

He lifted his weight off her. She didn't even move, looking positively ravaged, and sprawled like a virgin sacrificed on a stone altar. He realized he'd been pounding her bottom against the stone block.

"I'm sorry, Tru. I don't know what happened."

Her eyelids fluttered open and she focused on him with some difficulty. "Sorry for what?"

"For taking you on hard stone, for taking you too fast." He gave a great sigh. He couldn't believe it, he was rock hard again. "And most of all, for wanting to do it again."

Tru licked her lips. "Forgiven. But I'm on top next time."

"No next time. At least not here," he said, glancing around, angry with himself for taking such a risk. Someone could have sneaked up on them, found them . . .

He pulled his pants back up, ignoring his unshakable hard-on. He had to get down from this pyramid before he lost control again. No other woman had this effect on him.

Tru sat up, looking disheveled, and gave him a beautiful, content smile. The kind that could make a man want to take off his pants again.

"We have to go," he said gently, helping her with her own clothes and boot. He snatched the now completed pyramid from the center of the platform and shoved it in his pocket, gritting his teeth against the surge of energy. If they didn't find the Collection, they could always market the damn thing as an aphrodisiac.

Silently they descended the pyramid, the moon lighting their way on the treacherous stone as they scooted down each step on their buttocks. Rayce watched the guards making their rounds, heard an occasional verbal exchange out of sight while his internal worry list grew quickly.

Three courses from the bottom, he stopped and dropped flat on his stomach with Tru beside him. Voices grew louder and there seemed to be guards everywhere. He glanced at the time. They needed to move now if they wanted to get back to the ship before daybreak.

Motionless and silent on their bellies, they watched the guards gather in front of them. Rayce counted eight armed men, more than he would have liked. He hoped that was all of them. They seemed to be taking a short break, talking, laughing, smoking and drinking.

Finally after about fifteen minutes, they dispersed. Rayce waited until there was no movement in sight before signaling Tru and climbing down the final steps.

They'd just taken off in a dead run into the desert to the south when he heard the shouts.

"Hello! Hello!"

Chapter Fourteen

Tru gasped and turned to the voices. A guard ran toward them waving his arms and repeating the command, which she assumed to be something like "stop."

"Damn," Rayce said just before he yanked her to a halt.

"Should we run?" she asked as more guards appeared out of the night.

"The ship is ten klicks away. I don't think we'd outrun them in the sand and I'm not sure how willing they are to shoot us," he whispered back.

The first guard ran up to them, speaking in a choppy, terse dialect she didn't recognize.

Rayce put his hands up in an effort to calm the guard and began talking to him in what she assumed to be English. The word "American" caught her ears and the guard nodded, but then pointed an accusing finger to the pyramid. Rayce shook his head.

Her eyes followed the conversation as more

guards joined the fray and began arguing with Rayce and the other guards. The bickering quickly escalated and Rayce reached into his pocket. She froze, knowing he would be carrying a weapon.

Instead two bright lights blinded her and she recognized them as free-floating lightballs. The guards likewise covered their eyes and screamed as the lightballs floated into the air before their eyes.

Some ran, some swatted as the lightballs did what they were designed to do: follow a human around.

The next thing she knew, Rayce was yanking her by the arm toward the dark desert, leaving the guards shouting and flailing at the persistent little lights dipping and diving around them.

"Good idea," she gasped, running as fast as she could beside him.

"I know how much you hate weapons," he said, and turned his head to the action behind them. "Let's just hope it keeps them busy for a while."

Suddenly, loud pops rang out and Tru spun around to see one of the lightballs explode. More shots and Rayce gave a pained grunt and fell to his knees in the sand.

She stumbled to a stop and ran back for him, just as he got to his feet, holding his right arm. Dark fluid oozed between his fingers.

"You're wounded," she said, a flood of horrible thoughts running through her head.

He took off at a run, hauling her with him as they chugged through the heavy sand.

"I'm fine. I think it went clean through," he replied between gritted teeth.

"Does it hurt?"

"Only when I breathe."

She remembered the long walk to the pyramids and panic set in. What if he bled to death before they reached the ship? What if he became unconscious? What if . . . she lost him?

They were a couple kilometers from the pyramid before he slowed down to a brisk walk and a slight stagger.

"I want to see your arm," she insisted, noting that his jacket sleeve was soaked in blood.

"Not until we reach the ship," he snapped. "Keep moving."

She winced at his surly tone. He wasn't angry with her. He was in pain and he was as scared as she was.

He tossed her the datapad. "Make sure we are going in the right direction."

Her hands shook as she activated the unit and checked their bearing. She pointed to the right, "We need to change course that way."

He nodded, concentrating on the ground. The final kilometers seemed to stretch forever. More than once he leaned on her. But there was no more talking. She checked the datapad again.

"It should be right in front of us."

"Deactivate mirage," he rasped.

The ship appeared directly in front of them.

"Open hatch," Rayce said wearily.

The door obeyed and he climbed in, leaving blood smeared on the doorway. Tru entered after him and closed the hatch.

Rayce walked unsteadily to the front of the ship and dropped into his seat with a groan. Tru slid into hers and got her first good look at his blood-soaked arm and his pained expression. Her stomach rolled. He'd lost a lot of blood.

Minutes later, Earth and its pyramid were a distant memory as the ship exited the atmosphere and jumped to hyperspace.

As soon as they were en route, Rayce's head dropped forward and Tru gasped. She unharnessed herself and wrapped her arms around him as he leaned into her, spent. His breathing was shallow and quick, his skin gray beneath the film of dust.

"Rayce," she said, fighting back the fear.

"Bed," he mouthed, his expression twisted.

She pulled, pushed and muscled him to one of the bunks where he promptly collapsed. Panic began to set in in earnest.

She went to the back and rifled through the small storage cabinets until she found the med kit. She dumped the contents on the foot of Rayce's bunk.

Cutters sliced through his jacket and shirt. She gave a little cry when she saw the exit wound—a small bloody hole in his upper arm. As she pulled the fabric back, she felt the entry hole on the other side. Whatever it was had gone clean through.

The med-vid film indicated no bone damage, no major artery damage. He was a lucky man.

"Aritrox," he said in a whisper.

She glanced at his grimacing face. "Hold on." She found the labeled injection and applied it close to the wound. Then she took an antiseptic and rinsed the two punctures well as he hissed in pain. White patches went over the clean wounds.

"So what's the prognosis?" he mumbled.

"You'll live," she said, hoping she knew what she was talking about. "The Aritrox should be able to replace the lost blood within an hour."

"You're the prettiest medic I ever had." He smiled to no one in particular.

"I'll bet you say that to all the girls who patch you up." She smiled back, tears burning her eyes.

"Naw. Only the ones I want to reach critical mass with," he said, his eyes closed, dark circles beneath them.

"Here." He reached into a pocket with his good arm, pulled out the plate, now a full-fledged pyramid, and held it out to her. The silver miniature gleamed in his blood-encrusted fingers.

"Your Charter," he said and then slipped into tranquil sleep.

Tears streamed down her face as she took the precious key in her shaky hands. Emotions engulfed her as she sobbed uncontrollably, unable and unwilling to do anything else.

After long minutes, she tossed the pyramid on her bunk and wandered wearily to the lav to retrieve a wet cloth.

She returned and began cleaning him up, just like he'd done for her after Rostron. He slept deeply, unaware, as she swabbed the dust from his face and body. She removed his shirt and jacket, and stripped off the rest of his filthy clothes.

Then she covered him in a clean blanket and dropped into her seat, turning it to face him. And with nothing to keep her busy, the guilt crept back in.

His chest rose and fell gently. He could have died on Earth, died for her and her mission. In that split second when he'd stumbled to the ground, her heart had stopped. And nothing, not even the Col-

lection would have started it again if he hadn't
struggled to his feet.

And what if he hadn't brought the lightballs?
They could have been arrested and trapped on
Earth forever.

She'd lied, coerced and threatened him into helping her. And now she'd nearly killed him. For
what? For her own selfish gain. Nothing she'd done
so far had been for anyone else but herself. She
didn't even make him partner because she gave a
damn about his spaceport. She did it because it was
the only leverage she had to get what she wanted.

In her quest for her Charter, her great gift to man-
kind, what had she become?

The thought spun around in her mind as she
watched Rayce sleep, the bandages white against
his golden skin.

He thought all Majj were greedy and self-
centered. And she'd proven to him that it was true.
Where were her noble intentions and her humanity? Was Rayce right? Were all Majj like her? Did
their goals, their thirst for knowledge and con-
quests turn them into heartless monsters? Is that the
way the rest of the galaxy saw them?

She narrowed her eyes. No more excuses. It was
time to get some answers, even if they weren't the
ones she wanted.

She activated the ship's computer and flashed it
up on the holodeck table. Now she would find out
if Rayce's hatred of the Majj was justified.

He felt warm hands on his face, heard a soft voice
in his ear and rose out of the blackness to find Tru
standing over him.

Beat the hell out of waking up to his homely medic. But the worry lining her face and her sad eyes didn't escape him.

He reached for her hand and kissed the palm. "Miss me?"

She smiled weakly. "I have to admit, it's been awfully quiet."

"How long?"

Her smile faded. "You've been sleeping for twenty hours. We'll arrive at the spaceport in eight hours."

He nodded, flexed his arm and winced. Still some work to be done, but otherwise, he felt pretty good considering he'd survived another near-death experience. He struggled to sit up.

"I can't believe they fired on us," Tru said as she helped him.

"They didn't," he replied, steadying himself on the edge of the bunk. "They were trying to shoot the lightballs. I happened to catch a lucky shot."

"It *was* lucky. It could have been much worse," Tru said, her voice breaking.

He glanced up at her drained expression. A great sadness weighed in her voice and he couldn't figure out why. "I'm fine, Tru. It's all part of the job."

"Risking your life for me was not part of the deal," she said, refusing to look at him. "I don't want you to do it again. We won't be taking any more risks."

"Not even for your Charter?" he asked, confused.

"Not even for that," she declared with a determined shake of her head.

He studied her. Something had changed while he slept. And he wasn't sure he liked it. It was as if someone or something had snuffed out her light. Gone was the drive, the excitement, the single-minded determination.

"What happened, Tru?" he said softly. Her eyes met his with a flash of mourning.

For a moment, he thought she might actually tell him, but then she shook her head and said, "Nothing. I just don't want either one of us going through this again."

She looked tired as she brushed the hair from her face. He'd find out one way or another, but for now he'd let her win this one. She wasn't ready for a battle of wills today.

"Fine."

He swung his legs over the edge of the bed, wrapped in a blanket and realized he was naked underneath.

He eyed her. "So you undressed me?"

She crossed her arms and gave him a semi-serious glare. "You are in no shape to reach critical mass."

He beamed. "I recover extremely fast."

A reluctant smile brightened her face. "You're insatiable."

He slid off the bunk and let the blanket fall around his feet. Her eyes widened as he moved in to kiss her.

"Only with you," he whispered against her lips. Then he turned to the lav, leaving her smiling. Good. Maybe she was finally getting it. There was no way for him to disguise that he wanted her. She was more than a Majj; she was a desirable, sexy woman. He'd prove it to her if it killed him.

He headed straight for the shower and planted himself beneath the soothing mist. He let his head drop back against the wall and closed his eyes, the Aritrox blurring his mind.

Why was she talking about risks now? They'd never scared her before. Twenty hours ago, she'd have sacrificed everything to get that Collection. So why the sudden change of heart?

Whatever had happened, she wasn't ready to talk. He'd bide his time but he wanted to know what kind of force could slow Tru Van Dye down from the biggest, most single-minded objective of her life.

Rayce's spaceport appeared out of the nothingness of hyperspace, beautiful and bright against black space. The layers, the shape, all so eloquent. A pang of guilt ate at her. She'd threatened to take all this away from him. How could she do that to the man she loved?

"Home at last," he said next to her.

She nodded numbly. His home. His right. His Charter.

"Tru?"

She turned to find him eyeing her curiously, a fringe of black hair dropping over his forehead. She smiled. She was in love with him. Full-blown, full-tilt, full-fool love.

Too bad she'd never be able to tell him.

"Elvis is probably dancing circles around Gil as we speak," she said.

"Then he's doing it for you," Rayce huffed, turning back to dock the ship. "I think he's going to desert me for you."

"Maybe what he needs is a mate."

Rayce nearly choked. "Forget it. One dog is plenty."

She warmed to the idea. "It's really unfair to him, probably unhealthy, too. He'll never find a compatible mate out here. Don't you think he deserves to be happy?"

"He *is* happy. Hell, he's the happiest animal I've ever met. He doesn't need to *be* any happier," Rayce said, annoyed.

"Having a steady mate and regular sex might calm him down. I've noticed it seems to have that effect on males."

Rayce's hands froze over the controls and he turned to her slowly, fire in his eyes. Heat broke over her, just like that, followed by devastating sadness. How could he want her? How could he ever want a Majj? How could anyone? She'd never realized how much he'd overcome to make love to her. If she'd only known . . .

"You may have a point," he conceded with a sly smile.

She smiled back and looked away. She couldn't bring herself to face him. Now that she finally knew what he knew.

They touched down in the landing bay and exited to find Gil and Elvis waiting. Elvis was beside himself, as expected, jumping on Rayce, licking everything he could reach with his tongue. He spared Tru one crotch sniff and then hugged Rayce's legs like a shadow.

Gil gave Tru an unexpected hug.

"We are almost there," he said, bursting with anticipation. "Next stop, the Curzon Collection."

Tru nodded and followed the men out of landing bay. "It looks that way."

Gil clapped his hands together. "I can't wait to

get my hands on it. Hell, if it's worth as much as legend says, we can buy out our investors. Right, boss?"

"Right," Rayce replied and added in a soft voice, "And what will you do with your portion, Tru?"

She stared down the long corridor. "I plan to return to the Institute with my discovery." And she turned to Rayce. His reaction was a hard glare, just as she expected. There wouldn't be any forgiveness, and she understood that.

At an intersection in the hall, Tru stopped. "If you'll excuse me," she said to them. "I think I'll retire early."

"You don't want to celebrate?" Gil asked, surprised.

"I'll celebrate after we find the Collection. We aren't there yet." She gave Rayce a nod. "Good night."

He didn't say anything, just looked back at her intently.

She headed to her quarters alone. The giant vase of fresh flowers awaited. She leaned in and inhaled deeply. So sweet. Perfection. Or at least, close enough.

She poured herself a drink, settled in a chair in front of the comm unit and using her Majj clearance, she ordered the computer to establish a comm link to one person she knew would take her call. Seconds later, a familiar face appeared on her viewer.

"Greetings, Odell," she said with utter composure. "If I'd known you were such a prick, I never would have gone out with you."

Odell's candid expression was precious and she

wished she'd recorded this little communiqué. It waffled somewhere between shock and rage and annoyance. He was shaken.

She smiled. Sweet retribution.

"Tru. We've been concerned for you," he replied in that condescending way he had.

"Like hell you have. You don't give a damn about me, Odell. You never did. Luckily, I didn't give a damn about you either, so we haven't wasted any energy on each other."

He recovered from his initial, unguarded reaction and leaned back, self-possessed as usual. "I see. Well, I'm afraid it's a little late for flattery. As an administrator, I'm required to inform you that you are being formally disassociated."

She took a sip of her drink. "I see. And that holds even if I bring in the Curzon Collection?"

His smug smirk dropped, replaced by a fleeting glint of worry, before he finally laughed. "You don't have it."

She ignored his patronizing tone. "I will shortly. Are you saying the Institute would turn down the find of the millennium?"

"Of course not. We would gladly accept a gift from an outside contributor, Tru."

Prick. "I'm afraid, as an outside contributor, I would have to ask for some sort of compensation."

His face hardened. "What kind of compensation?"

She ran a finger around the rim of her glass. "Enough to make me give up credit for the Collection so *you* could take it instead, because you will. Enough to pay back all the credits you administrators squeezed from the very people we Majj were supposed to be helping. Enough to make up for thirty years of destroying the good name of the Majj. How much do you think that's worth, Odell?"

For a moment, he said nothing. Then he smirked. "You can't do a thing to us. You can't get to the Majj. You will never set foot on this Institute again. And when I'm through with you, no one will believe a word you say."

"You picked the wrong Majj to go up against," she said, taking a sip of her drink.

Odell just grinned. "You are history, Tru. Without the Majj to hide behind you are nothing."

"You're *wrong*," she said, resolve in her voice. "I'm more than woman enough to bring you down."

He leaned into the viewer. "If I go down, then you *and* your father's sterling image go with me. Who do you think started this policy?"

She breathed in, out, and spoke clearly so that even a bastard like Odell could understand every word. "My father used me and he used the Majj. He deserves neither my respect nor my honor. And neither do you. I thought you were a smart man, Odell. Don't you know better than to threaten a woman who has nothing to lose?"

"Don't you know when to quit?" he snapped back.

"As a matter of fact, I do. It'll be right after I expose you and the rest of the administrators."

"You do and you will be committing professional suicide. You'll never find work anywhere in the galaxy. I'll see to it myself," Odell sputtered.

She countered, "And neither will you. The Majj won't take you back and no one on the outside will touch you after they find out how you administrators have overcharged them. If I were you, I'd start worrying about your own future."

Then she smiled at his livid expression and cut the communication.

Her quarters were silent as she finished her drink. Well, that felt good. Unfortunately, Odell the Prick had some valid points. No one on the Institute would take her seriously after she was disassociated. But she didn't need to convince everyone. The Majj understood and trusted facts. So that's what she'd give them—the thousands of accounts where the administrators had sold the Majj's hard-earned discoveries, cures and technology to the highest bidders, leaving the less fortunate to suffer. Desperate appeals that fell on deaf ears of the bastards who trashed the Majj name in the process, against everything they believed in. Her eyes misted over.

They'd ruined more than the Majj; they'd destroyed honor and humanity and decency. And unfortunately, there had been no attempt to distinguish between the administrators and the Majj in the eyes of outsiders. To them, they were the same. So the administrators filled their pockets under the guise of the Majj.

And her father's name had prominently appeared in those transactions. And why not? After all, he'd masterminded the change in policy some thirty years ago. The same man who told her repeatedly that she could do better, that she could be perfect only if she'd worked harder. The man who had monopolized the past twenty years of her life so he could build his own reputation and never gave her so much as a nod of appreciation. He had played them all for fools. And the naive Majj went along happily in their own shielded world, oblivious to the mountains of fortune the administrators were accumulating in their name.

Tears rolled down her face. Her own father. He'd soiled the Majj, used her for his own gain, and betrayed everything that meant anything to her. Every dream, every truth, every promise was shattered before she was even old enough to do anything about it. It had all been right there in the archives. Archives that were censored at the Institute, that no Majj had ever seen.

She hadn't wanted to see it herself, but somewhere in the back of her mind, she'd known something wasn't right. Rayce had known all along. She dropped her head back on the chair. He'd been truthful about everything, about the greed and the cold-bloodedness.

He should know. He'd suffered it first-hand. Miranda was no ex-lover. She was his younger sister who died of a disease that shouldn't have killed her. A disease that had a treatment. Tru knew, because she'd worked on that project for her father twenty years ago. One of her first, the first of many for a man who didn't care for the sanctity of human life. Tru knew how the Sykes Fever killed, how it indiscriminately tortured its victims until they suffocated in their own fluids. And so did her father. It just didn't bother him.

If Rayce knew she'd worked on that project, he'd never be able to forgive her, never be able to forget. Every time he looked at her, he'd remember her hand in his sister's death. He'd spent twenty years feeding his hatred. That kind of anger wouldn't disappear overnight. The last thing she wanted was to be around when he found out.

Rayce knew what the administrators had done. And she'd walked in and fed right into the image the administrators had laid out. He had every right to hate her, but instead he'd never once told her how the Majj had hurt him. He could have. Humiliated her, humbled her, thrown her out of his life. Instead, he'd shown her more respect than a Majj deserved, loved her as if he cared, even bled for her. And he hadn't asked her for anything. What could she possibly give him in return?

Staring at the ornate ceiling of her luxurious quarters, she found the answer. The Collection. His dream. Yes. That much she could do. This spaceport would become reality.

And somehow she had to find a way to get back to the Institute, pass along the information so that the Majj would understand that they'd been deceived. What they did from that point would be up to them. She wouldn't be around to find out. She would not become a Majj. The realization brought tears to her eyes. She didn't belong there. She never had.

A calm numbness stole over her that she knew would not go away for a long time. For the first time in her life, everything felt right.

She, alone, knew the full truth. Her father had brought disgrace to the honorable Majj and to the Van Dye name.

It was up to her to resurrect them both.

"Well, it's about time you checked in." Quin Coburne feigned worry and Rayce grinned. His father could never stay serious for long.

"I take it Mother has been driving you crazy?"

On the small comm view, his father chuckled. "Damn right. It's a good thing I love her to death. She's relentless. I know where you get it from now."

Rayce leaned back in his chair. "Any news over there?"

"Naw. Things are quiet." His father eyed him. "And with you? How's your lovely Majj client?"

He smiled reluctantly. "She's fine."

His father's expression changed to surprise and then he grinned. "I knew it. She's got you."

Rayce huffed. "She doesn't *have* me."

"The hell she doesn't. You've met the woman who is going to get you into trouble."

"I don't need any help getting into trouble, thank you."

"Not that kind of trouble," his father said. "I'm talking the life sentence."

Rayce stared grimly into the viewer. "I don't plan on stepping into that. Ever."

"You won't have a choice," his father said like a man who'd tried and failed. "Because life won't be worth living without her. No other woman will do, and you know why?"

Rayce didn't even want to ask but, "Why?"

"Because she's going to be the only woman who makes you face and conquer your biggest fear." His father nodded as if he'd just explained the miracle of life itself.

Rayce looked at him, dumbfounded. "I have no idea what you are talking about."

His father laughed. "Sure you do, you just don't want to admit it."

Rayce leaned forward. "Enlighten me."

"It works this way. What's your biggest fear?" his father asked.

"You coming to live with me."

His father waved him off. "Worse than that."

"Not from where I sit," Rayce muttered. "I have no other fears."

"Every man has fears, Rayce. What's the one thing that scares you so much that you don't even want to think about it?"

His father waited.

Rayce stared at him for a while, Miranda's final cries drowning out any thoughts, the crush of helplessness and hopelessness. "I'd rather not say," he said so softly, he didn't even think his father had heard him.

Quin nodded in quiet understanding. "Miranda. Yes. Why?"

Rayce scowled and rose to his feet. "This is ridiculous." He paced his office restlessly. "What does Miranda have to do with Tru?"

His father sobered, a rare and mesmeric event. "Because Tru is the one who is going to make you face that and, if you survive, she will have made you the man you want to be."

Rayce stopped in his tracks. "What? That's the craziest thing I've ever heard you say. I *am* the man I want to be." He crossed his arms. "And if you believe all this, then tell me what fear Mother made you face?"

Quin smiled blissfully. "Waking to the same woman day after day, the same face, same laugh, same temper. My greatest fear was that one day I'd want to wake up to a different face."

"Have you?" Rayce asked.

"Not once." His father shook his head. "She's my challenge, my conscience, my strength. And in return, she's made me a better man than I ever thought I could be."

"Well, you're stuck with me the way I am. Tru isn't going to be around long enough to make any changes. She's heading back to the Institute as soon as we finish this mission."

Quin grinned wide. "Is that so? Did I mention that this kind of trouble goes both ways?"

Chapter Fifteen

Frustration.

Rayce tapped the controls on *Miranda* sharply as he rechecked their course for the solar system, AR-3346A. They were halfway there and he was a frustrated man. And not just from lack of sex, although it didn't help. He'd had plenty of long stretches without sex.

No, this frustration was dealing with a woman who'd re-erected a wall around herself that he thought he'd knocked down. A silent woman. As much as she drove him crazy when she did talk, this was far worse. All that silence, all that time for her brilliant little mind to be plotting and planning or doing whatever brilliant little minds did.

Not that she had said or done anything particularly unkind. She'd been more than nice. In fact, she'd been downright polite, treating with him as if he was some . . . some hired guide.

And then there was the conversation with his father. Crazy talk. The man needed therapy. Tru wasn't going to change a damn thing with his life. Hell, she was barely speaking to him.

He banged the navigation panel again.

"You're going to break it," she said, glancing up from her datapad, her seat swiveled toward the back.

Behind him, being coddled by Tru, Elvis whined in agreement. Rayce glared at the traitor dog.

"You want to drive?" he asked her.

There was a beat of silence. Then she spun her seat around to the front of the ship and replied, "Actually, I do."

He turned to look at her, stunned. "What?"

She shrugged. "I think it would be a wise move, considering you are the only qualified pilot on this mission. What if something happened to you?"

He squinted at her. "So you want lessons?"

"Exactly," she said with a pleased nod and a wide smile. "I've already read all the manuals."

He laughed. "Then you are probably the only one who ever has." He rubbed his neck. She had a valid point. He still didn't want to think about what would have happened if he hadn't made it back to the ship on Earth. It wouldn't hurt for her to learn the basics.

"Okay. We're in hyperspace now but I can set the navigation panel to manual flight simulation. I'll flash the panel up on your side and we'll start."

The flat black panel in front of Tru lit up with the labyrinth of controls it took to fly *Miranda*.

He spent the next three hours teaching her the fundamentals, which she memorized quickly and completely. Then he let her fly a simulated mission, which she did without a single flaw. They moved quickly through the basics to the advanced levels and by the time they were done, he was beginning to think he wasn't such a great pilot after all.

"So that's it?" she said, leaning back in her seat.

"Pretty much," he said, rather disgusted. "Some practical experience would help. You can take over once we reach AR-3346A."

"Fine." She pointed to the upper corner of the console. "Are these the controls for miraging?"

He eyed her. "Yes, but none of the planets in the AR-3346A system are inhabited. We won't be needing it."

She nodded. "Do all your ships have miraging capabilities?"

"Most of them. Why?"

She tapped the navigation panel. "Just wondering if it's standard equipment on small ships."

"It is on mine," he said, stretching his arms over his head. "It's nearly meal time—"

"I'll get it." She exited her seat abruptly and headed for the galley with traitor dog in hot pursuit.

Rayce watched her disappear into the back and shook his head. This was going to be a very long ride if things didn't change.

He followed her into the narrow galley made for one person. Elvis made it three, although he was glued to her leg. She didn't look up from meal prep.

Rayce moved up behind her until their bodies pressed together. "Talk to me, Tru."

She whispered, "I can't."

"Did something happen at the Institute?"

"No."

"Did Odell contact you?"

A pause. "No."

He took a breath and a step back. "Then it's me."

She spun around, her eyes wide. "No. No, it's not you." She brushed hair from her face and sighed. "As a matter of fact, I think you are the only person I trust at the moment."

He waited and watched as emotions played across her face. Finally she looked him in the eye and said, "Have you ever discovered that something you believed in your entire life wasn't what it appeared?"

He thought about the Majj and the hate. And how Tru had blown his image all to hell. "Just recently. What have you discovered?"

She flinched and shook her head. "Nothing I can't handle." She turned around, leaving him to face her wall.

"Kiss," he said softly to her back.

She froze, turned and peered at him forlornly. "How can you want me? I'm a Majj."

Not yet, she wasn't. "You're a woman and my partner and we had a deal."

She smiled a little. "Yes, we did. Actually, I think you missed a few days."

"Two-point-three days," he said, clearing his throat. "Not that I've been counting."

Her smile grew. "In that case, I owe you something special." She moved in, wrapped her arms around his neck and kissed him with a desperation that made him a very happy man. So it wasn't him. That made him feel mildly better. What was it then?

He would have pursued that very point if she hadn't rubbed up against him, reminding him just how long two-point-three days had been.

Because life won't be worth living without her. His father's words spiraled through his head and he let them. So he cared about her. So what? It wasn't like he wanted to spend forever with her. That's what he told himself, even as Tru filled his senses, flooded his mind, completed him.

She pulled back and great sadness flitted through her eyes and he didn't know why. Then it was gone and she smiled demurely. "So, have you ever reached critical mass in a galley before?"

Now she knew why solar system AR-3346A didn't rate a real name. It wasn't much to look at. The red sun filled *Miranda*'s viewer in the distance. They dropped out of hyperspace directly in front of a lone planet—a giant ball of azure blue gas. A colony of small moons circled its massive girth.

"Let's hope the Collection isn't on Big Blue," she said aloud and pushed Elvis's snout off her armrest.

Rayce spun his chair around and brought up the holo table. Within seconds AR-3346A's satellite moons appeared.

"Extensive gaseous atmosphere. Mostly methane," he said. "And damn cold. We'll concentrate on the moons. Park us for a while."

She entered the proper sequence to bring the ship to a stop and then turned her chair around to face the deck. Thirteen tiny moons floated around the main planet.

"I seriously doubt the Curzons would have picked a volatile or extreme climate in which to hoard their priceless Collection," she told him.

"True. Computer, clear out moons with environments inhospitable to known sentient beings."

To Tru's surprise, eleven planets dropped out. All that remained were two moons called AR-3346A*M003 and AR-3346A*M008. She glanced at Rayce who explained, "Luckily, there are few planets that can support life as we know it." He leaned forward. "Computer, give climate comparisons of two remaining moons."

A digital table appeared and two columns marked M003 and M008 scrolled down slowly. Tru scanned the data.

"M008 is entirely water. No solid land masses," she commented.

Rayce nodded. "M003 it is. Human habitable. We won't even need environment suits. Comfortably cool days, cold nights. Moderate rains. No reports of sentient life forms."

She huffed. "Don't count on that. Bring all the weapons you've got."

He grinned. "Set course for M003. Time for landing practice."

Her eyes widened. "You can't be serious. I've only landed in the simulation exercise. We could crash."

He spun his chair around to face the front viewer. "I have complete faith in you."

"Well, that makes one of us." She reluctantly turned back to the navigation panel with its hundreds of controls and she suddenly couldn't remember what any of them did.

Rayce leaned back, folded his arms and closed his eyes. "Take us in."

She shoved aside the image of the ship as a flaming ball crashing to the ground and entered the commands to bring the ship into orbit around

M003. The moon loomed large in her viewer, brown and green with white cloud cover, and rather nondescript as moons go. Probably why the Curzons chose it.

"Oh, and it's your turn to hold the pyramid," she said as the ship shuddered through the moon's outer atmosphere. Elvis staggered between their seats.

"Decrease your entry angle," Rayce commented calmly without even opening his eyes. "You think it'll act like a beacon again?"

She winced as the ship bounced hard a few times and Elvis gave a little yip. Things began to fall off the shelves behind them. "I certainly hope so. Otherwise, we'll spend the rest of our lives scouring M003 searching for where they hid the Collection."

Rayce looked at her then. "You don't think it'll be another pyramid?"

The ship leveled out smoothly. She gave a sigh of relief and patted Elvis's head to calm him. "I don't know what to expect. But don't you think someone would have spotted a pyramid on this moon by now? It's not like this is an uncharted system."

He hummed agreement. "Bring us down to fifty thousand klicks."

She complied as he exited his seat and headed to the back. He returned moments later with the silver pyramid in a protective bag.

"You're going to have to take it out of the bag," she said, stifling a smirk.

He gave her a heated look because he knew what she was saying. Let *him* deal with the blast of sexual frustration.

"You could be in serious trouble," he said, slipping the pyramid out into his hand.

"Uh-uh, I'm driving."

"We have to land sometime," he reminded her, leaning toward her with a grin.

"Just point the way," she said, trying to keep him focused.

"Keep flying in the grid pattern laid down. I'll let you know when things start to heat up."

She concentrated on *Miranda*'s navigation panel. When they broke through the thick clouds, M003 became a lovely planet, rich in plant life—a sprawling jungle of green between long fingers of russet mountain ranges, deep crevices and an occasional strip of water. It took over an hour of flying low over M003 before Rayce said something.

"Slow down," he murmured with a bit of a groan.

She quickly adjusted their speed. "Do you have a sense of direction yet?"

He didn't say anything for a few moments, his eyes focused on M003's surface. "I think we passed over it." He checked the ship's current position and locked in a landing coordinate. "Bring her down."

Tru brought the ship around and headed for a rocky mountain ridge surrounded by a sea of green. With an unflattering thump and screech of metal, she landed the ship on a flat rock pad atop the bald mountain ridge. Elvis ran straight to the back of the ship, wagging his tail.

Tru peered out the viewer and over the valleys below. "See anything alive out there?"

Rayce shoved the pyramid back into its bag. "If there is, Elvis will find it. Or water or mud or something dead. I swear that dog has built-in sensors."

Tru wrinkled her nose. "Dead would be fine with me."

Rayce exited his seat. "Where's your sense of adventure?"

"I don't have one. I never did. And I don't want one now," she muttered, climbing out of her own seat.

Rayce shoved a full pack toward her. "We are on foot from here. I packed enough supplies for three days. If it takes longer than that, we'll have to come back to the ship to restock."

She hiked the pack over her shoulders. "How strong was the pyramid's magnetism?"

He pulled his own pack on. "Strong enough to make me want to forget this damn mission and take you to bed."

Her fingers froze on her harness and she looked up at him. "Really?"

Rayce grinned back. "Really. Actually, I don't even need the pyramid for that."

She just smiled. "We couldn't spend our lives in bed. We wouldn't get anything done."

"No, but we'd both be really happy people," he said with absolute confidence.

It was then she realized that she'd never find another man like him. No other man alive could make her want to forget why she was here. No other man would set her on fire. But this was no longer her mission. It was his. The Collection would give him everything he needed and deserved, small compensation for all that the Majj had taken away from him.

She watched him sling a laser rifle easily over his

shoulder and stuff a handgun in his holster. Strong muscles moved beneath his shirt. For a split second, she was tempted to slide her hands inside and feel his strength and heat again. It was a temptation she would need to curb soon. Her days were numbered.

She followed him to the back, where Elvis pranced impatiently. Rayce activated the door and cool air rushed in. Elvis launched himself off the deck and onto the brown rock surface.

Rayce glanced around and then jumped down himself. She exited and stepped up behind Rayce, who was making a slow sweep of the ridge. Elvis ran from rock to rock, sniffing each one.

"So far, so good," she said. Her words sounded loud in the unreal silence. Atop the mountain, she scanned the stunning views and the lush forest below. "It's beautiful here. I wonder why this planet isn't inhabited."

Rayce frowned. "Now that's a question I'm not sure I want an answer to."

Tru turned to him in alarm, and he raised a hand. "I know. You hate it when I say that. If you see anything suspicious, just let me know."

"In the meantime," he continued, handing her the pyramid. "Your turn. I need to have my hands free."

Their fingers brushed as she took it from him and a potent charge passed between them. His free hand slipped around her waist and pulled her tightly to him as he kissed her. The pyramid buzzed in her hand, its energy rising with each kiss. Passion roiled within her, owning her, driving her. She wanted nothing more at this moment than what Rayce could give her. Nothing else mattered. It was a need so basal that it rivaled air itself.

He pulled back and gazed at her with eyes of banked fire, as if one soft breath could ignite it with ease. For a fleeting moment, she wondered if he felt the same way, if he understood the risk and was willing to take it. But in the end, it wouldn't matter. When he found out about her link to Miranda's death, he would never look at her this way again. She didn't want to see that happen, didn't want to be there when he turned away and banished her from his memory. Nothing could be worse than that. Not even living without him.

"Ready?" he asked.

She nodded, unable and unwilling to say what she was ready for. Rayce would get his dream.

"See if the pyramid can give us some direction," he told her.

She held it out and felt the surge pull through her. Then she stepped around in a circle and the energy died. "Due west."

"We'll walk along the top of the ridge as long as possible," he said, leading the way. "Come, Elvis."

Tru turned to see the dog abandon the rock he was pushing around with his nose. She'd somehow taken a liking to the crazy animal. He trotted happily along beside them, occasionally veering off the path to explore as they negotiated the rolling crest.

She glanced up at the cloudy sky. "How long before sundown?"

"According to the computer, about six hours. If we don't find the Collection by then, we'll have to camp outside." He glanced back at her. "But I'd rather not."

They walked for thirty minutes, until the pyramid began burning in her hands, pulling her toward the edge of the ridge. The sexual energy was gone now, replaced by a new and strange urgency.

"Rayce, I think we need to go down there." She pointed to the green valley below them.

Rayce nodded and started the descent. About halfway down, Tru noticed that the rocks were different. The texture was more refined and the color a darker brown. She wondered why.

Suddenly, Elvis stopped directly in front of her with his ears perked high and whined softly. Rayce halted, too. The dog didn't move, concentrating his entire black body on something in the valley below them. A strip of thick fur rose on his back.

Tru looked at Rayce, who was frowning. "What is it?"

He shook his head. "I don't know, but Elvis has excellent hearing."

"So this is bad, right?" Tru said, nervously.

Rayce swung the rifle around and into his hands. "Maybe. Let's keep moving."

Tru followed silently, trying not to look like a good target for whatever was bothering Elvis. They continued their descent, the green forest drawing closer until Tru could make out the bizarre trees with their stringy branches and leaves. That's when the smell hit her.

She nearly gagged as an offensive stench stung her nose. Elvis stopped with her and whined as he hid behind her legs.

"Rayce, what *is* that?"

For a moment, he didn't answer. "I'm not sure I should tell you."

She retrieved a cloth from her pack and held it

to her mouth and nose. "I want to know before it kills me."

"It smells like decaying flesh."

The bile rose in her throat. "Flesh? I thought there was no life here?"

"No record of humans, but there could be animal life."

She reached down and rubbed Elvis's head. "Do you think Elvis is safe?"

"I think Elvis can take care of himself. I'm a lot more worried about you and me." He looked out of over the canopy of trees just below them. "Can you tell if we are heading in the right direction?"

She pulled the pyramid out and felt the strong surge. Stronger than before. "Closer." She swept the area with it. "North. Over there."

Rayce took a few steps away and surveyed the rocky terrain between them and "north," where a wide rift in the rock face blocked their path.

"We'll have to go down and around."

Tru scanned the down part. It would take them into the jungle below. A shiver ran down her spine. Intuition, maybe, but it didn't help that Rayce had his rifle ready as they descended the rocky slope. Elvis stayed by her side, no longer running ahead happily and doubling back as he had earlier. She could hear his soft growl every so often and the fur on his back stayed high.

Bare rocks gave way to small, scraggly shrubs and brown, thick, spiky grass before plunging into a jungle of surreal trees. Tru's fear eased as her eyes adjusted to the limited sunlight filtering through the odd canopy.

"Flowers," she gasped. Unexpected but welcome.

She stepped up for a closer look at a nearby tree along the edge. A great fountain of stringy branches arched from the top of the red tree trunk, flowing down. Each branch was covered with round, glossy leaves and rainbow garlands of giant flower heads. Pure perfection like she'd never seen before, nearly too perfect to be real.

"How beautiful." Mesmerized, she reached out to touch a pale blue blossom.

"Don't move any closer," Rayce warned sharply. Tru stopped and turned to look at him in confusion.

"It's just a flower."

He was looking up into a nearby tree. Elvis stood beside him snarling softly, his black eyes fixed on the same place.

With great trepidation, her head slowly followed their twin gaze. As her eyes rested on the blood-red tree trunk, something moved in the mass of greenery at the top. Something large. And in pain.

A guttural rattle emanated, tortured and weak, but leaving no doubt what it was: a captured animal.

"Rayce, the tree—"

"Now we know why this planet is uninhabited."

She swallowed. "Carnivorous trees. What next?"

"I'm beginning to think the ancient Curzons were a little on the sadistic side."

"Brilliantly sadistic," Tru commented. "They didn't want to make this easy. Or even tempting."

Rayce stepped up behind her. "Let's move along before we discover any more surprises. And stay away from all the vegetation. I have a feeling the entire planet is hungry."

Tru's stomach rolled as the digested beast in the tree moaned pathetically.

"Can you at least kill it so it won't suffer?" she pleaded.

Rayce pursed his lips. "I suppose." He raised the rifle and fired into the green ball of branches.

Suddenly there was a squeal from the tree itself and those around it. Branches flailed, and the branch nearest Tru lashed out. One tendril snapped around her wrist and yanked her tight. She stared at the lethal restraint covered with its perfect flowers.

"No!" she screamed, tugging on the tightly wound binding, the vine piercing her skin.

A flash of light whizzed by her face and severed the tendril with one slash. Rayce pulled her away from the tree, wielding the laser blade for any other attacks. The jungle around them thrashed and wailed.

"That really burned them," he noted grimly as he ripped the strand from her wrist and cast it aside. She winced at the series of tiny bloody marks it left behind.

"And I thought the other planets were bad," she said, wincing as he wrapped a Aritrox bandage around her wrist. "*Something* better be easy on this mission."

Rayce smirked. "If it were easy, someone would have done it by now." His gaze swung around to hers, eyes clear and bright. Eyes she could look at forever. The kind that wouldn't fade with time, wouldn't lie to her, wouldn't lose their luster. For a moment, all the dangers around them disappeared and all she could see was his beautiful eyes and the way he looked at her like she was the only woman in the universe. If only they could stay that way.

Elvis bumped his leg, breaking the moment and Rayce patted his head. "We're going, boy."

Rayce took her hand and guided her around the gnashing trees. Tru followed, her eyes watching every movement and shadow. Elvis brought up the rear. They walked on, careful to avoid anything that looked remotely alive and ravenous.

Just as they cleared the deep ridge, she felt the pyramid leap in her pocket. She slipped it out, barely able to contain it in her hands.

Ahead of her, Rayce stopped and turned. "Close?"

"We must be right on top of it. I've never felt such a strong energy surge." She pointed it around her and ended up facing the deep slash in the mountain, shrouded in darkness. "In there."

Elvis trotted toward the fracture in the rock, sniffing rocks and moving on. Then Tru watched as he disappeared into the mountain.

"A cave. It figures." Tru took a deep breath. "I suppose this means we have to follow him."

"It's probably safer in there than it is out here."

She glanced over at Rayce. "You really believe that?"

He turned and grinned at her. "No. But I know how much you hate it when I tell you what I really think."

She shook her head. She was going to miss him. A thousand times a day, in a thousand ways.

Rayce reached into his pack and pulled out two

lightballs. They immediately came to life and took their positions beside their masters.

Then Rayce hefted his rifle and they headed into the shadows.

Chapter Sixteen

He didn't like it. Didn't like the smell or the murky cavern with all its hiding places. His lightball stayed close, illuminating an otherwise lightless cave. Old bones and whole animal carcasses littered the floor between giant stones. Even Elvis left them alone. A datapad sweep showed no life, but things hadn't been going their way this mission. Anything was possible. They continued to move forward into the darkness while Elvis crisscrossed in front of them.

"A lot of bones," Tru whispered. "What do you think it means?"

He whispered back, "It means they're all dead."

She wrinkled her nose at him. "Bite him, Elvis."

Elvis whined in confusion and Rayce laughed.

A few moments later, Tru said softly. "You saved me again back there."

He shrugged, peering at the black shape ahead. "That's what partners are for. We have a doorway. Definitely man-made."

They stopped before a large rectangular opening cut through the stone wall of the cave, bordered by a series of intricate carvings.

Tru stepped up. "They look similar to the artwork on Earth. Did the Curzons invent the style and pass it to the Egyptians, or did the Egyptians teach the Curzons?"

"Good question. One I'm sure we'll never get an answer to. Let's see where it leads." He surveyed the doorway for traps and stepped through. "We need to be very careful from here on in. My acquisitions friend couldn't come up with anything in the way of information on this find."

"That's comforting. Is he a good friend?"

"Only the kind you risk your life with."

"I bet you have a lot of friends like that," Tru said. He could hear a little sadness in her voice.

"It pays to have friends who will die for you but are good enough not to. The air is getting stale."

"I noticed. And cooler."

The lightballs lit a tunnel hewn through the solid stone of the mountain. Rayce held his rifle ready as the tunnel took a sharp right and then continued to another sharp right.

Behind him, Tru commented, "We're heading up."

"How's our little key doing?"

"It's vibrating. And it feels lighter. Almost weightless now. Like it could float if I let it go."

"Hold onto it. I have a feeling we're going to need it."

The tunnel took one last turn and finally ended in a small three- by three-meter room with no other outlets. The floor was perfectly smooth, the only noticeable difference from the tunnels.

Tru placed her hands on the rough stone walls. "This makes no sense."

Rayce scanned the room with the datapad. Nothing.

Elvis whined just as a great rumble filled the tiny space and the floor tilted under their feet, giving way to an impossible angle. They fell on their backs and tumbled through the inclined floor as it became part of a narrow, smooth slide. Rayce grabbed for Tru, trying to keep her from getting banged around and at the same time, aiming his rifle on whatever was waiting for them below. Elvis yelped all the way down before they were unceremoniously dumped in a heap into another small room.

"Are you okay?" Rayce asked, helping Tru to her feet.

She brushed off her pants and muttered, "I swear, if I'd known, I would have done my Charter on something boring and completely inane like the mating rituals of Berkerain beetles."

"I'll take that as a 'yes,'" Rayce said, glancing around. Elvis shook himself and headed toward the small door in an otherwise empty room that looked very much like the one they had been tossed out of. They were all alive, he still had his rifle and both lightballs were intact and present. Things were great.

He heard a low rumble above them that lasted a few seconds, and then silence. The floor had closed back up. Not so great.

"That would be our exit," he said grimly.

Tru gazed up into the mouth of the slide. "Do you think that's the only way out?"

He didn't want to answer that question. The thought of being buried alive under a mountain on an uninhabited planet was more than he cared to share with Tru. Already his internal warning system was on full alert.

"There are probably other exits," he said casually, heading for the door.

Tru followed him as the room opened up, and then they stopped in unison.

"Oh my," she said, her voice hushed in reverence.

Before them lay an enormous chamber, brimming with art and artifacts, heaped and piled atop one another. The lightballs shone between rows of thick stone columns and over mounds of treasure, haphazardly stacked between them. Precious metals, earthen pots, jewelry, scrolls, statues, and coins lay strewn across the floor. The walls were lined with two tiers of shelves, overflowing with artifacts.

"It's real," Tru whispered, moving around him. She hurried to the nearest shelf and picked up a slim, crystal vase.

"Wsu Marnian. Priceless."

Then she set it down and reached for a small, brown statue. "Elgarian. Exquisite."

She glanced up at him, excitement flushing her face. "It's more than I imagined. The history, the art, the craftsmanship. This is the best of the best. Some of these pieces are the only surviving works of their respective cultures."

Standing in the shadow in her lightball's soft glow, she was lovely. He almost hated to tell her that something was very wrong. They'd spent the last ten days building that damn pyramid in her pocket. For what? They didn't even need to use it. They'd waltzed in here like they'd been invited. The Curzons had planned everything out so carefully, made it nearly impossible for someone to find it, and yet made this so simple. Easy. Too easy.

His alarm grew as he wandered through the maze of objects and massive columns, walking the perimeter with the datapad. No exits located. Not a single doorway except for the one they'd already come through. The one that had closed up behind them.

Elvis trotted up to him with something in his mouth. Rayce wrestled it from his jaws. A bone. A human femur bone. Elvis turned away. A few seconds later, Rayce found him hovering over the remains of a human body huddled in a corner of the chamber.

Rayce kneeled down and examined the remains. The clothing had mostly disintegrated, the body nearly mummified in the constant temperature underground.

On the other side of the chamber, Tru gave a steady commentary on each piece she found, where it came from and its significance in the Collection. Rayce put the bone back, stood up and walked over to her as she appraised yet another item, completely engrossed and oblivious to the fact they were trapped in a tomb surrounded by a treasure they might never share with the outside world.

He stopped behind her. "Tru, we have to figure out how to get out of here."

She halted mid-recital and looked at him, startled. "You said there were other exits."

"I lied."

"You're serious," she said in astonishment, setting the artifact down.

He stared back at her, the feeling of helplessness growing in his belly. "We need to find a way out. Now."

Her eye widened and she nodded in simple reply, moving quickly beside him. "Any ideas?"

He pointed to the far side of the chamber. "Start over there. Examine the walls for anything that looks like a doorway or a hatch. If you find something, call me."

She nodded and set off. Elvis whined at his feet.

"Go with her," Rayce said to the dog. Elvis cocked his head and then trotted off to follow Tru.

Rayce began his search, running his hands along the polished stone, looking for something the datapad scan had missed. Seams were few and far between and nothing looked like a doorway. After two hours of intense searching, he ended where Tru had left off. She had already finished up and was standing behind him when he turned around and leaned back against the wall.

She held her hands up helplessly. "Nothing."

He ran a hand through his hair. "Okay, Plan B." He motioned to the depictions high on the walls over the stone shelves. "See if you can make any sense of these paintings. They might give us some clue."

He pushed off the wall and headed back the way they'd come in.

"Where are you going?" she asked.

He glanced over his shoulder. "To see if this laser

rifle can cut through solid stone." He caught the look of doubt in her face and shrugged it off. She was probably right, but he wasn't going to die lying down.

Tru shivered in the cool chamber. Elvis nudged her hand and she patted his head absently as she peered into the dark corners where her lightball didn't shine.

Rayce was worried. Deeply. He didn't have to say it, but she knew they were in trouble.

"Come on, Elvis," she said softly, her voice piercing the silence. They navigated the stacks and rows, following the perimeter of the room. Tru barely noticed the precious, priceless history around her, only the present.

After an hour, she was back where she'd begun. Then Elvis's soft whine brought her gaze down to a dark, dead body, curled up in a corner.

The air caught in her lungs as she froze, unable to turn away from the sunken eye sockets and the cocked head. He had to be a thousand years old. In his hand, he clutched a valuable crystal cup.

She backed away from the man who'd never found freedom. Tears stung her eyes, blurring the treasure within reach.

"I should have warned you about him."

She jumped and spun around to find Rayce behind her, looking weary. Her response was slow to form. "He's been here a long time."

Rayce nodded pensively. "And we might be here for a while ourselves. Find anything?"

She wanted so much to fix the deathtrap she'd led them into, wanted to free Rayce to follow his dream but all she could do was shake her head. "You?"

He put his hands on his hips. "I tried shooting the laser rifle back up the slide. I tried cutting a hole through all the walls. Then the floor and the ceiling. And I swore a lot."

"And?"

He dropped his hands. "The swearing made me feel better."

She smiled a little, even if her heart wasn't in it. For a moment, they just stared at each other, both understanding the situation. Finally, Rayce took her hand and led her to the only part of the massive room that had an empty floor space in the center between four colossal columns.

She sat on the floor and settled her back against one of the stone pillars that formed a small square. Rayce dropped against the opposite pillar and Elvis tracked back and forth between them before choosing Rayce to lay next to.

She looked out through the columns. "It appears that each wall depicts life on all the planets we've been to as they were 5,000 years ago." She pointed to the walls in turn. "Curzon, then Arête, Rostron and finally Earth over there."

Then a strange realization struck her and her mind spiraled deep into thought.

"What?" Rayce's question jolted her back.

She frowned. "It's rather odd but I think the Curzons may have been using the Five Ancient Elements."

"Keep going." Rayce prodded.

She licked her lips. "Maybe it's just coincidence, but Rostron used to be mostly water, so that would have been the Water Element. Arête has its eternal winds, which would have been Air. Earth, if it was called that 5,000 years ago, would have been Earth Element. And Curzon would have been Fire, with its ancient burning pylons."

"So what was the fifth element? Death by vegetation?" Rayce asked.

She winced. "Thankfully, no. Just everything in between."

Rayce chuckled and shook his head. "Well, that's about as clear as anything else."

She followed her thoughts. "Actually, it was called Dark Matter by some cultures. They considered it to be the space between the other elements, binding them together, yet giving them room to be separate entities. The contradiction of logic—intangible, yet real. Even invisible, it is the force that binds us, gives us commonality and balance. An energy force of unknown origin and great power."

"Which means what to this puzzle?"

She gave a great sigh. "I don't know. Maybe the Curzons didn't mean it literally, but more like a concept or an essence. Or a lesson."

Rayce's eyes narrowed. "You're getting pretty philosophical for a Majj."

She smiled a little. "I've discovered that science doesn't have all the answers." Too late, she thought.

"What about our pyramid?"

She pulled the small silver object from her pocket and bounced it lightly on her palm. "Nothing on the walls about this piece. I always thought of this as a key to get the treasure. But all it did was act like a homing device. Doesn't make sense."

She set the pyramid down and rubbed her hands

along her thighs. "I'm sorry, Rayce. I thought I had it all figured out. It seemed so clear-cut when I started, but nothing has turned out the way I planned."

He laid his head back against the pillar and closed his eyes. "Not many people would have gotten this far, Tru. Not many people have your courage. I don't blame you."

She blinked at him. How could he not blame her? How? This entire mission had been her idea and she'd dragged him into it against his will and now they were going to end up like the dead guy in the corner.

The administrators had cost him his sister, made his life miserable and now she'd taken the rest. The least she could do was apologize. For a lot of things, but one thing in particular. Not that she could change the past, but maybe she could ease some of his anger and pain.

"I'm sorry about Miranda."

He snorted lightly. "The ship is fine. I don't think you damaged it on that landing."

She took a deep breath and wrapped her arms around her legs. "I'm not talking about the ship."

For a moment, he didn't move. Then he leveled his gaze at her. "How do you know about Miranda?"

Her eyes flickered to his and then down at the floor. "I did some research. She died from the Sykes Fever and she shouldn't have."

His voice was hard. "You're right, she shouldn't have."

Tru flinched. "What was she like?"

"What?" he asked with a shocked expression.

281

Her eyes begged him. "Tell me about her. I'd really like to know."

He closed his eyes and shook his head.

"I know she meant a lot to you. She must have been very special," Tru coaxed him.

"She was. She lit up the room." It sounded like the words were ripped from his throat.

Tru said nothing, just waited.

After a few silent seconds, Rayce continued, "My first memory of her was the day she was born and she threw up on me. From that point forward, she never let me forget who ruled the house. She tormented me mercilessly and got away with it because she could. One sweet smile and I would forgive just about anything."

A smile touched his lips. "But she had the biggest heart I've ever known. Any stray animal that passed by our house never went hungry. Even if she had to give up her own meal."

Tru knew how Rayce's family had struggled. And she had finally found a definition for *gruners*. The poor and destitute. The Inferiors.

He stared at his hands. "Once she stayed up all night with me when I was sick and my parents were working. Every time I woke up, she was there, waiting. She'd give me some smartass remark that I was only faking so I could miss school for a few days and I better not get her sick. Then she'd wipe my head and sing some old song over and over again until I fell back to sleep. I can still remember that song."

Elvis nudged his leg and Rayce rubbed his big black head.

"You were there when she died," Tru said softly.

He nodded and his expression tightened. "I was there. It didn't matter. I couldn't help her, couldn't save her."

"She suffered," Tru whispered. "I'm so sorry, Rayce."

He absently stroked Elvis's fur. She wanted to tell him so much more, somehow make it right but all she could offer was "sorry." It seemed a poor substitute for someone you love.

Finally he said, "I doubt you could have done anything about it. You were too young."

Tru swallowed and stared at the floor. *Too young. Wrong.* She'd been there, been part of the process.

"You left home after that."

He eyed her. "I had a lot of anger to vent. And I did. Enough to almost get myself permanently incarcerated. Luckily, I picked up a few sane friends."

"You did well for yourself, Rayce."

"I need to do better."

She caught his determined expression and felt the simmering rage beneath it. A rage he had carried all this time. Was it the anger that had driven him this far? Or had it held him back?

Very softly, she asked, "Tell me, has your anger done you any good?"

His piercing gaze met hers. "I have the right to be angry."

"But do you have the right to be angry on Miranda's behalf? Would she have wanted that?"

His eyes burned into hers. "I don't know. She's not around to ask."

Tru pursed her lips. "Are you mad at the Majj or at something else?"

He didn't say a word, just glared at her intensely.

She pushed. "I'm not saying the Majj are perfect. They aren't. But if you found out someday that the Majj weren't who you thought they were, who would you have left to be angry at?"

"I blame the Majj," he snapped.

Tru didn't back down. "Is that how you honor Miranda's memory? With all that anger?"

She could feel his rage from where she sat. Even Elvis had moved away from him nervously.

She waited. Waited for him to tell her how evil the Majj were, to tell her all the things that she now knew were true. All this time, he'd never said anything, only assumed that she knew exactly what the Majj were and was willing to become one of them. As disgusted as he was by her being a Majj, he'd never once accused her directly. Now would be the time. When he had nothing left to lose.

"I think this conversation is over, Tru."

She watched him get up abruptly and storm out into the shadows. Her mind spun around the realization that he hadn't lit into her. He could have. He *did* have a right to hate the Majj. She couldn't deny that. But he didn't hate her.

She laid her head back against the pillar. She should have told him about her involvement. But what would it solve? Nothing, only add more pain and she'd already done plenty of that. Besides, it was obvious he was incapable of forgiveness. If he hadn't found it in his heart to forgive yet, nothing she could say or do would change that.

She swallowed the hard lump in her throat. She should have just kept her mouth shut. They didn't have much time left together. So what if he had a misdirected hatred of the Majj? It didn't matter anymore. Nothing mattered except that they were probably going to be spending eternity in this place.

Half an hour later he reappeared, looking markedly calmer. Without a word, he pulled his pack over and withdrew some food rations. He ripped open a pouch for Elvis who inhaled it in three seconds flat and proceeded to stare at theirs with hope in his eyes.

Tru frowned as Rayce tossed her a ration. "Seems rather pointless, don't you think?"

"I'm waiting for that brilliant brain of yours to come up with something."

She gave a muffled snort. "Now you're asking for trouble. I'm not having the best mission of my life."

He shrugged and tossed a bit of his food to Elvis. "Take your time. We have three days of food and water. You've done pretty well until now."

Her eyes met his in marked surprise and her expression dropped. "I had help. A lot of help. I couldn't have done it without you."

He smirked. "I'm not sure I've helped very much. It's your theory. I'm just along for the ride."

She was bewildered by his answer. "Is that what you think?"

"And my good looks."

That drew a big smile out of her. "And your modesty."

"Don't forget my sexual prowess," he added promptly.

She laughed out loud at that one. "Excellent point."

"Glad I'm good for something." He finished his ration and let Elvis lick it clean. "So you know what my childhood was like. What was yours?"

Her mood darkened immediately as she poked at her food. "Normal, I'm sure."

"I seriously doubt that anyone can have a normal life at that Institute."

Not hungry, she gave her portion to Elvis, who wolfed it down and proceeded to chew on the tray. "I was born there. I grew up. There's really not much to tell." She looked up at the dark room outside their small, lit circle. "It was all pretty mundane."

"Were there other children at the Institute?"

She nodded. "The most promising candidates around the galaxy are taken from their parents at a young age and educated on the Institute. When a candidate reaches twenty, he has to pass the stringent selection process. Failure means expulsion. If the candidate passes, he becomes an honorary member and begins work toward a Charter."

"But you were born there," Rayce noted.

"Yes, but that didn't give me any special rights. In fact, it made it more difficult. Births at the Institute are very rare. Forbidden, in fact. If my father hadn't been so prominent, we probably would have been asked to leave."

"And if you had failed you would have had to leave your parents behind?"

She eyed him. "Other candidates did. I was no different."

He looked disgusted. "Lovely place. So explain to me again why you want to spend the rest of your life there?"

"You're assuming I *have* a rest-of-my-life," she murmured.

"I am. So tell me."

She bit her lip, cast her gaze off somewhere far away. "I guess because it's home. I know it's not perfect, it doesn't have to be. Home just has to be somewhere . . . where there is love."

Rayce squinted at her. "Was there?"

Faded, delicate memories wrapped around her, warming her as they always did. Aged, tiny scraps that she held onto for dear life. They were all she had. "A long time ago there was. I don't remember many details of my mother but I know there was love."

"Nothing from your father?"

She stifled a shiver. "Nothing like love. I don't believe he understood what it meant. He didn't need it. He didn't see why anyone else did either."

She fought back tears. She'd finally found love again. Too bad she couldn't keep it.

"It's not supposed to be that way," Rayce offered.

"And people you love aren't supposed to suffer and die."

Rayce rolled his shoulders. "So what does it all mean?"

"I don't know. Maybe it's not supposed to mean anything. The universe doesn't see reason or logic or justice. We do. We put meaning to events, try to tie them all together into something we call our lives. So maybe the universe goes along blissfully the way it has for eons and we just need to make the best of what it hands us."

He considered her random thoughts. "Or maybe we're just pawns in a game played by giant aliens who treat us like toys."

She gave him a sardonic look and he laughed. "Too much for you, huh?"

Then he removed a large pad from his pack and spread it on the floor between them. He stretched out and gave her that sexy grin. "Since the universe is ignoring us anyway." He patted the empty space next to him.

She shook her head in wonder. "Do you *ever* worry about tomorrow?"

He propped his head on his pack. "I can't do anything about tomorrow until it's here."

Elvis promptly made himself comfortable at Rayce's feet as the lightballs positioned themselves above them. Tru gazed at Rayce's long, solid legs, slim hips, broad chest. But his heart was what drew her to him as she crawled the short distance and stretched her body over his. And it was his heart she wanted as she kissed him tenderly.

His palms went to her face, wrapped around her and drew the tears from her eyes. She loved him. She wanted him. She couldn't have him. The universe didn't care.

"No tears, Tru," he spoke softly against her lips. "I'm here." He rolled them both over, settled himself comfortably on top. His warm lips kissed her jaw and throat in long, lingering, loving ministrations.

She gave a deep sigh and looked up at the lightballs slowly dancing over them. A strange design on the ceiling between the two lights caught her eye. Rayce whispered something so wicked in her ear, she nearly lost track of her thought. Then the lightballs separated enough for her to see the ceiling clearly.

Her hands clutched Rayce's arms. "Yes!"

"That was fast. I'm just getting started," he murmured, taking a gentle nip of her earlobe.

"No, the ceiling!" She shoved at him until he rolled off, scowling at her.

She jumped to her feet and pushed both lightballs to the side. On the ceiling, in the middle of their small square space was a giant "X;" and in the center, a small, pyramid-shaped indentation in the stone.

Next to her, Rayce studied the ceiling. "You think it'll fit in there?"

"I'm counting on it."

"And then what?"

Then what, indeed, she thought. They were already inside, what more could the little pyramid do? Unless . . . Of course!

"Rayce, I don't think the pyramid was the key to get in."

"No kidding."

She turned and looked at him. "I think it's the key to get out."

His gaze snapped around to hers. Then a giant smile flashed across his face. "I knew you could do it."

"I haven't done anything yet," she said. "And I have no idea what will happen when we insert it."

"It's worth a try." Rayce walked over to an engraved chest and dragged it into the center of the room.

"You want to do the honors?" he asked. "It *is* your mission."

"It's your mission, too." He had no idea just how much. She handed him the pyramid.

He took it and hopped up on the chest. Even with the added height, he couldn't quite reach the ceiling, but as he held the pyramid up, it leaped from his hand, spinning wildly. Light from the lightballs glinted off the surfaces around the chamber.

"Rayce?"

He watched the pyramid above his head. "Hold on."

The pyramid hovered just below the indentation and the spinning began to slow. Suddenly, it stopped, spun in the other direction, then back. Streaks of light flashed as the tiny pyramid rose to the ceiling and locked into the empty space with a resounding click.

Then it was quiet. Tru closed her eyes. *Oh please, don't let this be the end.*

Elvis whined beside her, prancing around her legs nervously. And then the floor began to shake, lightly at first, before building to a great, rolling rumble.

Rayce jumped off the chest, pushed her against one of the columns and covered her with his body as the chamber reeled. A deafening roar arose above them and artifacts began to tumble from their 5,000-year-old resting places.

Tru covered her ears as the noise reached terrifying proportions, reverberating through her entire body, and the energy around them made her hair stand up. Wave after wave of what sounded like explosions rumbled above them, around them—so many that Tru couldn't tell where one began and the other ended. All she knew was that they were going to die and she'd never told Rayce that she loved him.

Dust engulfed them, burning her nostrils. Then, as suddenly as it started, it stopped.

She coughed into Rayce's chest as he lay on top of her.

"Rayce?" Her hands went to his body, checking to see if he was alive.

He gave a groan and raised himself off her, a layer of dirt falling off their bodies. He shook his head, creating a cloud. The lightballs barely pierced the thick haze surrounding them.

He gazed around. "Well, I wouldn't have guessed that outcome in an eon. You sure know how to keep this mission interesting."

Tru peered through the cloud. "What do you think happened?"

Rayce stood up and swatted his clothes. "I'm not even going to guess. We were already buried under a mountain. How much worse could it get? Where's Elvis?"

She felt around her. "I don't know. He was here a minute ago."

"Elvis!" Rayce yelled into the haze.

Long seconds passed before the dog came bounding back to them. He stopped in front to them, tail wagging and then stomped his paws on the floor before bouncing away again.

"Now what is he so happy about?" Rayce said with his hands on his hips.

Tru stood up and shook the settling powder off herself. "Isn't he always?"

"I smell something."

She glanced up at him in dread. "Nothing dead or dying, I hope."

"Fresh air," he said and then took off in the direction Elvis had gone. Tru followed him through the maze of jumbled treasure, back through the doorway, past the room they'd dropped into and out onto the moon's surface.

She gave a cry. "We're out!"

The night sky above was crystal clear and she spun beneath it, her arms open wide, scattering dust. Elvis yelped and frolicked around her. Cool air felt delicious against her skin and she inhaled it deeply into her lungs.

"Looks like we found our pyramid after all."

Rayce's comment stopped her and she spotted him standing a short distance from her, looking up.

She turned around.

Before them, their burial chamber had become a gleaming pyramid, its pinnacle silhouetted against a starry sky. Crumbled rock lay beneath her feet and in all directions around them as far as she could see.

"The pyramid was buried under the ridge," she said, stunned. "No wonder no one found it before now. The key must have created a repulsion chain-reaction on contact."

She smiled at Rayce and repeated her earlier words. "The fifth element. An energy force of unknown origin and great power. It was true."

Rayce surveyed the surrounding forest and the new raw rock face where the ridge now ended. "Whatever it was, it made a hell of a mess. I hope *Miranda* is intact."

"Should we check?"

He shook his head and walked past her to the entrance. "Not at night. Not in a place where everything wants a piece of you. We'll hike up tomorrow. Tonight we sleep inside."

She followed him to where he stood examining the open doorway.

"Do you think that's safe? There's no door to keep out animals," she glanced around. "Or other malicious vegetation."

"I was just thinking about that. Seems rather odd that the Curzons would design this to stay wide open."

He glanced over at her. "I guess we'll have to rely on my rifle and Elvis to protect us."

"You won't sleep."

He shrugged and entered the chamber. "It's the least I can do after you saved my ass."

The dust had settled considerably, she was glad to see as she followed him in. "I owed you a few."

"It doesn't work that way, you know," he said, shaking the dust off the floor pad before laying it back down. "We don't keep score."

She wrestled with the concept. Everyone kept score on the Institute, picking sides, winning at all costs. It seemed rather cutthroat now, but back then it was just the way projects were won and lost.

She glanced up out of her thoughts to find Rayce contemplating her.

He said, "You did a good job, Tru."

A lump settled in her throat. *Very good, little Tru.* The words emerged as soft and gentle as a blooming flower. Her mother's words, resurrected from the depths of her own childhood memory. Tru held onto the gift for a few moments as she stared back at Rayce. Why did they have to come again from the one person she couldn't have?

"Thank you," she uttered softly.

Chapter Seventeen

Morning bloomed cool and crisp on M003, a lazy fog floating through the woman-eating forest around them. Standing between the pyramid and where Rayce had relocated *Miranda*, Tru watched the sun rise over the ridge above her. Elvis leaned against her leg and she reached down to rub his head.

She was here. She'd succeeded, found the Collection and won. *Miranda* was now loaded up with some of the rarest, most prized artifacts in the galaxy.

She should be ecstatic, but all she could think about was good-bye. Elvis trotted along behind her as she entered the chamber and wandered through the Curzon Collection one last time. Each item was valuable for its history alone. But the few items she'd selected to bring back to the spaceport were the finest and the most prized. Enough wealth to finish Rayce's spaceport in style.

She stopped and examined a simply carved female figurine holding a single flower, a fine example of Dahah Shier stonework.

She scanned the chamber and a collection like no other. Enough history to fill a museum. Which was where every piece should be. Not split up, not sold off piecemeal and certainly not given to the administrators. But the fate of the Collection was no longer her concern. Rayce could do with it what he wished.

Still, her heart sank. Each and every artifact deserved to be saved, but with no door to protect the exposed pyramid and its contents, she doubted any of it would be here by the time Rayce returned with a larger ship. By the time she was gone.

"I don't think we can fit much more into the ship," Rayce said to her, carrying a large vase that she'd deemed worthy. He glanced at the figurine in her hand. "Are you taking that?"

She shook her head and set if down. "It's a Dahah Shier courtship gift. The male Dahah would have left it for his prospective mate to find. If she knocked it over, she refused him. If she picked it up and set it beside her, she accepted. The tradition continues 5,000 years later. This piece is exceptional but not particularly valuable."

She felt his frown before she saw it. Still she met his cool level gaze.

"Then by all means," he said, "leave it behind." And he brushed by her.

She rubbed Elvis's head and watched Rayce walk out into the morning sun. "I don't think he liked my answer. It's for the best. He might as well start hating me now. Again."

Elvis whined softly. She looked down at his sad

black eyes and smiled. Who'd have thought she could feel something for such an adolescent creature. "Let's go."

She followed Rayce out. Suddenly, a great rumble shook the ground behind her and she turned as a stone slab door swung down to block the doorway. Elvis stood right behind her with their tiny silver pyramid in his mouth.

"Elvis," she said, kneeling to take the drool-covered pyramid from his jaws. "Where did you find this?"

She carried the key back to the great pyramid and waved it in front to the entrance. The stone door opened. She walked inside and then back out and the door swung closed again.

"I guess we don't have to worry about thieves now," Rayce commented.

She nodded and walked past him, leaving it all behind. His Collection was safe.

So she was going to go through with it. Take her half of the Collection back to the Majj and become one of them. He laid in his bunk after what had been a mostly sleepless night filled with nightmares of being buried alive under black dirt. Trapped and suffocated. Kind of the way he felt now.

He wanted her to change her mind, to see how wrong the Majj were. And she wouldn't. Maybe she couldn't. He remembered her insistence that she was nothing without her work. He'd tried, but he hadn't banished that conviction from her mind. The pricks who'd drilled that into her had won. He'd lost. And he wasn't used to losing. Not these days.

He turned his head and looked over at her in the

other bunk, her back to him. Elvis laid at her feet. Smart dog.

Rayce loved the curve of her female body, the way her hair laid heavy across the sheets, the way she moved in her sleep, so sexy. He hadn't offered to sleep with her and she hadn't asked. Now he was sorry.

He rolled off the bunk and entered the lav, giving up on sleep altogether. The warm spray of the shower felt good against his neck and he let the water soak him but it did little to wash away the vision of her in bed. He wanted her. Just once more before she became something she wasn't.

Then he heard a noise behind him and turned to find Tru standing naked in the mist.

She'd heard him get up, heard the water running, felt the ache without his touch.

So she'd slipped inside and watched him, relaxed and all male. Water ran rivers down his head and big arms, across broad shoulders, sliding between the muscles that cut across his back. She followed the long V of his torso, down his spine to slim hips and a beautiful set of buttocks. Unable to help herself, she had groaned.

Hearing her, he pushed off the wall and turned around suddenly. She gasped. He was full, thick, pointing right at her. Her legs gave a little. She looked up into his face. Eyes stared back at her—hypnotic and intense.

"I was just thinking about you," he growled low. "Come here."

Excitement fluttered in her belly. He wanted her. He had no idea how much that meant.

The pang of guilt was quickly pushed aside. She'd spent her life giving. This time she was taking. This would be the last time that she'd feel his heat. The last time she'd feel alive. And there was no excuse good enough to stop her.

Mist swirled as she slipped into the small shower designed for one. Rayce wrapped around her, pulling her under the hot water. His fingers circled her jaw, lifted her face to his and he gave her a lover's kiss.

She heard moaning. She was pretty sure it was her own.

Her fingers spread out across his chest, slick with water. She found tiny, perfect nipples, big shoulders she could barely get her hands around, biceps that flexed under her touch. She pressed her body to his, her hip trapping his erection. He spread his legs further apart, letting her grind against him as he let out a long hiss.

She pulled her lips from his and kissed, licked, sucked her way down his throat to the center of his chest, lingering on his nipples before making her way lower. All the while, she was dragging her hands down his back, slipping around his buttocks and tense legs. And lower still.

He pushed his hips into her with a long, guttural groan as she explored him with her hands, water dripping between them. She wanted to taste him but he had different ideas. His hands closed around her head, pulling her to her feet.

"Your turn," he rasped.

"Mine? But I wanted to—" She never finished the sentence. He'd started sipping the water off her shoulder and she lost track of her mind.

He pressed her back to the wall. Even under the warm water's caress, her body shivered, knowing what was to come. Then with just his fingertips, he reached out and touched one nipple, tracing around the hard tip and out to the dark areola. As she watched, his fingertips made wide circles around her breasts, then moved down her belly, stroking, teasing with a whisper of a touch. She felt the sweet torture all the way to her center. He had too much patience, too much control but he knew her limits and finally moved his fingers down to the neat tangle of hair. She looked into his eyes, her lips parted, waiting. A small smile crossed his lips as his fingers slipped below. Her breath was coming in hard now. She couldn't help it, didn't care.

He bent, wrapped his lips around a nipple and sucked, keeping rhythm with the movement of his fingers. He moved leisurely to the other breast, never breaking the tempo. Her hips rolled to him, completing the dance. She could feel the tension begin; tremors shot through her legs. Then his lips were nuzzling her thighs. She never even noticed that he'd moved.

"Spread your legs a little more," he whispered against her, his fingers still on her, still working. She moved, even though she could barely stand as it was. The heat of his mouth slid down and flooded over her. Her hands went to his head, pulling him closer.

While his tongue was making love to her, his fingers plunged deep inside her, pulling a surprised scream from her. Her head rolled back and forth. She wondered if a woman could die from over-stimulation. Little shocks rolled through her, tension building. She was so close.

Then her breath pulled hard, once, twice, filling her lungs, fuel for the explosion. Every muscle in her body tensed, tighter and tighter, until she felt like she was going to split open. Mercy finally, as screaming release shattered her, wave after wave. Her cry echoed within the walls of the tiny shower. Her legs gave out and he scooped her up, holding her while the aftershocks racked her and she tried to put herself back together. He stroked her back until her breathing calmed and her legs stopped shaking.

She lifted her face to his. They kissed, deep and long, letting passion build yet again. He pressed his body against her, pinning her to the shower wall. She could tell his patience was waning. It was about time. She wanted the animal unleashed.

"Wrap your legs around me," he said roughly. It was more of a desperate order than a request.

Confused, she whispered, "It's too small in here."

"Obviously, you have a lot to learn about physics."

He gripped her waist and lifted her as she wrapped her legs around him. Their eyes locked as he slid her down his body, impaling her on him. She let out a long moan. Her back against the wall, she was caught between a rock and a hard place.

She linked her arms around his neck, squeezed her legs around his torso and held on as he thrust up, the animal finally let loose. Time and time again, he tunneled up and down, filling her to the brim. She whispered little wicked snippets in his ear, telling him how beautiful he was, how she wanted more, until there was so much heat she could barely breathe. Faster, harder, deeper. Then he drove into her one last time and roared. Head back, neck muscles corded, he looked like he was in pain, but she knew better. She had just been there.

For a long time, all she could hear was water trickling and his heart beating. She savored their last time together, the heat of his skin and the way his strong hands held her. No man would ever feel like this, she was sure of it. But she didn't want any man. She wanted Rayce.

He never saw her tears mingle with the water.

When he finally recovered enough to put her down, he turned off the shower. They dried, wandered back into the cabin naked and collapsed on the bed.

Savoring her contentment, she nestled against him.

"I like the way you teach physics."

"Maybe I'm in the wrong field," he said lazily.

Gil nearly ripped Rayce's arm off the minute he stepped out of *Miranda* and into the shuttle bay.

"You did it!" he bellowed, slapping him on the shoulder. Even Elvis got a rub on his head and then Gil grabbed Tru off the ship's platform and whirled her around.

"Hey, get your own woman," Rayce said with a grin.

Gil set a startled Tru down and beamed. "This calls for a celebration. Something special. I want to hear all about it."

Tru gave him a smile. "I can show you what we brought back."

Rayce watched Tru and Gil disappear into *Miranda*'s cargo hold and the cold feeling he'd had in his belly over the past few hours grew. Her mission was completed and time was running out. He thought maybe she'd changed her mind about the Majj on the leg home. A few times, he'd caught her watching him. He could have sworn she wanted to tell him something, but she never did.

Moments later, Gil exited through the cargo door and helped Tru out.

"That's one impressive haul." Gil clapped him on the back. "Well done. I never doubted you for a minute."

"Like hell you didn't," Rayce said with a grunt.

Gil smiled at Tru. "Naw. Not with Tru to keep you focused."

Rayce glanced at Tru. She had a sad smile on her face and then her gaze met his and the smile faded entirely.

"Well, I'll let you two celebrate. I have some matters I need to attend to." She turned and walked out of the shuttle bay.

Elvis whined softly. Rayce patted his head. "Go ahead." The dog took off in a dead run after her.

Gil shook his head. "I think he's in love."

Rayce stared at the floor. *In love. Maybe.*

"Come on," said Gil with an obnoxiously happy smile. "Let's hear it."

Tru entered her room. Fresh flowers beckoned. She touched the delicate petals and inhaled the sweet scent. She would miss this. In fact, she'd miss the spaceport. She'd grown surprisingly fond of it, strangely proud of its progress. It would be a jewel in the sector when completed, but to her it almost felt like home.

For a moment, she indulged herself in her own future. The one where she had no home and no career. But somehow she would find work outside the Institute. She just needed a planet to begin on. That would require research and she could do that, but there was no point in worrying about tomorrow until it was here.

Besides, right now there were other priorities. The plan she'd formulated over the past few days would take preparation and timing.

Phase One was complete. The Collection was found and Rayce had his dream. That was the easy part. Now to Phase Two—to free the Majj.

Getting back onto the Institute grounds would require some tricks she'd learned from Rayce. She shook her head. Who would have thought that a Van Dye could have learned how to sneak around?

She sat on the bed and retrieved Noa's special comm unit from her bag. Then she pulled out a datapad she'd borrowed from Rayce and linked the two together. They bleeped compatibility and she transferred Noa's program and communication codes to the datapad.

Then she tossed the comm unit aside. The transfer rate would be slow but adequate through the datapad, and Noa's security clearance should still work. After all, he wasn't the one who'd been disassociated.

A pang of bitterness swept through her and she summarily dismissed it. Justice didn't play into this anymore than it had when the fever killed Miranda. The universe didn't care.

She took a deep breath and continued with the next requirement—a ship. She tapped her fingers on the datapad. If she asked Rayce, he would probably insist on bringing her back himself. That would never do. She couldn't face him, not with what she was going to tell the Majj. No, this would have be a solo flight. Gil's bright smile flashed in her mind. Yes, he could be persuaded. But she'd have to move fast or Rayce would find out. The last thing she wanted was him coming after her.

She could handle the piloting, thanks to Rayce's instruction, but entry onto the Institute itself would be a problem. Landing at the main transport area was out of the question. She'd never make it past the transport controllers without appropriate authorization. So that meant she'd have to land somewhere without them. The central courtyard should be big enough to accommodate any ship.

The ship's mirage would protect her entry and landing but she needed something else—a way to scramble the Institute's standard scanners like Rayce had used on Earth. She would download the necessary program from *Miranda* or the spaceport's central computer.

After that, she wasn't sure. How to call the Majj together? How to prove her point to the thousands of Majj and have them believe her after the damage that Odell had no doubt already done to her reputation? Contacting Noa would be too dangerous now. There had to be another way.

Well, she'd worry about that when the time came.

Then she smiled at herself. *A woman without a plan.* How did that happen?

She repacked her few belongings into her bag and her fingertips touched the VirtuWav cartridge. Her eyes closed as the memories flooded back.

The cartridge felt warm in her hand as she held it, knowing that she shouldn't keep it. Having him virtually would no longer do. It wasn't right. She had to let him go.

The feeling of loss was overwhelming. She'd never see him again, in reality or virtually. Perhaps it was just as well. Perhaps in twenty or thirty years, she'll have forgotten all about him.

Tears stung her eyes as she plugged the cartridge into the datapad and watched Noa's program begin on the tiny screen. Her heart clenched as she saw him at the bar in the saloon.

A warning flashed up. PROGRAM MODIFICATION. She frowned. No one had modified the program, not even her.

In disbelief she watched a second Rayce Coburne enter the program and dismiss the first version. Her jawed dropped as she saw herself, heard her own voice saying, "I hope you don't mind, but I need you again."

She shook her head, her heart aching painfully in her chest. It couldn't be. He wouldn't have done that to her. She shut the program off when the bed chamber materialized. She already knew the rest.

Her hands shook and her mouth went completely dry. Pain tore through her, bringing tears to her eyes. There had to be a mistake. Had to. Otherwise, it would mean that he'd lied this entire time. He wouldn't have done that to her. He couldn't hate her that much.

Then she clutched the cartridge in her hand and headed out to VirtuWav banks.

"Incredible," Gil repeated for the tenth time since they parked themselves in Rayce's office to split a bottle of Safin. "Just incredible. And there's still more there?"

Rayce took a swig of his drink and nodded. "A room full. Even half is more than enough to use as collateral and buy out all the investors."

"That's the best news I've had in a long time."

Rayce eyed him. "You don't have to work for the rest of your life if you don't want to."

Gil shot him a toothy grin. "You mean we don't have to *do* the work. I kind of like the giving orders part."

"It will be nice for a change," Rayce agreed. He ran a finger along the rim of his glass. Everything had changed. And not all of it for the good.

"So, what about Tru?" Gil asked, reading his mind.

"What about her?"

"Well, for one, is she staying or leaving?"

"Leaving."

Gil stared at him as if he'd lost his mind. "And?"

Rayce poured the rest of his drink down his throat and let it burn. "And what?"

"And you aren't going to stop her?"

"No." He looked at the bottom of the empty glass and poured himself another. "I'm not. I told you before, all she wants is that Collection. She wants to be a Majj and I can't change that."

Gil stuck his face in front of Rayce. "Did you ask her?"

Rayce glared back at him, getting more annoyed by the second. "I don't have to. She's a big girl. She's made her decision."

Gil rolled his eyes and leaned back in his chair. "You're just afraid she'll say she wants to stay."

"You know, you are starting to sound like my father," Rayce said, disgusted with both of them. "And you're both crazy."

"What would you do with her if she stayed?" Gil asked smugly.

"I'd probably ask her to shoot you."

Gil snorted. "You don't have an answer, do you? You haven't gotten past the sex part yet."

Rayce grabbed his drink and stood up. "If I want this kind of abuse, I'll call my family." And he stomped out of his office, leaving Gil to snicker alone.

He didn't slow down until he'd reached the atrium. Elvis was expending some dog energy by running from one end of the vegetation habitat to the other, chasing something only he could see and trampling flowers and plants as he went. Rayce shook his head. Tru would have a fit if she could see this.

The thought was sobering despite the drinks. His life without Tru in it. Not that it would be all bad. No Majjs, no crazy missions, no death-defying feats. No warm bed, no one to set him on fire, no sexy whispers in the night. He stopped himself before it got any more depressing.

The bottom line was that he couldn't compete with the Majj. She hadn't said a word on the trip back or given him any indication that she'd changed her mind. In fact, she'd made sure they selected the most valuable pieces from the Collection to bring back with them on the first trip. No doubt to impress the administrators or whatever they were at the Institute.

He swallowed the last of his drink and set down the glass. Elvis spotted him the minute he stepped into the atrium and bounded at him at full speed. Rayce sidestepped the wild-eyed dog and grabbed a stick to toss around. As he played with Elvis, he realized his life was fine just the way it was, anyway. What more did a man need than a successful business, enough credits to keep his family comfortable, and a dog? And casual sex. Right. There would be plenty of that once the spaceport opened.

So what did he need Tru for?

She certainly didn't need him.

Chapter Eighteen

Tru wandered numbly through the halls of the spaceport. The floor blurred through the tears.

The VirtuWav archives had confirmed her worst fear. Rayce had entered her program not once, but twice. Twice. Just to be sure he'd made a complete fool of her. She had trusted him, believed that he really cared about her. Would die for her. Would risk.

All the time they'd spent together and not once did he confess. She could have confessed, too, but she hadn't. It only proved that they didn't trust each other enough.

It was her own fault, of course. If she hadn't been such a failure with men, she never would have needed to use the VirtuWav. She'd used him, too, in a way.

His voice echoed through the pain and she looked out over a balcony into the flower garden below. Rayce held onto one end of a stick with the other end in Elvis's mouth as they fought for possession. Dazed, she watched Rayce play with Elvis. Just like he'd played with her.

He was her hired guide. She shouldn't have expected any more than that and had been foolish enough to let herself think otherwise. He hated the Majj and he hated her. He'd used her for sex and she'd used him. He'd earned his spaceport credits; she'd accomplished her mission. As far as she was concerned, they were even.

She turned away from the balcony and down a corridor to a computer bank. "Computer, locate Gil."

Gil's location flashed up—Rayce's office—and she headed there.

It was just as well, of course. She couldn't have him anyway. If anything, this made it easier to leave.

But she was going to miss the dog. She might consider getting one. At least she knew they were loyal, no matter what a bastard their owner was.

By the time she walked through Rayce's doorway, the tears were gone, leaving behind a heart that was unfeeling and empty.

Gil glanced up at her in surprise and then grinned wide. "Tru. What a nice surprise."

She smiled back politely. "Greetings, Gil. I'd like to purchase one of your small transport ships."

He blinked. "Really? Well sure, but we'd be happy to take you wherever you want to go."

"I appreciate that, but this is personal."

"Do you know how to fly?" he asked, sounding very confused.

"I do."

Gil scratched his head. "All right. I'll ask Rayce which one he—"

"Rayce already knows," she lied. "He said a Class Two ship would be adequate and told me to make sure it's a ship with miraging capabilities."

"Rayce knows," Gil muttered, shaking his head a little. "Fine. When do you need the ship?"

She smiled. "Now would be perfect."

"Sorry to bother you, boss, but I thought you ought to know."

Rayce glanced up from his datapad to find Hencke filling his office doorway. The distraction was welcome, if a little unusual. Rayce set the datapad down and rubbed his face, his brain drained from a full day of reviewing the spaceport finances. Coming into a small fortune was a lot of work.

"Ought to know what?"

Hencke shuffled forward, his massive shoulders hunched over. He placed a VirtuWav cartridge on the desk.

Rayce eyed him. "What's this?"

"It belongs to Tru Van Dye. It's *her* program." Hencke gave him a critical look. "The one you went into twice."

"And?"

Hencke's broad face carved a deep frown. "She knows."

A prickle raced down his back. "How do you know that?"

"She came into the VirtuWav and checked the archives. Then she gave this to me and told me to tell you to enjoy it." He took an angry breath. "And she was crying."

Rayce swore under his breath. This was not good. "Thanks, Hencke. I'll take it from here."

The giant didn't move. Rayce looked up at him. His eyes were narrow and challenging. "She's a nice lady, boss. I don't like to see her cry."

The man wasn't stupid. In his simple mind, he knew the difference between right and wrong. Even *he* understood what Rayce had done.

"Yes, she is. I'll apologize to her."

"I like her. You should, too."

"I do," Rayce said gently.

Hencke nodded approval and with that, the big man lumbered out of the room. Rayce picked up the cylinder and breathed a quiet, "Oh, shit."

Rayce stormed into Gil's office, clutching the blasted VirtuWav program. "Where is she?"

Gil's eyes widened. "Tru?"

"Who the hell else?" Rayce planted his hands on Gil's desk. "I checked the computer and she's no longer on the spaceport."

"Well, no kidding. She left yesterday," Gil shot back hotly. "You let her go."

"What are you talking about?"

Gil rolled his eyes. "You told her it was okay to take one of our Class Two ships."

He shook his head in disbelief. "I told her no such thing."

"Well, she took the ship. I cleared her for takeoff about twenty hours ago. Where have you been?"

Rayce stood up and ran a hand through his hair. "Trying to get an appraiser in here to estimate the value of our little Collection so I can see how many investors I can shake loose."

"That took twenty hours?"

He put his hands on his hips and stared at the floor. "I thought she needed time."

"She did. To make her escape. She didn't even say good-bye," Gil said with a scowl. "What did you do to her?"

Rayce didn't say anything. He couldn't. What he'd done to her was too cruel for words. "I screwed up."

Gil nodded as if that was no surprise. "So you're telling me that she won't be back."

"No." And he would never get a chance to apologize. Hencke may kill him for that, alone.

"So what about the Collection?" Gil asked, leaning back in his chair.

A cold thought brought Rayce's head up. Tru had the pyramid.

"I'll be back." He walked out of the office and headed for her quarters. Just how mad was Tru when she left? Mad enough to take the pyramid and go after the Collection herself? Mad enough to claim the whole damn thing for the Majj? Mad enough to ruin him?

By the time he entered her former quarters, he was fuming. What he saw next drained the anger from his soul.

In the middle of room sat her share of the Collection. He moved closer and counted the items. It looked like every single piece was present and unharmed. His gaze traveled to the silver pyramid laying in the center of her bed. For a long time, he stood there disbelieving his own eyes.

Not only had she not ruined him, she'd left everything behind. Why? What would she bring back to the Institute? How would she earn her Charter without the Collection?

A new thought intrigued him. Perhaps she was planning on coming back. Relief flooded through him. Yes, that must be it. That's why she didn't say good-bye.

He scooped up the pyramid and tossed it lightly in his hand. He'd still have his chance to see her again.

Tru touched down in the dark main courtyard with a solid thump. She cut the engines and waited until they had stopped whining. Rain pelted the small ship as she looked through the main viewport at the Institute buildings she knew so well. In the distance, the Van Dye building stood brightly lit, as it was every night.

Miraging the ship meant that no one could see her or the ship but she could see others. Not that anyone was outdoors at 3 A.M. in the rain. No, everyone was probably hard at work in one of the research buildings.

It amazed her that it didn't hurt more sitting here in her old world. But she was too numb to care anymore and she had more important matters to tend to.

She slipped to the back of the ship and pulled her Institute rain garment on. The hood hung low enough over her eyes to hide who she was to the casual passerby. It should be enough to get her to Noa's place.

A driving rain met her as she stepped out of the safety of the ship. She mentally memorized the nearly invisible ship's location and then ran across the courtyard to the housing complex.

He answered the door on the first knock, but she almost didn't recognize him. He'd aged in the past few weeks.

"Noa, it's me," she whispered through the rain drops falling from her hood.

He blinked several times before breaking into a giant smile. With a grip stronger than he looked capable of, he pulled her into his quarters and gave her a powerful hug. She hugged him back, tears mingled with the rainwater.

He held her away from him. "You look tired."

She laughed. "I flew straight through from Rayce's spaceport to here. I've been up the entire time downloading data."

He helped her off with her soaked jacket. "How did you get here? The controllers have strict orders not to let a disassociated member through security."

She refused the drink he offered and explained, "I flew in alone using a ship I bought from Rayce, scrambled the Institute sensors, miraged the ship so it couldn't be seen and landed it in the middle of the main courtyard."

He gaped at her. "No kidding?"

"No kidding. You can thank Rayce for my new-found skill set."

"And how is our mercenary?"

"He's got the Collection," she said, following Noa into his austere quarters and collapsing on a chair. "All of it. I'm not bringing it back here."

Noa took a seat opposite her. "Why would you? They wouldn't take it from a disassociated member anyway."

315

She suddenly felt weary. "Oh yes, they would. Odell would. And he'd take the credit for it. I'm not about to let that happen."

Noa looked at her with his old eyes. "I'm truly happy to see you, but if they find you, they'll make a public scene and toss you out. Why are you here?"

She took a deep breath. "It's absolutely critical that I talk to the Majj. I just need a forum and the Majj. And *no* administrators."

Noa's white eyebrows arched. "What could be that important?"

She closed her eyes. "My father did something terrible and I need to correct it."

"Odell has destroyed your reputation," Noa warned her. "Your word won't be worth much, even with the people who know you."

"Don't worry. I have more than enough proof to support my allegations. And I spent most of the past ten hours downloading it into the Institute archives." The information that should have been there all along, she seethed. Now it would be.

"Will this get you reinstated?" Noa asked hopefully.

She shook her head. "No. And I'm not sure I want that anyway. But it will change everything." Her gaze met Noa's. "I need to do this now, Noa. Right now. I don't have much time. Can you help me?"

The old man squared his shoulders. "I may not carry the clout I used to but you'll get your chance, Tru. I'll assemble the Majj if I have to drag them there myself."

"Thank you."

Then he gave her a pathetic look. "Uh, I killed all your plants. I'm sorry."

Tru chuckled softly at his sad expression. "It's all right, Noa. They are only flowers. They die. Besides, no one is perfect."

An hour later, Tru walked into the crowded Training Center as several hundred suspicious eyes turned to her. She could hear the muffled whispers, most of which were probably about her disassociation and how she'd managed to come back when no other Majj had. But the Majj had never met Rayce Coburne. Her chest gave a mighty squeeze at the thought of him and the big hole he'd left where her heart used to be. Even through it all, she still loved him. She would not be here if it weren't for his fearlessness, his ease with risk and his confidence in tomorrow. She never would have found the courage to face a day without the Majj.

She ascended the podium of the grand lecture hall, its series of austere arches like rings echoing in the distance. Every seat boasted a computer station making the venue perfect for training and mass lectures, as well as important announcements of the latest advances. None of those announcements would be as important as this one.

Noa followed her to the podium and the room hushed. They didn't leave their research or their warm beds for *her*. They were here because they owed Noa and it was time to pay up. She heard his footsteps behind her and drew strength from them. He'd handled the bad news about the administrators well, with anger and quiet rage and resolution. And then he'd gone to work. In a short time, he had assembled the most powerful Majj at the Institute. She'd been surprised by his persuasive conversations and his commitment. It was a side of Noa she'd rarely seen and he seemed perfectly comfortable doing it.

Disheveled and sullen, the Majj shuffled to take their seats and a polite, if indifferent, silence settled over the room.

She gazed over the familiar faces. These were colleagues she'd worked with for twenty years, but she still felt like a stranger. Different. Imperfect. She smiled at the freedom that brought her. Tru gripped the sides of the podium for strength but she knew she wouldn't get it. What she needed to say could only come from her soul.

"Thank you for coming at this late hour. It is of great importance and urgency." She looked out over the scowling faces. "I'm sure you are all aware of Odell's accusations of my breaking Institute rules and the subsequent disassociation." She took a deep breath. "And I'm here to tell you that the accusations are true."

A collective gasp followed.

"I'm also here to tell you what I've learned outside. It concerns the survival of the Majj."

She swallowed the hard lump of humiliation, but this was not about her pride. These were the Majj that she loved, the belief that she held true. She would not fail them, no matter what it cost her.

"You have been used," she said clearly. "Your minds, your work, your lives have been manipulated. Your inventions sold to the highest bidders in the galaxy."

There was a stunned silence.

"Used by whom?" A question rose from the back of the room.

She pursed her lips. "My father and the other administrators."

A resounding laugh rolled around her and more than a few Majj rose from their seats ready to exit.

"If you don't believe me, check for yourself. The computer archives don't lie. Access the transaction records for your inventions. See who they went to and how much they sold for. Discover what the rest of the galaxy thinks of us."

The Majj murmured among themselves but didn't move.

For a moment, she thought they would not check the files. Would they want to know the truth or would they only want the safe world they'd always known?

Beside her, Noa stepped up. "What are you waiting for? We live in search of the truth. So search."

Tru smiled at him, at his firm and commanding presence. Maybe he was her only friend, but he was a good one. A few Majj settled behind their computers and began their inquiries.

Tru leaned toward Noa. "Do you think they will believe me?"

"They will believe what they see with their own eyes." He gave her a misty look.

The room had grown very quiet with only whispered instructions for the computers.

Then the Majj began to talk. First to the ones closest to them and then she saw them moving from one computer to another, shaking their heads in disbelief.

Finally, a voice called out, "Noa, how do we

know this information is legitimate? We've never seen any of this before."

Noa responded. "Tru downloaded information from the outside that previously had been censored from us."

Another voice balked. "Censored? Our data isn't censored."

Noa nodded. "Yes. Yes, it has been for a long time. We just never knew." He threw up his hands. "How would we? We weren't encouraged to go outside. Look what happened to Tru when she left." He gave a great sigh. "And we didn't want to leave. Our isolation has made us complacent, lazy and vulnerable."

More questions arose and Tru remained silent as Noa handled them all. She'd done her part. The rest was up to the Majj now.

The Majj. As if they were an outside group that she didn't belong to. More than ever, she felt like an outsider. And she wanted it that way. She wasn't one of them; she never had been.

Voices drifted around her, growing louder and angrier. They *should* be angry. Angry enough to face the administrators. It was the Majj who made the Koameron Institute great.

Just then the door to the room flung open and Odell stormed in. He stopped and growled at the room full of Majj and then zeroed in on her.

"What the hell are you doing here?" he roared. He stopped in front of her, rage twisting his face.

Tru stared back at him and realized that he was as insignificant to her as an insect. And about as bright.

"Greetings, Odell. It's a little early for you to be up. Have a hot disassociation today?"

He glared at her and pointed to the paralyzed Majj. "What is this all about?"

Tru shrugged. "I warned you."

He stabbed a finger at her. "You are disassociated. No one will listen to you."

She smiled smugly. "They know, Odell. They know what you did."

His eyes widened and he turned to the Majj. Tru watched in dismay as they shrank back under his scrutiny. Maybe they weren't angry enough after all.

Odell sneered at her in victory. "So what? They know. It doesn't matter because they work for us."

Tru wanted to challenge him, to tell him to go to hell. But it wasn't her place anymore. She wasn't a Majj and she couldn't speak for them.

Noa stepped up to Odell, who towered over his aged body. The old man drew his shoulders back tall and square. "Odell, I think you're mistaken. *You* work for us. Or I should say, you used to work for us."

Behind him, the Majj nodded in solidarity.

Odell raised his chin defiantly. "You can't do anything to the administrators. We own you."

Noa laughed, a sound that Tru had not heard in a very long time. He shook his head.

"Odell, you are nothing without us. But we are still something without you. We made this Institute. We can shut it down."

Tru smiled as the rest of the Majj gathered behind Noa.

Odell blinked at them in disbelief. Then he

turned to Tru. "This is all your fault. Now you've disturbed our organization. It was running fine until you ruined it."

"Fine for you and the other administrators," she said coolly. "Too many people have suffered for you. Too many lives have been lost under the name of the Majj. I think that's about to end."

His eyes darted between her and the Majj, his concern now undermining his arrogance. If she only had a holo recorder.

He hissed softly, "You will never get away with this. I'll make sure you are apprehended and prosecuted on legal grounds."

Noa narrowed his eyes. "I don't think so." And he stepped between Tru and Odell. "Go, Tru. Get out while you can."

She knew he was right. Her presence here would be too disruptive in an already volatile situation. The Majj had enough to deal with without trying to protect her, too. Besides, her work was done, her duty fulfilled.

She was free.

"Thank you, Noa." She nodded to the other Majj and hurried out. She looked back once to see the Majj converge on Odell as he tried to follow her.

Then she was gone, out of the building, running through the downpour toward the courtyard. She twirled in the rain, let it soak her body and cleanse her soul. Hands turned up, face to the sky she reveled in her frightening freedom. When she reached the courtyard, she unmiraged the ship and boarded. The Institute fell away and the ship rose through the dark clouds and broke through the atmosphere into space.

She shivered. Her clothes clung cold to her skin. The ship hummed as she sat staring at the millions of stars in an infinite universe and watched the sun peek around the side of the planet.

Well, it was tomorrow. *Now what?*

Rayce wandered through the quiet corridors of Level Four, making mental notes of work yet to be completed now that he had the funds to finish the spaceport the way he'd always envisioned it. And with no one except Gil to tell him how or when. They could take their time and do it right.

Elvis trotted along next to him, veering off course regularly to sniff a newly installed item. Rayce liked the company, even if Elvis wasn't much of conversationalist. And he wasn't much of a kisser, either. Rayce scowled. He had to stop thinking like this.

She was gone. He'd tried numerous times to contact her ship, only to have his communications ignored. He'd checked all the major ports but found no sign of her. He'd even tried to hail the Institute and had been rebuffed at every attempt. He'd lost her and he had no one to blame but himself.

He found himself in the shuttle bay and stopped abruptly in front of *Miranda* for the third time in the past two days. This was becoming a habit.

He pulled up a container and sat down on it. Elvis plunked down next to him, nudging his hand. Rayce automatically rubbed the dog's head.

"I screwed up, Elvis."

The dog whined softly in reply.

Rayce looked into his black eyes. "Why would she leave it all behind? This was her goal in life, to

323

bring in that Collection. And she left it all for me. Even after what I did to her. Why?"

Elvis only blinked.

Rayce ran his gaze over *Miranda*'s silver frame. It occurred to him that Majj or not, Tru's heart was as big as his sister's. Was he the only one without a soul?

Tell me, has your anger done you any good? Tru's words flashed back.

He rested his head in his hands.

"It hasn't done anything," he admitted aloud. It hadn't brought Miranda back or honored her life or made him into a particularly good man. He hadn't done a single useful thing with all that energy. All he'd shown the world about Miranda was his rage. And he didn't have the right to portray Miranda like that.

If he wanted to honor Miranda, he could reveal her generosity and her caring spirit even in the midst of poverty. If she were still here, she'd have started a clinic of some sort, helping the poorest of the poor on his home planet, giving food and shelter. If she were here, she'd crusade for the *gruners*. But she wasn't here.

Then his head shot up. The answer came to him so suddenly and so easily, he couldn't believe he hadn't seen it before. But then again, he'd never gotten past the anger before.

Miranda wasn't here, but he was.

Now he had the credits to do something worthwhile. He could make a difference. A real difference. And maybe even save someone from Miranda's fate. Then and there, the vow was made. He would do what he should have done all along.

Elvis laid his head on Rayce's lap and gave him a soulful look.

Rayce nodded. "I miss her, too."

She'd poked and prodded him to see his own anger. She'd given him the monetary means to do what was right. She'd shown him that things aren't always what they appear. She'd fought for what she wanted and gotten it.

And along the way, she'd made him the man he'd always wanted to be. His father's words cut through him. He closed his eyes at the sting. Now he understood what his father had been trying to tell him.

So she was a Majj. He didn't care anymore. She was also the woman he loved.

"I need to get her back," he said to Elvis abruptly. The dog's eyebrows went up one at a time. "I can't do this without Tru. And I don't want to."

At Tru's name, Elvis gave a sharp bark and jumped in front of Rayce, tugging on his sleeve.

"What's wrong with you?"

The dog let go and went charging out of the shuttle bay at a dead run. Rayce could hear him running down the corridor.

"That dog needs some regular sex," he muttered.

Seconds later, Elvis came bounding through the door with something in his mouth. It was covered with the same dark soil they used in the garden, and dog drool.

Elvis dropped it at his feet and snorted dirt from his nose. Rayce picked up the small metal object and wiped it off. It was a comm unit, but not one of his.

He activated the unit. Within seconds, an old

man appeared in the small screen with a worried face, pale blue eyes and wild white hair.

"Tru?" he practically shouted.

Rayce frowned. "She's not here."

The old man donned a sour expression. "Coburne. I should have guessed."

"I haven't had the pleasure," Rayce replied with a sardonic smile.

"I'm Majj Noa Leeberfinger," the man muttered. "Where is Tru?"

"You are on the Institute now?"

"Of course I am," Noa grunted. "Where else would I be?"

"And you don't know where she is?"

Noa blew out a long breath. "No. I was hoping she went back to you after she left here."

"She was there and left?"

Noa smiled crookedly. "Yes. But not before she brought down the entire administrative body, exposing them as the greedy bastards they are." He grinned outright. "You should have seen her—armed with a mountain of information. She called the Majj together at the general forum and buried the administrators alive in their own mess before they could drag their lazy asses into the room. They tried but couldn't deny any of it."

"Deny what?" Rayce asked, completely confused.

"Didn't she tell you?" Noa questioned. "For the past thirty years, the administrators have been using the Majj to make themselves rich beyond measure. They sold every one of our inventions and discoveries to the highest bidders, regardless of humanitarian need. They censored our computer archives. They ruined our reputations. They worked us like animals and treated us like prisoners." Noa's face turned red with anger. "It's a crime, that's what it is. And until something is done to correct the situation, no Majj is lifting a finger on his or her projects."

"You Majj didn't know this was happening? How could you not know?"

Noa gave a great sigh. "We trusted the administrators. They have always protected us. It never occurred to us that they'd use us. But Tru downloaded all their dirty work to our network. All the information they've been censoring from us."

The old man looked as if he would cry. "People suffered and died in our name, Coburne. We didn't even know."

Rayce couldn't believe it. The Majj were innocent? That meant that Tru was innocent. He closed his eyes in disgust at himself. What had he done?

"Why wouldn't she tell me all this?" Rayce murmured.

Noa shrugged. "Her father started the change in policy. I wouldn't be telling a lot of people, either."

Rayce's heart clenched in his chest as he realized that he'd wasted so much time and so much energy on the wrong guilty party. And on Tru.

"What about Odell?"

Noa's eyebrows went up. "You know about Odell?"

"I know he's a prick who hurt Tru."

The old man's expression softened considerably. "Then you are more perceptive than I thought. She kicked his ass."

"Good," Rayce said seriously. "If she hadn't, I would have."

Noa grinned. "It was a beautiful thing. She destroyed them and cut the Majj free. And then left." His smile faded. "I knew she would. She never really belonged here, no matter how hard she tried. Her compassion rules her heart. She was meant for greater things than being locked away in an Institute."

"Do you have any idea where she would have gone?"

Noa shook his head. "None. You are the only outside contact she had, as far as I know. You haven't heard from her?"

"No." He was the last person she'd contact.

"I hate to think of her out there alone," Noa said sadly. "She's like a daughter to me. I knew her father used her but I never imagined how much." Tears welled up in his eyes. "I love her."

"That makes two of us," Rayce said quietly.

Noa gave him a long, hard look and then nodded once. "Then go find her, Coburne. Find her and give her a real home."

Rayce looked up at *Miranda*. "My thoughts exactly."

He signed off and ruffled Elvis's furry head. "What we need now, buddy, is a plan."

Gil glanced at Rayce as he walked into the office with Elvis dancing around his feet.

"I want you to report Tru's ship as stolen."

Gil's jaw dropped. "What?"

Rayce crossed his arms. "Report the ship to the authorities as stolen."

"But she paid for it with her share of the Collection," he stammered. "Hell, she paid for a whole damn fleet of ships plus the shuttle bays and half of Level Three."

"Do you want her back here?" Rayce asked.

Gil looked mortally confused. "Well, yes but—"

"I think it might go a little faster if we had some help."

The realization dawned in Gil's eyes. "You're right." He turned to the ship's computer and began entering the request.

Elvis planted two big black paws on the desk next to Gil, Rayce moved behind him and the three of them stared into the computer.

"Make sure you specify that we want the assailant unharmed at all costs. And held in custody until I can talk to her."

"Right," Gil said, bobbing his head.

"And send the notification to me on *Miranda* when they find her."

Gil shot a glance over his shoulder. "Where are you going?"

"I have to pick up something."

"How about a mate for this crazy dog?" Gil muttered as Elvis licked his face.

Chapter Nineteen

She couldn't believe it. No sooner had she landed at the Pitcairn Station than she had been promptly arrested by the authorities. She glared at the space marshals escorting her down a long corridor like some common criminal who would suddenly go crazy and commit mass murder.

So this was life on her own. How comforting.

"I'd really like to know what I'm being charged with."

One of the marshals piped up. "Theft."

She gaped at him. "What?"

"Unauthorized use of a ship."

She worked her mouth but nothing came out. The *ship*? The ship she'd paid for in full? *That's* why they arrested her? Wait until she got hold of Gil. He was a dead man.

The marshals stopped at a door marked "Interrogation" and opened it for her. "These will be your temporary quarters."

"Until when?"

He shrugged. "Until the charges can be proc-
essed."

"I'm innocent," she contended.

The marshal nodded. "I'm sure you are. But for
now, please wait in here."

She took a deep breath, which did nothing to
calm her nerves, and stepped through. The door
shut behind her. It was a small, square of a room
with a bed, a tiny lav and a sitting area.

Lovely. She dropped into one of the chairs. Obviously she'd be here for a while. Not that she had
any particular place to go. The only reason she'd
docked was to refuel. It wasn't like anyone wanted
to hire her. Not after Odell had put the word out
to the sector of her disassociation, along with a few
depositions about her state of mental health. No
reputable place would want her now, certainly not
in her field. She'd be lucky to get a common server
position.

She dropped her head back and stared at the
metal ceiling.

Well, Odell had received what he deserved, too.
It had given her great pleasure to watch him squirm
and sputter useless reprisals and threats when he
realized that she had him.

She might have destroyed him in front of the
Majj, but he'd done more damage than she could
have imagined out here. And when word of her
father's policies got out, the name Van Dye would
be a disgrace. Not exactly the kind of association
she wanted to put on a job application.

Once she had this mess with the ship straightened out, she'd change her name. Her old identity
would be formally lost along with all her creden-

tials. The realization hurt even if it meant a new beginning. She was on her own now. The revelation was both exciting and terrifying.

Who was she now without the Majj? Never in her life had she had so much time alone with nothing to do except think. She wasn't sure she liked it at all. But then again, the universe didn't care.

Her return to the Institute didn't bring back any warm memories. She felt no longing, didn't miss a thing except Noa. It was when he'd asked her to stay that she realized she never really belonged there in the first place. Well, maybe she did belong but she certainly wasn't happy. She didn't laugh there like she had with Rayce or with his silly dog. And she wanted to laugh, wanted a life with choices and chances. Risk.

Tears stung her eyes. She missed Rayce and she hated him for it. If she ever saw him again, she wouldn't know what to do first: thank him for setting her free or kill him.

"This is highly unusual," La Mas, the security chief of Pitcairn Station, said to Rayce. "We've had her in custody for over thirty hours. You realize that's not even legal."

Rayce walked along beside the man through the station corridors. For a small man, he moved with military precision and speed.

"There will be no reprisals, I promise."

La Mas eyed him suspiciously. "I hope not. So why didn't you want her prosecuted?"

"I plan to make her my mate."

The thin man's eyes widened. "So you had her

arrested? Do you really think she's going to be happy about that?"

Rayce shrugged. "Believe me, that's the least of my worries."

The older man shuddered. "My mate would have my head if I ever did that to her. You're a brave man."

They stopped in front of a door and the chief used his handprint to open it. Tru was sitting in a chair reading a datapad when Rayce walked in.

Her expression switched from disbelief to hurt to anger in a split second.

"What the hell do *you* want?"

Behind him, the security chief whistled low. "Good luck, boy." And left.

Her pleasant greeting wasn't a good beginning. "I realize you aren't thrilled to see me but I need to talk to you."

Her eyes speared him and she stood up wearing generic street clothes, no more Majj uniform. She tossed the datapad on the table in front of her with a clatter. "Not thrilled to see you? I can't imagine why. You lied to me. You made a fool of me. You used me." She pointed toward the door. "And you had me arrested for stealing a ship that I paid for. I've been locked in here for an entire day. Why would I not be happy to see you?"

He couldn't help but smile at her passion. He'd missed her. Too bad she hated him.

She crossed her arms. "I'm so glad you find this amusing."

He sobered. The part where she agreed to come home with him was going to be the challenge of his life.

"I'm sorry about the ship. It was the only way I could find you quickly. Did they hurt you?"

"Not as much as you did," she said bitterly.

He wasn't backing down, no matter how mad she got. She deserved to vent some anger his way and he deserved to take it.

"And I'm sorry about the VirtuWav."

She flinched like she'd been shot and turned away from him. She whispered, "Why? Why would you do that to me?"

He grappled for words. He'd rehearsed this conversation a hundred times in his head on the trip here but no explanation came to mind except one.

"It was the only way I could have you without hating myself."

Her gaze swung back to his. "Was it that bad that you hated yourself when you were with me?"

"No," he replied in a second. How could he explain to her what she meant to him? "The first time was a mistake and a surprise. The second time I wanted to be there. I wanted *you*. I didn't want some virtual replica of myself doing something stupid and hurting you."

"Not when you could hurt me yourself," she added sadly.

"I took you any way I could get you, Tru. That's how desperate I was."

She looked at him like she didn't believe him. He ran a hand through this hair. Now what?

"Why are you here?" The wounded look in her eyes nearly brought him to his knees. She'd been through so much already. He wanted to make the pain stop.

"Come back to the spaceport with me. To stay."

She shook her head and said firmly, "It wouldn't work."

"Why not?"

She clenched her hands into fists and she seemed to brace herself. "Because . . . because I worked on the Sykes Fever vaccine project."

Rayce narrowed his eyes in thought. "But you would have been too young."

"No. My father started me on that project."

"So what does that have to do with you not coming back with me?"

"Because every time you look at me, you'll think of my role in Miranda's death."

For a moment, he just stared at her tense body. Her pain was his fault. All of it. He'd driven her away with his anger. How many times could he screw up in one lifetime?

"Miranda's death wasn't your fault or the Majj's. It wasn't even the administrators' fault," he said softly. "It just happened. I wasted a lot of energy blaming you and the Majj. And I was wrong."

She looked skeptical. "Just like that you're willing to give up twenty years of rage?"

"Actually, I'm still angry about her death. That will never go away. But I've decided to do something about it." He looked her in the eye. "And I need your help."

"My help," she repeated. Then she sat back down in a chair and peered at him solemnly. "So, you want me to return to the spaceport because you need my help."

He winced at her cynical tone. He was really making a mess of this. "No, that's not the only reason why."

She watched him silently, waiting for the next brilliant choice of words with which he was going to bury himself. For a moment, he was lost in her gray eyes. Eyes he couldn't live without. It all came down to this moment. If he blew it, he'd be lost, himself.

"I need a partner."

She didn't even blink. Wrong again. Damn, she wasn't making this easy. To hell with subtlety.

He threw up his hands. "Look, I want you by my side when I open the spaceport. It's as much yours as it is mine. And it's not like you have any place to go. Gil and Hencke are going to kill me if I don't bring you back. Hencke, especially, and let me tell you, when he's not happy, he's an animal. I need a curator for that damn Collection and you are the only person I trust to manage it right. I want to do some charity work for my home planet and I have no idea where to begin. I love you and Elvis misses you like crazy." There, that covered it. He'd given her everything he had.

Her mouth dropped open. "You love me?"

He blew out a breath. "I love you. Lord, I love you. You asked me once if I worried about tomorrow. I do now. And I don't want to live the rest of my life without you because I screwed up."

It was now or never. Out of the bag he'd brought with him, he withdrew the Dahah Shier courtship figurine and set it down on the low table in front of her.

With every ounce of his soul, he rasped, "You are my challenge, my conscience, my strength. Without you, the spaceport, the credits, none of it matters. Be my mate, Tru."

He heard her breath catch and watched the tears well up in her eyes. For a long, excruciating minute she blinked at the figurine and at him. Then she reached out and he froze, waiting for her to topple it and reject him from her life.

With great care, she picked up the figurine and stared at it for a long time. She couldn't believe it. He'd gone back to M003, back to the pyramid to get this for her. A woman's admiring face, the simple flower in her hand, a stone figurine meant to last forever, for a love that would last forever.

She looked up at his face and into his eyes. And there she saw the same fear she felt and knew he meant what he'd told her. If he said he loved her, then he did. If he said he'd forgiven her, then he had. If he said he needed her, he was telling the truth. His fear drove his words but love drove his heart.

Tru closed her eyes and felt the pain tear through her. So this was how it felt to love someone so much that it hurt. These were higher stakes than she'd ever faced before. More important than the Collection or the Majj or the name Van Dye. This was her heart and her soul. This was risk.

He'd risked, too. He didn't have to be here, didn't have to track her down and lock her up to keep her long enough to put his heart on the table in front of her. In the end, it didn't matter how he'd gotten here, just that he had. It didn't matter how long it had taken him to figure it out, he had.

She opened her eyes to find him still standing there, waiting. There was no hatred in his face, not even a spark. No condemnation, no painful memories to cloud his beautiful blue-green eyes. He looked at her as if she held his life in her hands. And she understood exactly how he felt.

He loved her. Not for what she had accomplished or her last success. She knew she didn't need to be perfect for him to still love her. All he wanted was her heart.

Relief and freedom flooded over her and she let it. Love in all its forms consumed and owned her, caressed and besieged her with its promises, its pain, and its rapture.

Tears spilled down her face as she placed the figure next to her.

He let out a huge breath and reached for her, pulling her up and into his arms where she belonged.

Epilogue

"Where is he? This *is* the grand opening." Gil hissed in her ear as he fidgeted with his formal shirt.

Tru smiled at another guest passing through the giant arch of the spaceport's majestic entrance.

Through her smile, she replied, "He said he'd be here."

Beside her, Gil snorted. "And you believed him."

"He wouldn't miss this for anything, Gil."

"At least he took Elvis with him. That was one less worry these past two days. You know, the Collection was supposed to make our lives carefree and easy." He ran a hand through his disheveled red hair and gave a great sigh. "I've never worked so hard in my life."

Tru nodded, remembering the long days and sleepless nights leading up to the grand opening. There had been so many details, so many people involved, so many meetings and logistics to contend with.

"It's worth it," Tru said softly.

Gil grinned proudly at her. "Yes, it is."

Wild, white hair and a familiar face in the non-stop parade of guests caught her attention and Tru rushed over to hug Noa Leeberfinger's narrow shoulders. He looked nervous but happy to see her.

"Welcome to the Miranda Foundation, Noa," she said to him. "I'm so glad you came."

Noa gave Gil a nod and turned back to Tru. "As if you gave me a choice."

"You are the Majj commissioner, Noa. And since this is now part of your research complex, you should at least take a tour," she reminded him.

He shoved his hands in his pockets and surveyed the teeming ballroom with a scowl. "Too many people."

She laughed. "You might make some new friends."

Noa shook his head and gave her a soft smile. "I have one good friend. That's all I need."

She took his hand and pulled him with her down the central corridor away from the crowd. "You can never have too many friends. How's the organizational restructuring going?"

The old man fell in step beside her. "The original administrators are all gone now, including Odell."

Tru smirked. "I wish I could have been there."

"He didn't take kindly to being disassociated," Noa said with great satisfaction. "Amazing, since he never had any qualms about doing it to any of us."

"And how are the Majj adjusting to their new administrative roles?"

Noa shrugged. "It's not quantum science. We'll get by. Our biggest problem now is that the credits the administrators stole from us will be locked up in the courts for a long time. It makes me sick to see the extravagant way they lived, wasting so much," he said in disgust. Then he gave her a rare grin. "Luckily, we have one generous backer to keep most of our projects running."

"Don't worry. We'll get every bit of the Majjs' credits back, too," she replied firmly.

"I understand the new Majj researchers are onboard and already settled in," Noa said.

"Yes. Their quarters were completed a few days ago. I'm looking forward to working with them. One of the first projects will be to finish cataloging the Collection onboard and the rest still at the M003 site. I haven't been able to devote much time to it lately."

She ushered Noa into her favorite place on the spaceport—the gardens in the center atrium. Balconies bordered the atrium which was the full height of the complex and open to the stars above.

Tru pointed to the exposed levels. "Care centers on Four. Research on Level Five. The entire sixth level is quarters for the Majj *and* their families."

"Families," Noa repeated with a smile. "That will take some adjustment but I'm glad to see it happen."

"No more isolation," Tru stated. "The Majj will be working with the people they are here to help. A much better incentive than fear of disassociation."

Noa nodded thoughtfully. "It's a generous gift you gave the Majj, Tru."

She smiled as a group of children ran through the flowers and plants. "Not me. This was Rayce's idea. He wanted to bring the Majj advances to the people who needed them most."

"Rayce could have made a fortune by catering to the rich," Noa noted.

She turned to her old friend and smiled. "The Collection is more than we need, even after we sold some of the pieces to a few good museums to complete the station and cover operating costs. We have enough to ensure this facility will run for our lifetimes and beyond. Plus we have financial freedom from investors or anyone else who might try to undermine the integrity and direction of our goal to help the needy."

"Like the administrators," Noa added sadly.

"Exactly."

Then she heard a familiar barking behind her. Tru turned just as Elvis raced into the atrium with a second black Labrador dog behind him.

"Good heavens, what are those things?" Noa gasped.

Elvis ran excited circles around her along with his new friend. Then he gave a petrified Noa a complimentary sniff in the crotch. Tru laughed and reached down to pet both excited dogs.

"Do you like her?" Rayce's voice brought her head up. He walked toward her looking tired except for the fire in his eyes. In the past few months, those eyes had never ceased to stop her heart. All the love, all the future she needed were in them.

"She's beautiful," Tru said, pushing past the dogs to wrap her arms around him for a long kiss. She could feel his raw desire, the way his body absorbed hers.

"Miss me?" she asked against his lips.

He gave a soft growl and rubbed his hands along her back, pressing her against him. "You have no idea. I've been stuck in a ship for two days with dogs. I need to reach critical mass in the worst way. Care to join me?"

She humphed. "And here I thought you loved me for my mind."

He nuzzled her ear. "I'll get to your mind later."

Tru turned at the sound of children squealing and laughing as they played with the two hyper dogs.

"Where did you find her?"

"Tess hooked me up with a lady who needed a new home for the dog," Rayce said. "Luckily, Elvis fell in love with her on sight. Her name is Louise."

She smiled up at Rayce who still held her tight. "Has Gil seen her?"

Rayce's eyes gleamed. "Unfortunately, yes. Don't go near him for a while. I think he's about to have a breakdown."

Tru laughed and kissed him again as the dogs danced around them and children laughed. In the center of it all, she held onto the man she loved.

It was a perfect moment, one she would never forget. All was right with the universe.